BLIND FAITH

ALEXA ASTON

OLIVER
HEBER
BOOKS

Created with Vellum

PROLOGUE

CALIFORNIA 1854

*S*unday.

Supposedly a day of rest. At least that's what a preacher man would think.

Jeb Foster's only concession to Sundays was he didn't take a drink until noon. Or a quarter of, at the earliest. Living in hell gave a man a powerful thirst.

He laughed aloud as he cast his line into the still waters of Lake Margarita. At least that's what he called the body of crystal blue water. The sun reflecting off it blinded him with its brightness, much as Margarita's beauty had the first time he saw her.

Hell. Any time he saw her.

Jeb shifted on the bank. *When had he started down his path to meet the devil?* He'd been a right stinker from the start. Sticking fingers into freshly made pies. Swiping an apple or piece of sweetmeat from a neighborhood kid. Slipping a penny from the collection box at church. A thousand things Mama told him he'd done. That is, before she up and left.

He couldn't blame her. She'd lost a husband and had two little mouths to feed when she hooked up with that Black Irish charmer. Married him when Jeb must have been three or four. He had no memories of his real father— only ones of that whoring drunk who'd made all their lives miserable. Mama finally cleared out one day. Her eyes stayed blackened more often than not. Her body had become a rainbow of bruises piled one atop the other, all hidden under layers of tattered petticoats and cheap gowns.

But did she have to run off and leave Anthony and him with the whoremonger?

That started him on his descent into hell— and his sins piled up over the years.

The pole almost shot out of his hands. Jeb tightened his grip and stood, drawing the line from the water. The fish hooked on the other end put up a strong fight. He watched it struggle, whipping its body from side to side. Finally, the hook tore and the fish flopped onto the ground, straining to reach the water.

With a swift motion, Jeb speared it to the ground with his dagger. Instantly, the impaled fish went still. Its eyes, cold and dead, stared back at him.

Reminded him of his charming stepfather's.

But that was a long time ago. Jeb had moved on. He'd killed other men. Done things no man should be a party to. Lost Anthony along the way in a barroom brawl. A bit more of him had died each day.

Until he'd met Margarita.

He smiled. Just the thought of her beauty could bring a grown man to his knees.

Suddenly, the quiet of the day was interrupted. Something thrashed through the forest. A wild animal being chased? In flight for its life?

Jeb knew better than to mess with a bear in the midst of his kill but the thought of fresh bear meat made his mouth water. He raced to the nearby tree and reached for his rifle, propped against the trunk.

Whatever it was would be here any moment. Jeb cocked the rifle, ready for what would spring from the dense woods. He was a decent shot, and at this close range he couldn't miss.

"Jeb!"

The anguished cry tore through the air. He lowered his gun and placed it on the ground as Alena shot out from the trees. He met her halfway. She flung herself into his arms.

"Jeb, Jeb, Jeb," she cried over and over, tears streaming down her cheeks.

He cuddled the small child and rocked her like a baby, whispering calming nonsense as he stroked the raven hair.

Alena raised violet eyes to his, brimming with tears. Her bottom lip trembled. Jeb saw confusion and sadness in her face. And he knew who put it there.

Kevin McClaine. Her sorry excuse for a father.

"Don't talk, Sweetie Pie. You're safe with old Jeb."

Gradually, Alena's trembling ceased. Her breathing slowed and the tears dried from her cheeks. Jeb vowed this time he would do it. He'd wring Mc-Claine's neck and throw him in the lake. No, he'd stake him to the ground and let the buzzards gnaw him to death. Jeb wouldn't let Margarita talk him out of it.

This time, he would kill Kevin McClaine. They could rot in hell together as long as the Black Irishman kept to a different side of the eternal fire.

Alena touched her small hand to his face. "Jeb?" she whispered. "You need to help. Mama said to come find you if we ever needed help."

He smiled gently at the beautiful child in his arms. Oh, she was Margarita's, all right. The smooth, satin skin. Large eyes. Delicate chin. Long, straight hair that hung to her waist. This one would grow up to be as breathtaking as her mother. Maybe more so.

"Well, here I am." He stood and gave her a slight, re-

3

assuring squeeze before placing her on her feet. "Let's go see what your mama needs help with."

Alena swallowed. Her mouth turned down and then her face crinkled up again.

"Don't cry, Sweetie Pie. Jeb'll fix it, whatever it is. You know that."

Over the years, he had painted the McClaine barn. Birthed their cows. Fixed the plow. Repaired the fence. Sharpened knives. Whatever Kevin McClaine left undone before he disappeared on one of his frequent benders, Jeb Foster completed.

"You know there's nothing I wouldn't do for you or your mama. Come on, little girl. Let's go."

He took the child's hand. They set out for the neighboring homestead. The land had been Kevin McClaine's payoff after his service in the Mexican War. Jeb was used to having next to nothing, but he shuddered every time he saw the McClaine place.

Margarita came from fine stock, one of the landed ranchero families of California. Her family disowned her after she fell for the dashing American cavalry officer. Now she lived in abject poverty, with only little Alena as the single bright spot in her life.

As they came closer, Jeb determined to settle things, once and for all. He'd wanted to possess Margarita from the moment he met her. Only Kevin McClaine stood in his way. Funny, he'd killed in anger. Dispassionately. For money. For revenge. Yet in his thirty years, he'd never killed for love. Maybe he'd waited because he knew the love Margarita had for him would die if he shot her husband. He'd stood by and watched that bastard chisel away at Margarita long enough. Now, Alena was terrified. He'd give McClaine a chance to go peacefully.

If he didn't, Jeb would do what needed to be done. Either Margarita would forgive him— or she wouldn't.

He was ready to take the risk. Whatever the outcome, her life would be better with Kevin McClaine gone from it.

The ramshackle cabin appeared in the distance. A trail of smoke rose from its chimney. Jeb hoped he could find McClaine and make it happen fast. He would force Margarita to realize she couldn't go on living the way she had for the last seven years. He could save her from her husband's acid tongue and heavy hand. They would be a family, as he'd dreamed of time and time again. Maybe they'd even have a child or two of their own, playmates for Alena.

Alena drew up sharply as they entered the clearing.

"What's wrong, Pumpkin?"

Her grip on his hand tightened. She looked around, shy as a doe. Jeb knew she was looking for her father.

"Daddy kept hitting Mama, harder and harder. She cried and cried." Alena looked up at him. "Daddy's so mean to her. He kicked her. Mama just crumpled up in a heap. Daddy yelled for me to get out. I ran and hid in the barn."

His gut tightened. McClaine had always mistreated Margarita. Jeb had seen the telltale bruises from the time they arrived. At first, she'd lied and made excuses for how they'd happened. But Jeb knew. He'd seen it before and heard every story, chapter and verse, in his own mother's book. Finally, Margarita admitted the truth to him.

"Then I'm glad you came to get me, Sweetie Pie. That was the right thing to do."

"I couldn't fix things this time." Alena sniffed. "Mama lets me brush her hair when Daddy's been mean to her. She says it makes her feel better. But she wouldn't wake up. That's why I came to get you."

Jeb clamped down on the panic that surged through him. He ruffled the girl's hair. "Why don't you go wait in the barn, sweet girl? I'll check on your mama. Leave it to Jeb. I'll fix things."

Alena skittered off, pausing to look at him somberly before closing the barn door behind her. Jeb waited until she was out of sight before starting toward the house. He had a bad feeling.

The fire burned low. A pot of stew simmered in the grate. Margarita had been a terrible cook when she'd first married, servants having prepared every meal for her in the past. She was a quick learner, though. Now her apple pie and biscuits ranked with the best of them.

The stillness caused his heart to race. It didn't feel right, not at all. Alena's words echoed in his head.

She wouldn't wake up this time...

He moved past the simple furniture, some of it overturned. An empty whiskey bottle lay on the floor. Jeb kicked it out of the way. He might enjoy a nip every day, but he never drank to the depths Kevin McClaine did. McClaine was a mean drunk.

He moved toward the bedroom. He'd imagined himself and Margarita in there a thousand times, making sweet love in the late afternoon light. Or when moonlight spilled into the room. Jeb set his jaw. That would be a reality soon. He was bound and determined to remove McClaine from their sight. It was time to take a stand.

For love.

Jeb entered the small bedroom and squinted. The curtains were drawn tight. Only dim light peered over his shoulder from the fire and window in the other room.

Then his foot hit something soft. He knelt. Margarita lay before him. He rushed to the window and tore the curtains down. Light spilled in bright waves across the room. He returned to her side. A blanket covered her, and a pillow was partly under her head.

Alena's work. Margarita's lip was split. Dried blood ran from her mouth in a jagged line. One eye was swollen shut and yet she still looked beautiful to him in her sleep, so peaceful.

Jeb cradled her cheek with his palm and stiffened.

Cold.

His mind screamed as he gently lifted the blanket. She was nude beneath it. The perfect flesh marred with bruises of various shapes and sizes. Some weeks old. Others much more recent. He stroked the swanlike neck, held the tiny, perfect hand in his.

Lifeless.

The bastard had finally killed her. Jeb warned her this would happen. She had laughed, that musical tinkling that gave him the good kind of shivers, and assured him Kevin would never go that far. That his Catholic conscience was even stronger than hers. Beat her, yes. Kill her? Never.

Now, it was too late. Too late for holding her in his arms. Knowing she was finally his. Drinking her intoxicating kisses. Joining their bodies as one.

Jeb pressed his lips to hers, in their first and only kiss. He had loved her from afar. Now, he would mourn her in the only way he knew how. It came easily to him. Maybe it had been born with him.

"Goodbye, my love," he murmured softly and raised the blanket over his Margarita.

Then he went out to find that no good, wife-killing whoreson.

In the end, it took only a moment. McClaine's eyes showed the fear Jeb needed to see. He'd buried the body and then returned for Alena. She was his responsibility now.

And no one would ever come between them.

CHAPTER 1

CALIFORNIA 1868

" $\mathcal{L}$ et's get out of here!" Dingus shouted, alerting his band of outlaws it was time to depart.

He scrambled from the stopped train as the others scurried after him, their hostages in hand.

Quickly he leaped upon the back of his horse, securing the payroll bag to the saddle horn before looking up to make certain every man had made it out safely. Several mounted their horses in order to make a swift getaway as Jimbo Simon appeared, the last to step outside the car. Jimbo had to be the dumbest man Dingus had ever encountered. The fool clumsily jumped from the train to the ground and landed on his ankle wrong. The three hundred-plus pounds he carried likely contributed to his being off-balance.

A bad feeling rippled through Dingus as Jimbo hobbled to his horse and swung into the saddle.

Sure enough, a bespectacled man poked his head from the train and fired a wild shot, disappearing again inside the train as several gang members returned fire at him.

He watched as Jimbo fell like a ton of bricks to the ground. A bloodstain appeared instantly in his upper back. Dingus made the decision not to wait around. If

Jimbo was still alive by some miracle, he would never survive the rough ride to the canyon hideaway, the gang's base of operations for years. If the criminal did live, he wouldn't talk. Jimbo Simon might be as dumb as dirt, but he wasn't stupid. No one from the Marker brothers' gang had ever talked.

"Sammy! Put the senator on Jimbo's horse," he called out, watching as Sammy quickly bound the man's wrists together and tied them to the saddle horn.

Sammy slapped the horse and Jimbo's paint took off at a gallop, Senator Braden Reynolds hanging on for dear life.

Before Dingus could issue another order, Cletus swept up the boy with him. The bookish little fellow— small, pale, his eyes huge and round behind wire-framed glasses— made nary a peep. No one ventured a backward glance at Jimbo as the gang hightailed it away.

They rode for several hours, first at a breakneck pace and then slowing some in order not to tire their mounts. As they rode, melancholy invaded his soul.

How had he ever wound up in charge of such rabble?

Dingus cursed the day the last of the Marker brothers and their various cousins were jailed, shot, or hanged. The remaining gang members should have had the good sense to call it quits with the brains of the group dead or locked up. But this bunch of crazy out-laws lacked common sense.

His eyes darted toward Cletus, the nominal leader when Dingus wasn't around. Cletus ruled the roost by intimidation. If the others weren't so stupid, they would plot to overthrow the idiot and bury the bones the buzzards left behind.

Dingus realized he was tired of them all. Weariness blanketed him. His desire for the life the gang provided died long ago. His own life had been a rough one and he'd fallen in with the Marker brothers at a time when he needed companionship. They'd offered it and he'd been grateful for it.

He and Jacob Marker got along especially well, but nothing had been the same since the demise of the blood Markers. Dingus wondered if he might ever escape this association. He was getting old and tired of robbing innocent victims and sitting around in the middle of nowhere with dirty, bedraggled men bragging on their exploits.

That's why, over the years, he spent more and more time away. Jacob Marker had seemed to understand Dingus' need for solitude. In fact, Jacob even encouraged it. Dingus wished now that when Jacob was arrested and hanged that he had abandoned the gang for good instead of foolishly sticking around.

But now, sitting before him, might be his golden goose. The opportunity to make the break he so desperately desired. Americans everywhere knew the name Braden Reynolds as one of the most powerful politicians in Washington. A self-made man who had acquired a fortune to accompany the power he wielded. Surely Reynolds' wife would pay dearly for the return of her husband and only son.

He looked over his shoulder again. The key to everything he wanted rode behind him. It would take cunning— but he intended to walk away with every dime from this kidnapping. No sharing. No splitting the ransom.

In the end, it was every man for himself.

~

THEY RODE the rest of the day and most of the night. No complaints voiced. Dingus learned long ago to give an order and stick to it. The men surrounding him weren't thinkers; they were followers. Only Cletus questioned him now and then. Sometimes with a glance, sometimes pulling him aside. But even Cletus knew of the treasure they held. He saw the greed in Cletus's eyes and wondered if it mirrored his own.

Close to sunrise, they made the canyon. If there was a God, He'd definitely claim responsibility for the canyon. It was beautiful, rugged, and dangerous as hell to reach the bottom. Untouched by man, except for the Marker brothers and their gang of outlaws.

The men abandoned their saddles in order to lead the horses down the steep, narrow path. One look at the child and Dingus knew the boy wouldn't make it. He thought maybe the senator's wife might have pulled a fast one on her husband. Any man would question this scrawny child being his. Braden Reynolds was a good six feet, broad shouldered, and looked in fair health despite the paunch nestled around his mid-section. This boy was pale, skinny, awkward, and hacked like he had the consumption.

"Put the boy back on your horse, Sammy," he said quietly.

Sammy nodded and lifted the child back into the saddle.

Along with the dark circles under the boy's eyes, Dingus saw the terror underscored in his young face. After so long a ride, the child was still fearful. He went over and placed a hand on the boy's knee.

"Hold on, son. We'll be there soon." He didn't think twice about the reassurance. His soft side came out every now and then and he could tell it soothed the boy.

Within an hour, as dawn broke, the party finished making their way down the canyon and climbed back onto their horses to reach the cluster of small cabins at the far end of the valley.

Dingus dismounted once they arrived and tossed his reins to Sammy.

"Rub him down." He went to lift the boy from the saddle, placing him on wobbly legs.

He bent low and whispered, "Buck up, son. You'll be here awhile. Make your mama proud. Be a good little man."

He and Cletus entered the cabin with Reynolds and the boy in tow. The other men would care for the horses and work on some grub, a routine they fell into long ago. He led the boy to a cot.

"Lie down. You look like you need some rest."

The child trembled but did as he was told. He rolled so he faced away from those in the cabin and curled into a small ball. Exhausted, he fell asleep immediately.

Satisfied that the boy was taken care of for now, Dingus turned to look at Braden Reynolds. The man's jaw was set in granite. His eyes narrowed as he glared at his kidnapper with disdain. His very posture, much less the defiant look he wore, worked Dingus up into a lather.

He had no patience with adults, just a notorious soft spot for kids. And especially no sympathy for a high-and-mighty senator. The cold bastard hadn't given his own son a glance that Dingus could tell. No reassuring smiles. No whispers that Daddy'd take care of things. Dingus judged Braden Reynolds to be a pompous ass. He would make this selfish politician sorry. He'd show him who was the boss.

In a quick movement, Dingus threw a right cross, knocking the senator off his high horse and onto the floor. Reynolds fell hard, his hands still tied. Cletus picked up the hostage and shoved him into a rickety chair.

"Dingus? Do you—"

"Not now," he growled. "Leave me be."

Cletus knew well enough to do as he was told and exited the cabin. Braden Reynolds stared up at Dingus now, a small trickle of blood running from the corner of his mouth.

"What do you want?"

He smiled. The senator had him some guts, after all. "I want as much money as I can get for your sorry carcass."

Reynolds turned as white as lightning against a dark sky. This intrigued him. Why did the thought of ransom make him so fearful?

"You realize you and your boy are worth more to me alive than dead?"

Reynolds swallowed. Dingus could smell the fear on him now. Reynolds had a nasty little secret.

Dingus aimed to find out what it was.

He thrust his hand into the senator's pocket. The money clip was almost laughable. For a man in the senator's position, it held a measly four dollars.

"Not carrying much these days?"

Reynolds snorted. "I don't have to. My traveling secretary handles expenses."

He reached in again and withdrew a gold pocket watch. Now this was a keeper. He clicked it open. Inside was one of the most beautiful women he'd ever seen. The picture entranced him. She had flawless skin and large eyes framed by long, dark lashes. A mass of hair was piled artfully on top of her head, but a few curls had escaped, making her look vulnerable. She could be a princess in a fairy tale.

He winked at Reynolds. "Maybe I'll get to do my business with your missus."

Dingus anticipated Reynolds' action. As the senator stood to charge him, he landed a quick punch to the

14

man's gut. A rush of air blew out as Reynolds crumpled. Dingus added a swift kick to the head for good measure. He didn't want his guest going anywhere. He licked his lips. He'd lost interest in the senator's secret for now.

Instead, he began to think of ways to meet Mrs. Reynolds.

CHAPTER 2

*J*ohn Harper took a bite of cold biscuit and washed it down with a swig from his canteen. The autumn day was crisp and clear, not so cold that the wind stung his cheeks, but it had that clean smell to it. A blue sky reigned as king, with wisps of white clouds dotting it. Cicero turned her head and nickered softly. He placed the remaining biscuit in his palm and offered it to the horse.

Her lips barely grazed him as she daintily took what was left of his breakfast and nibbled it with relish.

He stroked her between the ears, her favorite place to be petted. "Good girl," he told her, as he did ten times a day. She was the only woman he'd sworn to have a lasting relationship with. So far, she had given far more than she received in their three years together.

John wasn't much for women. Human ones, anyway.

He tightened the lid on the canteen and returned it to its place. His knees nudged Cicero's flanks gently. She responded with a nice trot. He didn't want to tire her. They had been on the road several days, his latest assignment taking him across northern California. He knew she would like to bed down in a nice, dry stable and have her fill of oats, but until he could find Senator Braden Reynolds and his son, that wasn't going to happen.

If he found them.

John's throat constricted. He swallowed hard to push the lump down. He had seen Johnny once, with his parents at a rally in Pennsylvania, just after Gettysburg had been dedicated. The little fellow would have been about three then and his eyes had held all the mischievous charm of any boy that age.

The senator, too, oozed charm— but of a different kind. John had stared hard at the politician. It was the first and only time he'd seen the man in person. Reynolds had that slickness and confidence that bewitched women and caused level-headed men to trust him. But the suave urbanity prompted John to keep his distance.

That— and the fact that Annabelle had walked up.

John hadn't wanted to see her, much less let her see him, so he had melted into the crowd and rejoined his regiment. He risked one last glance at her, though. Their eyes met for a brief moment which seemed to go on forever. He wondered if the pain and regret he saw were mirrored in his own face.

He'd never seen her again.

Now the government was trying to track down her and her stepdaughter, Olivia. Last word was they might be in Italy. Or had it been France? Either way, she would be found and told that her husband and son had been yanked off a train and were now being held captive in parts unknown. Maybe for ransom, maybe not.

It was his job to find them.

He wasn't the only U.S. Marshal looking. A half-dozen others were assigned to the case. Braden

Reynolds had a lot of pull in Washington. He would find them, though. He had to.

John rode several hours, reining in any stray thoughts of Annabelle Martin Reynolds and putting them under lock and key. What they'd had was water under the bridge and a long time ago. Her betrayal caused him to sour on all women. On life, really.

He approached the canyon that Jimmy Littlefoot tipped him about, flat in the middle of nowhere. He trusted Jimmy. The bronzed Indian's tips always panned out. Jimmy swore the canyon was home to the Marker brothers, an odd gang of misfits active in this part of the country for nigh on thirty years.

John doubted there were even any Marker brothers left. He could name three in jail right now, two that were hanged, and another two that died in a shootout before Mr. Lincoln's War ever began. Of course, cousins and friends and hangers-on made up a good part of the outfit. No one really knew who the Marker brothers were right now, but as sure as the sun rose every day, some faction of the gang either planned something illegal or were in the act this very minute.

John dismounted. If it really was the Markers who had Senator Reynolds, they would have lookouts. He loosely tied Cicero to a tree and scratched her ears.

"Now, I aim to be back, girl, but if I don't make it, you're not tied up much at all. Give me a few hours before you light out."

Amazingly, Cicero would do as told. John had never come across a horse with such keen intelligence. She spooked him at times with what she knew and how she acted. It was almost as if she were human. He held conversations with her all the time as if she could understand him.

He wouldn't bet against it that she did.

Stealthily, he made his way down. He saw a cluster

of four cabins at the back of the canyon. There was one visible standing guard. If they did have Reynolds and the boy, they must be fairly certain no one knew it, or that no one could track them here.

Smoke rose from three of the four cabins. He wondered how the gang was divided up. Would it be on seniority? Reputation? Or whoever decided to bunk wherever?

As he got closer, John shivered involuntarily. His childhood nurse, a superstitious Irish nanny named Maureen, would tell him someone just walked over his grave. He glanced down at the ground beneath his feet before looking up. If he wasn't careful, it would become his grave, unmarked and full of secrets.

He approached from the west, one cabin visible, the others behind it. A crow passed overhead, its mournful cry bringing another chilled shiver racing down his spine. God, but it was quiet. Too quiet. A bad feeling twisted in his gut. Still, he kept on. That's what a marshal did. Bad feelings didn't stop him at Shiloh or Fredericksburg when he was a soldier. They wouldn't here, either.

John crept toward the first cabin. A window smeared with mud would give him a chance to count heads. He peered in. In the dim light, he saw four men sitting at a round table filled with cards and chips and shot glasses full of whiskey. Two had their backs to him, but the two he could see full-on were armed. Another man stretched out on a bunk, his hat pulled over his face, his pistol at his side within easy reach.

Carefully, he moved underneath the glass. John crouched and pulled his gun. It didn't hurt to be ready. He rounded the corner after a quick check. The second cabin was empty, no men and no fire. He stepped lightly and eased up to the next cabin's lone window.

Pay dirt.

Senator Braden Reynolds, looking haggard and heavier than he had at Gettysburg, was tied to a chair that had seen better days. One side of his face was puffed up, with an eye swollen shut. John scanned the room. Three men were there, two looking like they were used to taking orders, while the third seemed experienced in giving them. They all stood over the boy.

Johnny Reynolds looked fatigued. Bluish shadows hung under his eyes. His lips were cracked. His lower lip trembled. He seemed scrawny for his age. Maybe it was the hulking men hovering over him that dwarfed him so. Their voices carried from the open window.

"You think your mama's gonna save you, boy?" One of the minions sneered at the child. "Hell, your daddy can't do anything and he's a high muckety-muck Washington man."

"Cease badgering the boy!" bellowed Reynolds.

All three men turned to gaze at the senator, sly smiles on their faces.

"Your issue is with me. Not my boy."

The tallest of the gang grinned, pure evil dancing on his features. "You bet your bottom dollar our beef is with you, Reynolds." He grabbed a fistful of Johnny's hair and tightened his grip. Pain shot across the boy's face.

"Let him go!" stormed Reynolds. "He's only a child."

"Yeah. One living a life of wealth and privilege." The leader turned to Johnny. "Didn't know your old man got his fancy house and those fancy clothes and servants from the wrong means, did ya, kid?"

Johnny squirmed, his eyes squeezed closed beneath his gold-rimmed glasses.

"Look at me, little feller," commanded the leader.

Johnny opened his eyes. A single tear slid down his cheek.

"We ain't no nursemaids, kid. Now, if your mama

will hurry and come through with the money, maybe you'll be outta here soon."

John's thoughts flew. So since he'd taken off, the gang had sent a ransom demand. He wondered how much they had demanded.

"My m-m-m-mama's in Eur-Europe now," the boy stuttered. "Sh-sh-she's not home."

The leader slapped the boy. Both Johnny's father and John flinched. One couldn't do anything and the other dared not tip his hand yet.

"Quit your bellyaching." The leader turned to the other two. "Maybe those lawmen think we're pulling their legs."

Both gang members shrugged. One twirled a toothpick in his mouth. The other spit a spray of tobacco into a corner of the room.

"Maybe we need to shake them up some, boys."

The leader's eyes gleamed unnaturally. John cocked his gun, ready to spring from his haunches into action. He didn't like the looks the leader passed from man to man.

"Hold him."

The men sank meaty fingers into the boy as the ringleader jerked the boy's hand down on the nearby table. Within seconds, he'd whacked off the boy's pinkie. Johnny's scream tore into the silent day. John heard muted laughter float from the card players' cabin as he gritted his teeth and forced himself to remain hidden.

"We'll send this to them government sissies." The tall man whipped out a dirty handkerchief and wrapped the finger up. "Let them know we mean what we say."

Johnny collapsed onto the floor, his agony ripping at John's heart. The boy's father strained at his bonds, though fear hung over him like a limp blanket. John wondered how he would react if he had been in the senator's place.

The gang members looked relaxed. Now would be the time to take them, but John didn't see how he could and get the man and boy out in one piece. The first shot he fired would bring the other five— if not more— running. Much as he hated to, he needed to go for reinforcements.

He moved around the cabin and decided to ascend from the back side. It was steep, though, and he kept slipping. He couldn't get a firm grip and slid down more times than he could count. He didn't want to chance going back down and around the long way again. He'd made it this far without being spotted. Besides, fifteen more feet and he would be at the top.

Suddenly, a bullet whizzed so close to his head, he was sure it burned his scalp. He turned and fired a wild shot over his left shoulder, not being able to focus on the target in such a quick moment from his awkward angle. The second bullet struck him in his right shoulder. Pain shot through him like a lit fire under Satan. He gritted his teeth and swung back to fire another shot. It went astray from the shooters. He'd spied two of them.

Knowing his life depended on it, John scrambled up the remaining way. He slid his revolver into his untrained left hand and fired random shots, more to keep them ducking below than hoping to hit anyone. A handful of men in his regiment had felt comfortable shooting with either hand, but he never could pull off that feat.

Grabbing a scrubby tree growing halfway out the side of the steep incline, he pulled with all his might. The injured shoulder roared in protest as he flung himself to the ground. He crawled away from the edge and doubled back to see if they were pursuing him. One did. John steadied the gun in his hand. With the ground and his left hand supporting him, he got off an accurate shot, though his hand spasmed badly. The man fell backward and slid down the side. He saw no movement from him after that.

He couldn't wait around for any others that might follow. He ran as fast as he could. The shoulder throbbed and oozed blood, but he didn't think it would kill him. At least it wouldn't if he could get out of here ahead of the others.

And then like a miracle from above, Cicero appeared, galloping to meet him. Damn, that horse was fast. And smart. She would've had to start running the minute the first shot was fired, as far as she had come. Had she been smart enough to unhitch herself and wait? He wouldn't question divine intervention at this point.

Cicero reached him and turned, ready to be off again. John jumped onto her and she took off, kicking up dust as she flew across the land. Then she stumbled, a strange warbling coming from her throat. Confused, John looked down and saw the hole in her side, blood dripping from it. Shooting him was one thing; shooting his horse was something far worse.

He turned to fire and felt the bullet graze his temple as he did. It threw him off-balance, as did Cicero's bucking. John hit the ground hard, his head snapping. A million stars burst across the horizon. He blinked furiously, not able to see anything. He reached out, feeling the jagged rock his head had hit. It was a wonder the blow hadn't killed him.

Another shot cut through the air. He staggered to his feet and somehow climbed back on Cicero. He leaned down to whisper in her ear.

"Get us out now, girl. Please. Get us out."

Cicero snorted indignantly, as if questioning his belief in her, and took off again. John clung to her mane as the sound of bullets faded into the distance. He still was having trouble seeing, a map of stars exploding with each jarring motion.

He wrapped his arms around his horse as his world suddenly went black.

CHAPTER 3

*A*lena pulled the quilt over her and nestled her face into the soft pillow. Outside, the October wind howled, bringing a music all its own. The wind had picked up throughout the afternoon, turning the crisp, fall day into a cold, blustery night. Now, the staccato sound of rain began tapping upon the window, harmonizing with the wind's wail.

She wondered where Jeb was. If he was safe. If he had gotten a good price on the paintings and quilts she sent with him. It had been hard to part with the one of the mother and her doe. Still, the money her art brought would buy much-needed supplies and the little luxuries, like Jeb's pipe tobacco and her peppermints.

It concerned her that he had been gone longer than usual. Maybe it had been more difficult to sell her work this time. He usually took the quilts to the nearest town and then to others along the way to Stockton until they had all sold. Then he would travel to San Francisco, where he sold her watercolors and oil paintings.

Alena wondered what he said when he sold her work in Rio Vista, the small community about seven miles from their place. She had only been there once, many years ago. She still remembered the stares and the pointing fingers of the townspeople as she rode beside Jeb in the cart that day.

"Don't worry, Sweetie Pie," he'd assured her. "You're different from them, is all. They don't know any better."

As a child, Alena knew she was different. She had studied herself in her mother's mirror. The reflection staring back showed a solemn girl of eight, with smooth, olive skin and luminous violet eyes. As she and Jeb had driven down the streets of Rio Vista, though, no child had her skin color or hair as long and black as her own. The women there were fair-skinned with golden or brown tones of hair, nothing like her or her mother.

She clung to Jeb as they visited the general store, the whispers and furtive glances causing her a physical pain. Did they know her papa killed her mama and ran off, leaving her behind? That Jeb now took care of her and had for the last two years? She had hidden her face in the folds of his coat and swore she would never come back again.

And she hadn't in all these years. What did she need people for anyway, except for Jeb? He was better than her papa had been. More patient with her, teaching her to hunt and fish and shoot. Mama had taught her to cook and sew before she went to live with the angels. Alena figured God must have taught her to draw and paint, because the first time she had picked up a brush, it all seemed to come naturally. She had everything she needed in their cabin. She saw no reason to go out into the world.

Ever.

Alena tried to stop worrying. Jeb always returned in his own time. He was father and brother and best friend to her. They played chess sometimes in the evenings and even poker. Jeb said most women didn't play poker. Alena hadn't understood why but she knew she was very good at it. Jeb said so.

The rabbit in the cage next to her bed was restless tonight. She sat up and unhitched the latch, drawing the timid creature into her arms and cuddling it. Her fingers glided over the silky fur. She held the rabbit for some minutes, and it calmed.

Alena placed it back in the cage with a little sadness. Tomorrow or the next day, the animal would be well enough to set free. Thanks to her salve, its wound healed nicely. The fox that had latched on to the rabbit's hindquarters had been a scrawny little critter, but its coat had made for a nice hat.

Alena lay down again, sleep overtaking her thoughts of Jeb and the fox.

THE WHINNY of a wounded horse woke her. Alena knew instinctively it was real. Sometimes, she dreamed about the injured animals that seemed to make their way to her doorstep— but this was no dream.

The wind still whined, whistling its mournful tune. The rain, now a steady downpour, drowned out any other noise. And yet she had heard the horse. Or could it be Jeb returning? She rose and threw a flannel shirt over her plaid shirt and pants and quickly lit a lantern before she unbolted the front door. She opened it only a crack so as to keep the rain out.

There it was again.

Alena had not been dreaming. Somewhere out in the rain and cold was a hurt animal. One that needed her attention. She retrieved her shawl and draped it over her head before picking up the lantern and heading outside. She scanned the clearing before the

ALEXA ASTON

cabin, adjusting her eyes to the dark, though it would
be light in another two hours or so.

This time, the neighing was a complaining whimper
and Alena set off in the direction it came from. She
tracked it to the front of the barn. A large bay stood
with a rider slumped in the saddle. Alena made a few
clucking noises of sympathy. The horse let Alena lead
her into the dry barn.

She held the lantern high and the horse blinked.
Walking slowly around the animal, she immediately
found the problem. A small bullet hole pierced the
horse's side. Alena grabbed the limp man's face between her hands and tilted his head up in order to
study him. He was covered in blood and was as still as
death. She thought she could save the horse.

She wasn't sure she could save the man.

Silently apologizing to the bay, she led her back out
into the rain, right up to their front porch. She would
do what she could for this man. Bury him if she failed.

The horse seemed to know what she needed, low-
ering herself to the ground. Alena's eyes widened in
surprise. It was if the creature read her thoughts. She
scratched her between her ears and the horse seemed
to smile.

She wasn't a large woman, but farm chores over a
lifetime had made her strong. She half-dragged, half-
carried the man into the cabin and deposited him on
the floor.

Lord, he was a mess. There was blood everywhere
she looked. She wondered how he had stayed alive so
long, but Jeb told her most men were mean and ornery
and lived well beyond their chosen time to die. This
one must be particularly vile to have lasted this long.

Alena didn't bother to check his injuries. She would
deal with him later if need be. Right now, she had a
horse to attend, which was far more important to her.

28

She gathered up her basket of necessities and then hesitated.

What if this were Jeb?

Would she want some stranger to care for Jeb's horse before she looked after him? What if minutes did count in this case? That might be the difference for this man between living and dying.

Torn, Alena hesitated. She had always had an affinity with animals and considered them her friends. Due to their isolation, she didn't know much about people, except for what Jeb told her and the few she spoke to that passed by their place. And she'd really rather check on the beautiful bay.

Still, it couldn't hurt to examine the unconscious man first. After all, the horse was still standing. Its wound wasn't life-threatening.

Before she could change her mind, Alena wheeled and knelt beside the still figure. He was lying on his side, so she turned him over onto his back. The man moaned, a haunting sound that gave her pause. She had to figure out where he was bleeding. She started her search at the top. Immediately, she found the large knot on the back of his head, swollen bigger than a good-sized hen's egg. She ran her fingers along his soaked hair and found the cause of the blood, or at least most of it. It was a scalp wound. Those were notorious for bleeding like crazy. Maybe he wasn't hurt as badly as she had first thought.

Alena skimmed her fingers down his neck and across his shoulders. Again, the man's face tightened in pain. She reached into her necessities bag and rooted around for scissors. Finding them, she cut the man's shirt carefully, pulling away large parts of it except for on the right shoulder. That's where he had been hit and the cloth stuck to the wound stubbornly. She rose and took the time to build a good-sized fire and put a kettle on to boil on the right side and a large pot on the left. The stranger wasn't going anywhere. A few minutes one way or the other wouldn't make a difference at this point.

She doubled a cup towel and lifted his head, placing the towel beneath it. That would be better than the hard floor, especially with the knot he had back there. She also collected the remnants of his shirt to toss into the fire. As she started to pitch them onto the flames, something sharp raked against her palm.

Alena opened the material carefully. Against the black cloth was a silver star, catching the light from the fire. It proclaimed the wounded stranger to be a U.S. Marshal. She wondered if outlaws had hurt this man. A chill blanketed her.

What if they tracked him here?

She pushed aside the thought. She had too much to do. An injured man and horse took precedence over worrying. She fed the remainder of his shirt into the fire and stood, uncertain what to do with the badge.

"Better safe than sorry," she told herself, and walked to her flour bin. She jammed the hand holding the star deeply into the flour and released the badge, making certain it was buried from sight. Dusting off her hand, she set about to more important tasks.

Alena went to what Jeb called a hope chest and lifted the lid. She pulled out several quilts and settled on an old one she didn't mind getting stained. She placed it over the unconscious man.

Well, she did after she studied him a moment. She had seen Jeb without his shirt on a few times over the years. Jeb and the stranger seemed put together by a very different Maker. Where Jeb was on the wiry side and had about three gray hairs on his chest, this man looked sculpted from stone. His chest was heavily muscled and matted with dark hair. It looked... almost beautiful. She didn't know a man could be beautiful, but the stranger's broad chest certainly was. That is, if all the blood and mud were cleaned from it.

Alena covered him with the quilt and waited for the kettle to boil. Just before it did, she removed it from the fire and poured water from it into a large bowl. She soaked a few clean rags in the bowl and then chose one to wring out. She placed this over the sticky cloth still on his shoulder for a moment and then worked on edging it around the material. Gradually, it loosened up enough for her to pull it away from his skin. He flinched and his eyelids fluttered for a minute, then he was out again.

Alena carefully cleaned the blood from the area so she could examine it more carefully. Her fingers were small and the bullet hadn't gone in too far. In fact, it had hit the fleshy part between the shoulder and collarbone. Alena retrieved it with little effort.

She applied pressure to stop the bleeding and then cleaned and dressed the wound. She also washed the man's face and swept the warm, wet cloth gently through his hair. The scalp wound began to bleed again so she pressed strong fingers against it and held it some minutes. Finally, she was able to clean that injury, too.

He was still a mess, though. She wiped his head and face and neck. Might as well do the rest. But as Alena touched the rag to his chest, she flinched. The contact was . . . well, she didn't know what it was. It was almost like touching a lightning bug and having it give you a quick buzz back. Only harder. Stronger. More intense.

She ignored the fluttery feeling touching a half-naked man gave her, and decided to set about her business. He was a man, just like millions of men that walked this earth. No different. No more special than the next.

But as she removed the blood and mud from his

torso, she found herself holding her breath. A giddy feeling danced up her arm and into the pit of her stomach. Alena shook her head hard to clear it and continued. Finally, he was cleaned up.

And Lord Almighty, did he clean up nice.

His hair was still damp from the rain and her rag but she'd smoothed it. No longer plastered against his head from the rain, it was thick and dark brown, wavy where hers hung straight. His face looked as chiseled in stone as his chest did. His tanned skin told her he spent a lot of time outdoors.

She wondered what color his eyes were or if he had a nice smile. She was curious about the line of hair that trailed down his flat stomach and disappeared below his pants. The thought intrigued her— and scared her just a little bit.

Alena shrugged. She might as well find out. The stranger's pants were soaking wet from the storm. He needed to get dry and warm. It worried her how clammy and cool his skin was to her touch. She also felt his throat. His pulse was rapid yet weak. She placed her cheek next to his nose. Warm, quick breaths tickled her. Yes, she needed to get him undressed and warm.

She swallowed hard and pulled at one leather boot. It took considerable effort but she was able to remove both. The pants were another matter altogether. They clung to his body like a suckling pig did to its mama's tit. Alena pulled and pushed and grunted and groaned and pulled some more.

Success came at last and with it, a surprising reward. The man was so handsome, so physically perfect, it made her teeth ache. A strange yearning washed over her, a longing for something she didn't know existed and wasn't quite sure what it was about. All she knew was the stranger was absolutely flawless.

And she wanted him. Something primeval sang in her blood, beyond her experience.

She wished to hell she understood what was going on.

The man coughed suddenly, bringing her out of the strange reverie. Lord, she had a naked man lying on her floor, an injured one at that. She needed to do something quick. Anything.

She tossed aside the blood and mud-stained quilt and covered him with a clean one, tucking it under him on one side. She rocked him until he rolled over and she was able to pull the quilt under him. Then dragging it with him on top, she hauled him into her bedroom.

Alena looked from the floor to the bed. She would never be able to get him up there. Instead, she removed the mattress, placing it on the floor, and lifted him onto that. She covered him with her own quilt and folded it about him. She went back to the hope chest and took out two more, returning to place those on top of him, as well.

Finally, she lifted his head and placed her own pillow beneath it. She stepped back to survey her work. His head was the only thing visible. Part of that was covered with the dressing she'd wrapped around it to cover his scalp wound.

He was the sweetest sight she'd ever seen.

Alena idly wondered if a man could ever taste like peppermints.

$\mathcal{A}$nnabelle Reynolds stretched lazily as the morning sun poured across the bed. She and Olivia had traveled in Europe for more than two months, first seeing London and then Paris. They had visited museums and churches, been to the opera and theater, and eaten every dish imaginable. Annabelle had never traveled abroad before this trip. She was enjoying herself immensely.

Italy proved an unexpected delight. Olivia had been all for Rome but Annabelle tired of big cities. She wanted to see the true Italy, not the false front put on for American tourists with money. She insisted they go out into the country. After one day, she knew she had been right.

She threw back the covers and picked up her dressing gown. Throwing it about her, she walked to the open window. Though it was the end of October, the land still looked lush and green. Maybe they would stay another few weeks before returning home.

Yet where was home? Was it Braden's family estate in Pennsylvania? He had inherited Windowmere from his uncle, but it never truly seemed liked theirs. At any given moment, it could be filled with his cousins or friends and their families. Just for once, Annabelle would like to find Windowmere empty of servants and sycophants.

Washington proved no better. As a senator, Braden maintained a residence in the capitol city. She found herself there more often than not. They had no family life since Braden's time there was consumed by political business. Thank God, the war had finally ended. At least it was safe to be out on the streets of Washington once again.

Annabelle brushed away a tear that fell without warning. As always, it was a tear for John. *He* was home. Wherever John was, her heart would always be with her first love. She regretted the doubts she'd had about him. Doubts her father used to drive a wedge between them and push her into Braden's arms. Of course, she went there willingly. Above all, she was a dutiful daughter— and now a dutiful wife. Besides, she had fallen in love with four-year-old Olivia Reynolds, motherless and eager for a woman's love. Annabelle would never regret the decade she had spent with Olivia, nor giving birth to little Johnny.

The door flew open. Olivia ran and bounced upon the bed, abandoning her newfound sophistication. At times, Olivia seemed little older than the child she had been when they first met a decade ago, yet given the proper clothing and hairstyle, she teetered on the cusp of young womanhood. The thought was enough to put gray into Annabelle's golden tresses.

"Don't you adore Italy?" Olivia ran and threw her arms around her stepmother.

Annabelle smiled. "I know I love the smell of the outdoors and the feel of the sun on my face. And I slept well."

35

"So did I," Olivia proclaimed. She released Annabelle and stepped to the window. "I think we should breakfast on the terrace and stay in our nightclothes until noon."

Annabelle grinned. "That is a marvelous idea. Come, let's tell... who was the housekeeper? I can't for the life of me recall her name."

Olivia took her hand. "That's because you're nearly thirty, Annabelle. Frightfully old. Old people forget things."

"Such as you wanting a pair of fine Italian leather boots?"

Olivia gasped. "Surely, you wouldn't forget that? I've only pestered you about them since Monday."

Annabelle linked her arm through Olivia's as they crossed the room. "If you help me remember the housekeeper's name, it might jog my memory about other things, dear." Annabelle said this in a high-pitched voice, thin and wavery as her own grandmother's had been.

Olivia laughed in delight. "Signora Mosseli." She paused before adding, "And I'd like the boots in black and another pair in brown leather. A rich mahogany if we can find it." She batted her lashes coquettishly.

"I'm sure we will be able to find both," she reassured her stepdaughter. "Let's go find Signora Mosseli. I am famished."

They located the housekeeper. Though the woman's English was limited, Annabelle thought she made it clear that they wished to eat now and would like the meal served outside. If these Italians thought them decadent Americans for breakfasting in their nightdresses and robes on the verandah, so be it. Annabelle was relieved to have left behind the constraints of the social scene in London and Paris for a quiet sojourn in the Italian countryside.

Pietro, the house boy, brought them coffee and rolls first. The coffee was a rich blend, with an aroma that caused her knees to go weak. Though a senator's wife, even good coffee had been hard to obtain as the war progressed from months to years. Annabelle never took a sip of the brew without remembering those hard times. She knew they had been harder for John, though. Far worse for a man serving his country, rising from a private to colonel in the long fight.

Why were thoughts of John interrupting her holiday? She could go for days and not think of him. Then she'd hear a song. Smell a flower. See a stranger on the street that would cock his head just so, and memories flooded her, making Annabelle wish things had turned out differently.

She didn't hate her life. Far from it. She'd married into the lap of luxury, had a husband and two wonderful children, and was active in charitable organizations. Her life was on an even keel. Yet, every day the sameness invaded her soul, the predictability of one day much like the day before and the one to follow. The years stretched ahead in this unending fashion.

It scared the hell out of her.

Would things have been any different if she'd kept her promise and married John? As children, each day had seemed an adventure. They grew up next door to one other and had been best friends almost from the cradle. John was smart and fun to be around. One day, he might play tea party with her, and the next, they would stalk the woods. They would swim at the watering hole and play checkers. Read aloud and act out what they had read. Ice skating, sledding, long walks—every day seemed a new quest.

Annabelle realized it wouldn't have remained that way. John would have gone to work in his father's bank. She would have remained at home with their children. Her life would more than likely be very much as it was today.

But would the nights have been different?

"Aren't you going to eat, Annabelle?"

She had been unaware that breakfast had arrived. She buttered a roll and idly listened as Olivia chatted about what they would be do over the next few days.

"Signora Reynolds?" Pietro hovered, his manner hesitant.

"Yes, Pietro?"

"There... there is man to see you. He say it... urbent."

"Urgent?" Annabelle prompted.

Pietro nodded. "*Si*. Urgent." He looked at them. "Should he wait inside, Signora?"

Annabelle decided their attire didn't matter. If the news was urgent, it could be about Johnny. She said a quick prayer, hoping her son was safe.

"No, send him out here, Pietro. *Grazi*."

Olivia's eyes widened. "Annabelle, we are quite indecent!"

"You have a nightdress that is buttoned to the throat and a robe atop it. Let us hear the message without dramatics, Olivia."

She saw the quick look pass over the girl's face. She didn't mean to sound harsh, but sometimes Olivia was too concerned about appearances.

"You may wish to be seen this way, but I don't!" Olivia threw her napkin onto the table and retreated into the house.

Annabelle sighed. Olivia had definitely hit a certain stage. Sweet and childlike one minute, full of theatrics and wild emotions the next. It was just as well that she was gone, not knowing what news this messenger brought.

A man stepped onto the terrace and cleared his throat. He was no errand boy, being in his late forties. And American. Annabelle tensed but ever the politician's wife, she indicated the chair opposite her that Olivia had vacated.

"Please have a seat, sir. Would you care for coffee?"

The man stepped forward and took the offered chair. "No coffee. Henry Smith is the name, Mrs. Reynolds." If he questioned speaking to a senator's wife while she dined in her nightclothes, his face didn't indicate it.

"What brings you here, Mr. Smith? Pietro said your message was urgent. I assume it concerns my husband or son." It surprised her how calm she sounded.

"Actually both, ma'am. There's no easy way to say this so I'll tell you straightforward."

Annabelle nodded, containing the inkling of fear his words brought. "That's always best, Mr. Smith."

"Yes, ma'am." He took a deep breath. "I am with the State Department, Mrs. Reynolds. The government has been trying to track you down."

Relief washed through Annabelle. Braden chose the oddest things to worry over.

"We weren't on any special itinerary. I've simply cabled Senator Reynolds our whereabouts as we've gone. We only arrived here last night, which is why I haven't sent him a message yet. I'm sorry if my being out of touch with the senator has inconvenienced you in any manner."

Mr. Smith remained stone-faced. "No, ma'am. What I need to say is... well, this is difficult."

The chill returned. The news must be very bad if a seasoned diplomat had trouble verbalizing it. "Then say it, Mr. Smith. The sooner, the better." Annabelle steeled herself for whatever would come.

The envoy nodded. "Your husband and son were taken off a train in California over a week ago. They've been kidnapped, Mrs. Reynolds. If you don't cable your husband's man of business to pay the ransom in a timely fashion, they will kill them."

CHAPTER 5

*A*lena gathered her shawl about her and slipped the basket over one arm and picked up the lantern. She braced herself against the wind and rain as she stepped from the cabin.

The horse waited for her, as still as stone. She cocked her head, as if questioning how her master fared.

"I don't know," she mumbled, and took the reins to guide the horse back to the barn. She followed Alena docilely.

Once inside, the horse seemed to take over. She walked to a place in the corner and actually lay down upon a bed of straw, her wounded flank facing up. Alena shouldn't be amazed. Having more experience with animals than people, she knew how well they could communicate. She rarely used words herself, preferring to let her hands do the talking for her, both through her art and her healing.

She located the bullet, thankful it was shallow, and removed it with little difficulty. Alena cleaned the wound, all the while stroking the horse reassuringly. The horse, her ears pricked up, seemed to understand she knew exactly what she was doing. She never flinched, holding more still than the pond on a calm summer's day.

Alena fetched a bucket of clear water and oats and placed it near the horse. She blinked rapidly several times, as if offering thanks. She thought she should place the animal in a stall, but she seemed to be comfortable where she was. Alena shrugged, happy the horse would be fine.

She walked back to the house as dawn broke. The rain had turned into a fine mist, tickling her eyelashes as she made her way back to the cabin. The wind had died down. Maybe that was an omen. Maybe the man would make it. She knew his horse would.

The mess on the floor welcomed her return. Thankful she had put the large pot on to boil, she got to work cleaning up the blood with old rags before splashing water on the floor and scrubbing it thoroughly. It took water, elbow grease, and some of Jeb's special concoction to get the wood planks right again. Still, the pine scent rose, comforting her. Pine evoked memories of Jeb. With the smell filling the cabin, it seemed Jeb was already home.

Alena tossed the last of the rags into the pot and added the remaining water from a nearby bucket. It didn't matter if the bloodstains came out. The cloths were old, but she didn't like to be wasteful. She washed her hands and wiped the sweat from her brow. The man and his horse were clean. She might as well look after herself and rinse the night's work from her body and clothes.

Still, she hesitated. She would look in on the man before her bath. It would only take a moment. Just to see if he was resting all right. She wouldn't have to stay.

But she did. Alena hovered in the doorway, staring at him. His chest rose more evenly now, not in the quick, shallow breaths he had forced in and out before. That brought her some relief. She crossed the room and touched his forehead. A little warm, but then fever was to be expected with a bullet wound. It could be a lot worse.

Alena reassured herself the man could be left alone for a spell and went to draw some well water for her bath. She was chilled from the rain and about as bloody as the man had been. It was a good thing they didn't have company drop by on a regular basis. She would frighten them to death.

In an hour, she was clean from head to toe, her hair smelling of jasmine. That was one of the treats Jeb allowed her. That and the peppermints for her sweet tooth. Lord, she was aching to suck on a peppermint after all she had been through. She went to the jar they were kept in and fished out the largest one left. She deserved it after all she had accomplished in the last several hours. Her eyes hovered over the jar, wishing she could eat two, but she counted only four remaining. Not knowing when Jeb would return with more, she'd have to make them last.

She wrung out the rags she'd used and her pants and shirts and hung them in a corner to dry, along with the man's pants. It might have stopped raining for now, but she didn't want to take a chance on having a thunderstorm soak the clothes again.

Some travelers who stopped by for a cool drink or directions gave her odd looks when they saw her attire. She vaguely remembered wearing dresses a long time ago. Pretty frocks that Mama sewed. Although Alena sewed as well as her mother, she had gradually turned away from such feminine things and begun to wear a shirt and pants like Jeb. He hadn't said a word about it, and so she had continued all these years.

Every now and then, she'd slip on a dress of

Mama's. Jeb saved a few things from the old days. The bottom of the hope chest contained three of Mama's dresses. A Spanish comb and mantilla, too. Alena would try these on at times when Jeb was gone, stealing a glimpse in the tiny mirror that fit into the palm of her hand. The clothes were tight, though. She didn't know how Mama had breathed in them. Give her a pair of britches any day over an uncomfortable dress.

A moan interrupted her thoughts. Alena hurried into the small bedroom and placed a palm on the man's warm cheek. That lightning bug buzzed at her again. It made not only her hand tingle but her stomach, too. She removed her hand from the man's face and rubbed it against her belly, trying to still the funny beating in there.

Then her ears pricked up. She heard horses. Alena went to the front room and looked out the window. Three riders approached in the distance. Rough-looking. The kind Jeb was courteous to, but at the same time, ones he didn't make much small talk with, hoping they'd soon be on their way.

A rush of fear swept through Alena. They were here for the man. She didn't know anything about the stranger, but once all the blood and mud had been removed and he slept, there was a quiet dignity about him. He wasn't like these men.

These men would be a danger to him.

She had maybe two minutes at most. It was time enough but she would have to move fast. She picked up the rickety chair, the one missing two slats. It was left that way on purpose to discourage anyone from sitting in it. She set it aside and lifted the rug that had been beneath it, revealing the trap door.

Alena opened it and set the latch. She ran to the other room and grabbed the mattress. She yanked hard on it, dragging it into the front room until she'd reached the trap door. She leaned in and pushed aside the bags. The space was a little under two feet deep, but it was close to seven in length.

She picked up the blanket over the man and threw it into the hole. No time to smooth it out properly, but at least it would keep some of the dirt off him. She didn't want dirt in the wounds she'd taken so long to clean.

Taking a deep breath, she grabbed the man's ankles and pulled him as close as she dared before she rolled him over. He fell with a thud into the space, landing on his side. She leaned down and twisted him around until he was mostly on his back. She couldn't risk any further time. She already heard the trio ride into the clearing. Their voices were muffled but they would knock any second.

She closed the trap door, praying the man hadn't been further injured by the short drop and praying even harder he wouldn't regain consciousness in the next few minutes. She slid the rug back to conceal the door as she heard boots step along the porch. As she lifted the chair back into place, a heavy hand struck the door.

"Open up in thar, ya hear? Open up now!"

Alena's heart hammered wildly as she hauled the mattress into the other room. No time to lift it back onto the bed frame. She closed the door, hoping she wouldn't need to think of a reason as to why it lay on the floor.

She tiptoed to the doorway and took a cleansing breath before she reached down and picked up the shotgun leaning against the wall. She flung open the door, her gun's barrel leveled at the knocker's chest. She cocked it and looked into the meanest eyes she'd ever seen. They were small and black, like a weasel's,

45

except they had none of an animal's goodness in them. This man lived hard and wouldn't hesitate to shoot.

"Hey, pretty lady."

Alena thought he remained remarkably poised, which worried her even more. If he had broken into a sweat or stammered his greeting, she would have been more comfortable. No, he stood there looking as cool as a spring breeze, not rattled in the least by having a shotgun pointed two inches from his heart.

It troubled her even more that he immediately recognized she was female. Many times, passersby mistook her for a young boy, due to her clothing. Alena realized quickly that her hair hung loosely around her face, though. She usually tied it back or sometimes even hid it under one of Jeb's old hats. She had left it down to dry after her bath. Now it left her feeling vulnerable. She clutched the gun and her resolve more firmly.

"Sorry if'n we scared ya." He took a step back so there was a little distance between them. Alena didn't take her gaze off him. He narrowed his eyes, studying her.

She remained silent. She had chattered like a magpie as a child. She could still remember making up stories and telling them to Mama, talking to the animals in the woods, sharing things that had happened to her while Jeb fished. As she'd grown older, and especially after Mama went to heaven, she grew quieter. Jeb, too, was a man of few words. After living with him for so many years, she found she rarely needed to speak. They knew each other well and could anticipate what the other thought.

Silence could be a powerful tool. Alena put that lesson to use now. She continued to watch the stranger as carefully as he did her. Finally, he stepped back a few feet.

"Can you understand me?"

He thought she was mute. Or stupid. He wouldn't be the first to make that mistake. She nodded her head and lowered the gun a bit. He didn't seem threatening at the moment. She knew it was because he wanted information from her.

"Good." He removed his hat and scratched his head. "My boys and I are looking for a man. Tall. Riding a big bay horse. You seen anyone like that 'round about here?"

She was about to deny seeing the man when one of the riders hollered out, "The horse is in here, Cletus."

Alena looked past the leader, whom she supposed was Cletus, and saw a short, barrel-chested man walking their way, gesturing at the barn.

She spoke before Cletus could. "I found the bay this morning, wailing like a lost child. Shot in the flank." She frowned. "Haven't seen any man, though." She wrinkled her brow for effect. "Thought it was kinda funny."

He took the bait. "What was funny?"

"That so nice a horse was running around without a rider." She shrugged. "That is, until I saw the bullet wound. I figured the rider got hit, too, and the horse threw him. Horses get spooked, you know. They don't like a dead man on 'em. Maybe it's the smell."

Cletus started to speak but she interrupted him, her tone angry. "Don't go telling me you're gonna take that horse. I found it and nursed it. We could use another horse 'round here."

Alena tapped her foot impatiently. Her gun was still in front of her, the barrel pointing slightly down. She could raise it and blast Cletus before he could make any move.

"Ya don't have to give up the horse. We ain't interested in it." He paused. "Could we come in a spell and have a cup of water? We been riding a long way."

Alena knew this moment would come. Cletus still didn't know whether or not to believe her about the man. Her talk about horses easily spooking had created doubt in his mind, but he was wily enough to want to follow through.

"Fine. Wipe your boots good, though. Jeb done tracked in a bunch of mud this morning. I spent a good hour cleaning my floor at the crack of dawn." She stopped as the other two men stepped onto the porch. "I don't like people messing with my floor."

Alena stepped back a foot, standing beside the door in order to let the others pass, not wanting to turn her back on the men. She left the door open. Jeb hadn't raised any fool.

The three men filled the space of the front room. One went and stood by the fire, warming his back. All of them looked around, seeing if there was any sign of the man.

"So tell me, gentlemen. Are you the law?"

Alena knew they were probably the furthest thing from the law, but she needed information from them. The other two puffed up like they were proud for being mistaken as lawmen.

Cletus, however, looked wary. "Why'd you say that?"

She shrugged. "I got a shot-up horse. You're looking for her rider. I assume he's wanted and you're the search party sent to find him." She looked Cletus up and down. "I'd say you were the one that probably wounded him. You look like you might know your way around a gun."

Even Cletus had his weak point. A smug look filled his face with her compliment. He bent closer to her. "I am the man that wounded him, ma'am. He's a vicious outlaw. Passes himself off as a sheriff. We're on special assignment. Gotta bring him in for questioning."

Alena's eyes went wide. "Questioning? My, that

sounds serious." She pursed her lips as if in thought and then asked, "Bank robbery?"

Cletus nodded. "That. And murder."

Alena went cold inside. Cletus' little black eyes did a funny dance. A sense of familiarity washed over her. She didn't see why. She would swear she never saw him before but she wanted him out. Now.

"Well, what are you waiting for? A murderer's on the loose, and you're taking time to shoot the breeze? Shame on you."

Alena did her best schoolmarm imitation. Not that she knew what a schoolmarm looked like, but she'd read a few books about them. They were all little and old and always disappointed in everyone. She did her best to look displeased with the trio in front of her.

They all had the decency to look ashamed. "Sorry to take up your time, ma'am. But be on the lookout for a wounded stranger. He's shot once. Maybe twice."

She shuddered. "I will, and I'll tell my Jeb to watch for him, too, soon's he gets back from getting cleaned up at the pond." She hoped that was explanation enough for Jeb's absence, especially since she had already ranted about her muddied-up floor.

They nodded their goodbyes. Alena went out on the porch and watched them ride away, shotgun still in hand. As they finally left her sight, she slid weakly down the post she was leaning against.

Lord, but play-acting was hard work! She'd used up enough talk to last a good three months. She thanked her lucky stars that Mama had loved to read, and hoarded books like Alena did her peppermints. She had spent many a lazy afternoon by the lake reading, stepping into other people's lives when reading those books. She hoped she had come off as natural.

She stood, a little shakily, and watched the horizon. She would wait another ten minutes or so before she

ALEXA ASTON

checked on the man. She didn't trust that Cletus one
bit. It would be just like his type to ride back and check
up on her. In the meantime, she would go see about the
horse.

And try not to think about the man.

Or was he a murderer after all?

CHAPTER 6

*H*is head must have exploded. That was the only thing he could think of. Loose pieces of it must be scattered about him. If the intense throbbing stopped, he might try to put himself back together.

Cramped. The smell of earth. Pitch black. He tried to lift his head. Searing pain shot through it. He muzzled the cry that formed on his parched lips. Instinct told him to keep quiet until he knew where he was and who else was nearby. To distract himself, he bit his tongue. Usually, saliva flooded his mouth. Not this time. He could barely swallow.

He was lying down. That much he knew. His shoulder burned. He reached up and touched it, only to find it had been dressed. In a far-off place in his mind, he heard gunshots. Maybe he'd been wounded. At any rate, someone had found him. He ran his fingers across the dressing and then up to his pounding head. It was swathed in something soft and tender to his touch.

His heart began to race at the jumbled images that came to him. A boy, scared. Hooves beating. More shots.

What had happened?

51

And then a paralyzing thought hit him.

He didn't know his own name.

Fear washed over him like a hard rain. He had known fear before. Somehow, he knew that. Again, images passed by. Yelling. Men running. Screams...

He had to get out from wherever he was confined. It would all make sense then. He had to get out.

He reached and felt the walls of earth next to him. A crumpled, rough blanket underneath him. Then it hit him. He had nothing on, not a stitch.

What in tarnation was going on?

He tried to raise his hands. Something stopped him.

Wood. Smooth. Maybe this was the way out. He fought the panic that he'd been buried alive. No, he wasn't dead. Not yet, anyway. He would just push on the wood until it gave way. Or holler. Surely whoever dressed his wounds had taken care to do a good job. Maybe they were still around.

Yet a sixth sense whispered in his ear. Listen. He couldn't see in the blackness of whatever hole he'd been placed. Had no matches in his pocket to strike because he didn't have any pockets. So he waited.

Voices. From a distance? He couldn't tell. He strained to make out what they said but they were too far away. He knew better than to lift his head. Not much room to try and sit up. And with the way his head pained him right now, he was better off lying there peacefully.

Think.

But thinking made his head hurt. Even his eyes ached. Was that from trying to see in the dark? He ran his tongue over cracked lips. What he wouldn't give for a sip of cool water.

Noise. Quiet. Listen. Footsteps. Above him. His hands immediately went for his guns but only grazed naked hips. His reaction was fast. Was he a lawman—

or a gunslinger? He realized in that moment, he might be either.

It was the loneliest feeling in the world.

More walking. There were three. No four. Three men. A heavier tread. That meant the other had to be a woman. Was she the one who'd helped him? Hidden him? And was she hiding him from these men? Why?

Muffled voices continued. They were close to him now. One man spoke. Low tones followed. The man must be having a conversation with the woman. He wondered what they were saying, if they were talking about him.

The ache in his head made deciphering their words impossible. They could be speaking Pig Latin, for all he knew. Nothing seemed to make sense.

And he was tired. He'd never been this tired before. He would rest his eyes just for a minute. Then he would be able to think and remember.

That thought comforted him.

HE HEARD A ROCKER SQUEAKING. The constant rhythm soothed him. He still had a queasy stomach and was a little woozy. It was like he'd had too much to drink or been in a fight the night before. Maybe both. He reached up and touched the smooth wood again. It was the way out but he was exhausted and weary beyond comprehension.

His hands grazed against his head again. It hurt. He lowered his hands to his sides. He was hot, so hot. His shoulder burned. A vague nagging bothered him. Something about the shoulder.

Shot.

That was it. He'd been shot. He heard the sound of a

gunshot, several in a row. Saw a hill. A horse. A boy's face. The boy was in pain.

He had to help that boy.

Maybe if he had something to drink.

He slept.

~

HE HEARD MUSIC, a low, sweet sound. He smiled. The angels had come to take him. He hoped heaven was cool. His body ached and burned. He longed for release.

Fresh air. He breathed deeply. Something silky brushed his shoulder. Mingled with pine was the faint scent of jasmine. Like his mother wore. Was his mother in heaven, too? He couldn't remember what she looked like. Only the smell brought a warmth to his mind. It brought him peace, washing him with relief. He would be safe now. The angels would protect him. They would take his pain away.

He distinctly heard more humming. The tune was wistful. The silky feel brushed over his chest and neck. He smiled. It only hurt a little to smile. Hands touched him, light and delicate. Wait. They weren't soft. Calluses. He was confused. Angels didn't have calluses, did they?

Pain consumed him. He was being lifted. Someone there. He cried out. The sound surprised him. The cry was as weak as a newborn. Had it come from him? He thought of himself as strong, hardy. He could do anything. What was wrong?

Flat again. Relief. He breathed heavily. Softer this time. On a mattress. The humming began again. He didn't trust it this time.

"Hot," he croaked out. Maybe he was in hell. Yes,

that was it. He'd done wrong and would now suffer for it.

"Shh…"

Hands touched him again, brushing away… what? A blanket covered him. A pillow slipped beneath his head. A wet cloth brushed across his forehead. His cheeks. Across his lips. His tongue reached out to meet it. He was so thirsty.

Read his mind. His head lifted. A cup touched his mouth. He reached a hand up, only to have it fall away. Must trust. He sipped. Water. Cold. Heaven.

"Slower."

The humming had stopped. He shook his head. "No." Frowned.

"Yes." A woman's voice. Low but kind. It held authority. He respected authority.

He drank again. Not as fast. Still good. He sighed.

"Better," the voice told him.

Eased him back down. Cool rag on his face again. He gave over to the comfort it brought.

He slept.

THE ROCKER AGAIN. The constant rhythm comforted him. He wasn't hot anymore. A dull throb had replaced the burning pain in his head. His shoulder was still stiff, but he somehow knew that would fade with time

His thoughts flowed better. Things weren't so jumbled. He took a deep breath and let it fill his lungs before exhaling slowly.

The rocking stopped. Footsteps approached. A woman, from her movements. He didn't hear the swish of petticoats but her step was light. The subtle scent of jasmine was still present. That, he remembered from before.

He realized the torment earlier had been her lifting him from the hidden space. He still didn't know why she'd placed him there but he knew the answers would come soon.

Her hand rested lightly upon his brow. She made a murmuring noise to show her pleasure. His fever must have broken since the last time he was awake. That would account for the soreness in his joints and the smell of sweat that surrounded him, not to mention the awful heat no longer radiated from him. He fought to open his eyes. To see the woman. To thank her.

Neither his eyes nor his mouth cooperated. His lids flickered a few times, but it cost too much effort to keep them open. Lord, he'd never been so tired. He tried to swallow and squeak out a word or two, but he was drier than Arizona in August. He sighed, a weak whoosh of air escaping.

She lifted his head again. This time, he trusted her. The cup brushed against his lower lip. He drank, slowly as she'd asked before. The liquid ran down his throat. He basked in its smooth coolness.

His stomach gurgled. He didn't know the last time he'd eaten. Maybe she would fix him something. Food would be so good.

She lowered his head again. He sensed her moving away. He lay there, content to know she would care for him.

The feeling was short-lived. As he heard familiar sounds and smelled coffee brewing, his spirits sank. He still didn't know who he was. Where he was. Or worse, who'd shot him and why. Uncertainty plagued him. If he had an enemy, he needed to be on guard. He wanted desperately to remember. If not, no one could be trusted.

Not even the woman who helped him.

He lay still, willing his memory to come back, yet he realized he couldn't force it to happen.

She came again. He sensed her presence and smelled the biscuits. He liked biscuits. With honey or butter, but especially swimming in gravy. Funny, he could remember his preference in biscuits and not his own name.

She came close and brushed a lock of hair from his forehead. Her touch brought a sense of calm. He would remember. If not today, then tomorrow. Things would be all right.

"You need to eat. The fever has passed, but you must gain your strength back. You lost some blood."

She sat him up. The blanket covering him fell to his waist. Cool air tickled his skin. His eyes flew open in a panic. He was naked in a strange woman's presence.

But where was she? It was as if he still lay in that hole in the ground. Darkness surrounded him. He blinked rapidly several times, willing it to lift. Nothing. He rubbed his eyes roughly, his heart racing, his mouth dry.

Nothing. Only darkness stole about him, enfolding him.

A sob escaped. Shame filled him.

He looked in the direction the jasmine came from.

"I'm blind."

CHAPTER 7

Blind?

Had she heard him correctly? How could a lawman— or even an outlaw— be blind? Cletus' words had bothered her more than she cared to admit. Ever since the trio left yesterday morning, Alena thought about whether or not the man she had aided was in fact a criminal, one only pretending to serve the public.

Yet Cletus and his gang of two looked far more disreputable than her mystery man. He had a firm jaw and a noble profile, much like the heroes in her books. She should know. She had studied him enough since he'd arrived. And she'd examined more than his face. Just the thought of his muscled torso brought heat to her cheeks. The man seemed perfect in every way. He couldn't be a common thief. Or murderer.

Alena looked at him carefully. His eyes were wide open, yet a haunted look filled them. Uncertainty rippled through his posture, even in the way he now held his head. He was a proud man, she'd bet. Confident and in control.

Until now.

His jaw trembled. A single sob escaped his lips,

still parched from his illness, but now he pressed them firmly together. He looked like a lamb lost from its mother. Alena hesitated to speak. She wanted to touch him, comfort him, but she didn't know how. She doubted anything she would say could soothe him.

So she waited.

Minutes passed. She barely breathed, afraid even the smallest sound would distress him. The panic that had flooded his face gradually receded. The terror that filled his vacant eyes slowly dissipated. His handsome face relaxed.

Alena watched this subtle transformation with admiration. It would take someone of great courage to assess such a dismal situation and become as determined as this man. She could read his resolve as easily as reading a well-loved book. His eyes stilled as if focused on a long-range target. He sat a bit taller, though he gripped the sides of the mattress between whitened knuckles. He swallowed once and breathed deeply, and then cocked his head slightly, listening to the sounds about him.

"I know I'm injured," he began slowly.

Alena nodded before realizing he couldn't see her gesture.

"Yes," she said quietly. "Your horse brought you here."

A frown crossed his features. He squeezed his eyes closed. His grip on the mattress tightened. She didn't know what to make of it, so she continued.

"You've been shot in the shoulder. Another bullet grazed your scalp, enough to make it bleed quite a bit."

"Head wounds can bleed like the devil," he interjected.

The information he offered startled both of them. He got a look on his face that Alena couldn't describe.

She wondered just how many head wounds he'd had. Or given.

"I was able to fish the bullet from your shoulder. You were lucky it didn't hit bone. You'll soon be on the mend."

He reached up to touch the dressing wrapped around his head. She placed her hands over his and lowered them. A warm rush caused her to let go quickly.

"When I clean your head wound today, I'll probably be able to leave off the bandage. Fresh air'll do it some good."

The man nodded. He sat silently, so still that it unnerved her.

"Your horse was shot, too," she blurted out.

He scrunched up his face as if trying to remember what happened to cause his horse to be shot.

"She's fine, though," she added. "She's very smart."

"She is."

The two words hung in the air. Alena wasn't sure if they had been a question or if the stranger agreed with her. He wasn't volunteering much, but then again, she needed to be patient. He was like any bird or hurt animal she'd cared for over the years. Patience healed as much as her hands did.

The man reached out and found one of her hands. It was dwarfed in his. His touch gave Alena a pleasant feeling.

"Thank you. For helping me. And my horse."

She thought she better pull her hand away. It didn't seem proper holding a naked stranger's hand, especially when she didn't even know his name.

She slipped her hand from his grasp and patted it once. "It wasn't anything I wouldn't do for anyone else. So, who shot you?"

"I don't know." The flat tone scared her. It controlled a deeply-hidden rage. She knew about that. Even all these years later, she remembered when her daddy became angry. This man sounded the same way. Instinctively, Alena drew away from him.

"Don't go." His tone softened. Not really pleading, but not frightening as it had been moments ago.

"I... you probably need to eat now. I'm sure you're hungry. I'm sorry the biscuits got cold." She hesitated. "And... I'll get you some clothes."

She blushed as he self-consciously tugged on the blanket.

"I'm sorry. I had to cut your shirt away to work on your shoulder. I took your trousers, too. They were soaked by the rain and the blood. I'll get them for you now. They're clean. A shirt of Jeb's, too. I thought it better to leave you be while you sweated off the fever."

Alena reached up and touched his forehead with the back of her hand. "It's gone now. You mend fast, that's for sure."

"Maureen always said that."

"Who's Maureen?"

The man frowned. "My... my nanny." His words brought a smile to his face. "My Irish nanny. She used to tell me the most wonderful stories. Kept me in line, too. I was a bit of a hellion in my youth."

She smiled, picturing him as a tall boy, full of mischief. She knew, too, what a nanny was. Thank goodness she read as much as she did, else she'd be thought eternally foolish in the eyes of others.

"Who's Jeb?"

The question startled her. How did she explain who Jeb was?

"He's... my husband. He's away on a trading trip now. He'll be back any day, though." Alena stood. "I'll fetch your pants now and a shirt of Jeb's. It won't fit properly, but it'll help cover you."

She backed away a few feet. "Your food is to your right. I'll be back." She walked from the room, a thousand thoughts raging through her.

~

HE LISTENED TO HER LEAVE, her light steps moving away from him and from the room. He tried to hear what she was doing in the other room but this was all so new to him.

He put out a hand to search for the plate of food she'd brought. He touched a biscuit and continued to search until he'd located the plate on which it rested. Carefully, he raised it in both hands.

Something fell. His fingers skimmed the floor next to him, for the mattress on which he sat must rest directly on the floor. He found a fork. Holding the plate on his lap in his left hand, he moved the fork around. Feeling sure he'd located eggs, he pushed a bite onto the fork and lifted the fork to his mouth.

"Ouch!"

That was the side where the bullet hit his shoulder. Gingerly, he switched his grip on the plate and moved the fork to his left hand. It was awkward but he managed to eat the eggs. The biscuits were easy. He could pick them up. And they were buttery. He sighed as he chewed, content to live in the moment. His worries would still be there two minutes from now. A man needed to enjoy his biscuits in peace.

His mind wandered, though. He was proud that he'd remembered Maureen. He had a vision of a stout Irishwoman with a fluff of dark red hair, and a tongue sharp as a knife. He had suffered a few tongue-lashings in his time from her. He was grateful now that at least one memory stuck in his head.

A vague impression of his mother rose again. It was

as if she were a shadow. His father, too. He couldn't conjure faces or names but he knew the shadows. Their outline. Their profiles.

By God, he would remember them.

Then there was the woman. She had lied about Jeb, whoever he was. He'd heard it in the little catch in her voice. He knew people. He could read their body language as well as their words. That talent had served him well in the past. He was certain.

So why did she lie? He tried to look at it from her perspective. Here was a wounded, nameless stranger who had arrived from nowhere. She had taken good care of him. He had a hazy impression that she'd protected him somehow. A memory of men's voices came to him, floating as light as air. They'd been a threat. She'd removed that threat.

But she knew nothing about him. No wonder she didn't want to share too much. He couldn't blame her.

He pushed the remainder of the last biscuit around his plate, soaking up the yolk. So he knew three things. He'd had an Irish nanny. A nanny meant that his family was fairly well-to-do. He liked buttered biscuits. He had a smart horse.

And he still hadn't a clue who he was.

A knock interrupted his thoughts.

"I have your clothes."

She walked across the room. He still didn't hear any petticoats. She might be one of those frontier women that didn't bother with them unless she went to town. Life in California was too hard and chores too difficult to be a slave to fashion, he supposed.

"California!"

He sensed her puzzlement at his sudden outcry, so he rushed to explain. "I'm a little fuzzy on a few things. I'm not sure exactly who shot me. I just remembered that I was in California."

She sat the clothes on top of the blanket. "You do have a nasty lump on the back of your head."

He brought his fingers up and gently searched for it. He found it immediately through the bulk of cloth wound around his head. That was the source of some of his problems.

"The lump probably caused the gaps in my memory. I must've been knocked unconscious. Head injuries can play havoc."

He located the shirt's sleeve and slipped into it as he spoke. "That may be why my sight's gone missing. I know I could see before this happened. I feel it in my gut."

He tried to bring the sides of the shirt together so as to button them. A gap of about three inches made that impossible.

"I figured you were bigger than Jeb. At least it's something to cover you for now." He heard her shift, a foot scrapping back and forth. "I'll leave you to get your trousers on. At least they'll fit you. Let me check your head wound before I go, though. I've brought some warm water to clean it again."

His heart skipped a beat as she drew near. He inhaled her scent. A silky feeling brushed his exposed wrist. Jeb had shorter arms than he did. It hit him that it was her hair. It must be long. He wondered why she kept it unbound.

She unraveled the material about his head and cleaned the injury. It was tender, but her touch was gentle.

"I believe we can leave that off. I should look at your shoulder again. I'm sorry I didn't think to do that before you slipped into the shirt."

He began trying to shimmy out of it but sucked in a quick breath. She placed a light hand on his forearm.

"You're still hurting. Let me help."

He held still while she maneuvered him out of the shirt and examined his shoulder. She redressed it and helped him back into the shirt. Despite his curiosity about her, where he was, how he'd lost his sight, he yawned.

"You should be tired. This was a lot to do."

He felt the weight of the trousers lifted from his lap. "Stretch out and let me cover you with the blanket. Get some rest, and then we'll see about getting those pants on you later."

He lay back as she pulled the blanket up onto his chest and gave it a quick pat.

"There. Go to sleep now. We'll talk some more when you've rested."

She left the room, this time closing a door. Though his body was weary, his mind raced. Something his unseen nurse had done or said caused an image of a woman to come to his mind. Actually, she was on the cusp between girlhood and becoming a woman. Maybe seventeen or eighteen. Delicate features. Golden blonde tresses. A face reflecting kindness that transcended words. He had strong feelings for her. Was she his sweetheart? His wife? And where was she?

He fought the panic that threatened to well up again. The confusion that roared throughout him in those first few moments when he realized he was sightless. He slowed his breathing, something he knew would dissolve the terror. All thoughts focused on this. Breathe in. Breathe out. In. Out. He'd think of the woman later. When he was stronger.

Exhausted, he slept.

CHAPTER 8

*B*raden Reynolds feigned sleep in order to listen for any information that Dingus Doolittle brought. The train robber arrived mid-afternoon and collapsed, snoring within seconds of his head touching the lumpy pillow. The others knew well enough to leave Dapper Dingus alone until he awoke. Braden observed any time Dingus rode out from the gang's hideout how gingerly the gang treaded when their boss returned.

He'd stirred a few minutes ago. Braden knew Dingus would be up and calling for food soon. He carefully opened his eye a slit and saw Dingus stretching. He'd learned quickly that Dingus ran the gang, whether present or not. That fool Cletus acted as shepherd to this unholy flock in Doolittle's absence, but he hadn't the brains or leadership to keep the men together for any length of time. It took Dingus Doolittle to do so on an irregular basis.

If Braden met Dingus in another time and place, he would assume the man was well-bred and thoroughly educated. The outlaw was meticulous in manner and dress, albeit his wardrobe was of a western variety.

Braden wondered how such a man had fallen in with a group of thieves and kidnappers.

Dingus sat up and scanned the room. Braden closed his eyes until he heard the squeak of the mattress and felt the slight breeze of the other man walk by. As predicted, Dingus complained of hunger. Within minutes, he sat with an audience about him, spooning in something between chili and stew, dipping biscuits in it. Braden hadn't quite figured out what the mixture was, but it was practically the only thing the gang knew how to produce, so it had been the staple of their diet since they'd been taken. He could eat anything, but Johnny's gimpy stomach gave him a hard time with the blend. It caused his bowels to move frequently. Oftentimes, the gang let the boy foul his pants. After unmerciful teasing, Johnny would be led outside to clean up and wash out his pants. Each time his son returned from such humiliation, Braden saw the boy retreat further from reality. On the rare occasions he spoke, Johnny succumbed more deeply into the stutter that had plagued him since he'd begun to speak.

Braden had never been so helpless in his life, being at the mercy of the Marker brothers. The interminable waiting caused his mind to be on the verge of snapping.

He knew what the delay was. He'd dreaded it from the moment he realized they were being taken, for he knew their disappearance would result in a ransom note.

And there was absolutely nothing left to pay it.

No money would mean certain death. These men held life in contempt. It would mean nothing to them to strike down a middle-aged man and his sickly boy. They would probably take pleasure in the act, leaving their bodies for the vultures. Braden wasn't much for prayer, but if anyone was listening, he asked that it happen quickly.

He was afraid the opposite would occur.

He deserved it— but his son didn't. He glanced down at Johnny on the dirt floor, his bony shoulders drawn in, lank hair spilling across his eyes as he slept restlessly. He had never made much time for the boy, especially since Johnny was so unlike him. Oh, he was bright enough and good-looking in a pale, scholarly fashion but he wasn't the son Braden dreamed of. He was too kind-hearted by far and needed to toughen up.

No, the boy favored Annabelle, with his blond hair and pale skin and small build. Yet he couldn't regret marrying her. She was still attractive after ten years. Sweet natured and pliable, she cared for Olivia as her own, leaving him time to climb the heights of the political ladder.

Yet what had his ambition gotten him? Without a doubt, the power that came with being a United States senator. If he only had the discipline to match. Instead, he had gone through his late wife's fortune and then through the profits of the companies he'd invested in. Those he'd been privy to, thanks to his position in Washington. After the bad investments began adding up, he turned to gambling to bolster the family fortunes.

Talk about a disaster in the making. Cards. Ponies. Dice. He became addicted to them as much as fine wine and silk shirts. He sent Annabelle and Olivia to Europe so he could sort out the mess in private. His line of credit still opened doors and he knew they would enjoy the trip. By the time they returned, he guaranteed himself things would be right. The trip to California held great promise if what Braden had learned behind closed doors held true. His back to the wall, all his eggs in one basket, counting on the connection in San Francisco to change his fortune.

Then the ill-fated day on the train arrived. The fools

took him and Johnny— and Braden knew it was all over. Now there was no time to change the sorry state of his finances. He and Johnny would die. Annabelle would be forced to declare bankruptcy. She might be able to keep the creditors at bay for a year at most. Possibly enough time to marry Olivia off and accompany the girl in search of a new life.

Or she'd return to that Harper fellow. The one whose packet of letters Braden found a year ago. It surprised him how much it hurt to discover the letters his wife's beau sent so many years ago, all tied up in ribbon and hidden away. Braden had no real love for Annabelle. She was simply a pleasant diversion upon occasion and dressing for his arm on social occasions. Yet she had earned his grudging respect over the years. She might be a pawn in his political game, but she played her part perfectly.

Still, he demanded she burn them all the same. He ranted about her disloyalty and questioned her love for him, though he knew she was too meek to ever give a thought to indulge in a love affair, as half of Washington wives did while their husbands kept long hours on Capitol Hill.

She docilely complied, burning the letters in his presence, and hadn't brought the matter up again. That was his submissive Annabelle.

He had the man looked into, though. Princeton graduate and Civil War veteran. Highly decorated. The reports Braden received glowed with praise for Harper's unselfishness on the battlefield. The times he had risked his life for others with no thought for his own. Harper had gone out West after the war. He was a U.S. Marshal now, posted in California.

Wouldn't it stick in his craw if he was one of the men assigned to rescue the senator and his son? Especially with what Braden knew about Harper, something Annabelle could never have dreamed of.

Dingus burped loudly, ready now to hold court. The outlaw wiped his mouth fastidiously and leaned back in his chair.

"Got the last robbery money all invested now, boys," he drawled. "Put it in railroads. They're the future of this country, I'll tell you."

"I hope you kept a little of it out for food," Cletus complained. "I'm tired of the slop we eat around here."

"Cletus, would it help to hear that I've hired a cook?"

Cletus brightened. "It would be sorely appreciated, Dingus."

"Then maybe I will. The next time I go into town."

The outlaws guffawed loudly. Braden saw Cletus turn a dull red as the men laughed at his expense.

"What about our ransom? How's it coming?"

Dingus wiped away a tear and grew solemn. "Not as good as I'd like, boys."

Low grumbles filled the room. "Now, hold on. We're new at this business, after all. I'm not saying it won't happen. It's just taking longer than any of us suspected."

"Why's that?"

Braden heard the challenge to Dingus' authority in Cletus's voice. He wished fervently that Dingus had better news for this gang of cutthroats. As it was, Braden would probably be used as Cletus's punching bag once Dingus was gone. He had already suffered a broken nose and lost two teeth as a result of Cletus taking his anger out on the nearest victim.

Dingus clucked his tongue. "These are hard times, gentlemen. Lots of fancy-pants men have their money tied up. I gather it's not easy for any businessman to get his hands on his own cash these days. All that stock market investing and limited liability and whatnot."

The gang leader righted his chair, his level gaze moving around the table, making contact with each man. "I promise it will happen. I went to a few gatherings. Heard a little gossip. The senator's wife and daughter are in Europe now."

Cletus guffawed. "That's what the snot-nose said."

Dingus nodded. "Well, you should've believed him. They'll have to head back to the States now. From what I understand, if the senator has things tied up tightly, his man of business may even need the missus' autograph before he can go freeing up the funds we've requested. It'll take her anywhere from ten to twelve days for her steamer to make it back to the States, so we'll have to dig in for the long haul."

His eyes gleamed. "But we will get our money, gentlemen."

Braden swallowed hard and rolled over, his back to the gang now. He idly wondered if he should rush the table of men and get it over with. He probably would if he could. The handcuffs fastened to the wall prevented him from taking the coward's way out.

For now.

CHAPTER 9

Warm summer sun blanketed him in contentment. Calm water made rowing easy. He took them to the middle of the lake and brought the oars inside the boat.

"Ready for lunch?" she asked, an impish smile tugging at the corners of her mouth.

"Are you on the menu?" he asked.

Her eyes sparkled, reflecting the water they floated upon. "You are a big flirt, John Harper."

He caught her hand and raised it to his lips. "But a charming one, Annabelle." He kissed her open palm, enjoying the trembling smile the gesture brought.

"Life is wonderful," he told her. "In another year, college will be behind me. I'll join Father at the bank. Why, this time next summer, we might already be married."

Annabelle beamed. "Are you asking me, John?"

He smiled lazily at her. "Asking you what?"

She tugged at her hand but he refused to release it. "You know what I mean." She blushed prettily and his love for her spilled over.

He took her chin and drew close, bestowing a light kiss upon her soft lips. "We are meant to be, Annabelle. We've always known that. I didn't know a formal declaration was *necessary. You know what's in my heart. It's been there since you were four and I was five."*

She screamed as the first shot whizzed by. He dove and hit the ground. The boat dissolved. He was at Fredericksburg again. God, the blood. The smells of gunpowder. The cries of dying men. Not again. Please, God, not again.

He took a wild chance and in a low crouch, sneaked out and pulled Thompson back in. One arm was nearly severed from a bullet. Then he heard Simpson and Main and Peters all calling. Their attacks had been repelled, but maybe he could save one or two of the lost souls crying for help in the mud and blood.

Despair filled him. They would lose today, just as he'd lost Annabelle. It didn't matter if he lived or died. Besides, it was a calculated risk each time he went out. Once, twice, six times. Six men dragged to safety. Four of them would live. Two of those would even thank him. But wait. There was one left. He had to go back. He had to. He crawled toward the wounded soldier and a shot rang out, louder than the rest.

"No!"

He awoke in a cold sweat, darkness still enveloping him. It was hard to breathe. Was it the pneumonia again?

Then he sensed another presence. The woman.

And he remembered.

He was blind. The war was over. He'd lost Annabelle more than ten years ago. Of all the memories to come back, that was the one best left dead and buried. Yet here his subconscious had resurrected it. The wounds felt as fresh as the day he learned of her marriage to Congressman Braden Reynolds.

"Are you there?" he asked.

"Yes." She laid a hand over his for a moment. The simple touch reassured him.

"What's your name?" He hadn't asked before. He'd been so concerned about not knowing his own.

73

"Alena."

He sensed her hesitation, as if another question hung in the air between them, like a balloon rising from their midst. He'd been fuzzy on so many things the last time he had awakened. She probably thought he didn't know his own name yet. Hell, he hadn't— until the dream.

"I'm John. John Harper."

He heard her sigh of relief. Could feel the tension leave her. She probably thought him some crazy, shot-up fool. Funny how aware he was of her. It was as if all his senses had come alive to compensate for the blindness.

She laughed, a musical note played in a sea of darkness. "Well, John Harper, I'd like to check your progress."

He nodded. Fingers as light as spun cotton candy unwrapped the dressing. She examined him carefully, bathing the injury in cool water. After rewrapping it, she checked his head wound, too.

"Both look much better today. You're a fast healer."

He perceived an awkwardness between them all of a sudden. He didn't want her to leave. In fact, he craved company at the moment.

"Stay. I'm in a talkative mood. I guess that's what comes from getting shot up and being unconscious or sleeping too long."

He smiled and somehow knew she did, too. "I'm remembering bits and pieces. Things are starting to clear up some. It's like Thompson."

"Who's Thompson?"

"Buddy of mine. Got kicked in the head by a horse near the end of the war."

"You were a soldier?"

He nodded. "Thompson and I were in the same regiment from the beginning. After he got knocked up, he

74

had a knot the size of an apple on the back of his noggin. It took a couple of days to remember his name. Then he kept telling everyone how he was the Spelling Bee champ of Wessex County and had memorized the books of the Bible quicker than anyone in his confirmation class. He knew all kinds of things that happened from years ago— but he couldn't remember the battle we'd been in two days earlier."

He quieted, remembering the rest. "He didn't remember getting a letter from his mama telling him his girl contracted the fever and died. We fought at Appomattox a week later, and Grant let everyone go home. I wonder if Thompson remembered the rest before he got there."

The thought sobered him considerably. He remembered college. Losing Annabelle. The war. He felt in his bones he'd come out West after that. Everything beyond that was a blank.

"What year is it?" he asked suddenly.

"Eighteen sixty-eight."

Alena watched John mull over this information. He nodded his head and then scrunched up his face as if trying to remember more.

"That means I've only lost a few years. The war ended in sixty-five. I came West after that. I don't know what I did— or what I do now— but that's not bad. It's coming back."

She nodded in agreement, then felt foolish. He couldn't see her. She longed to jog his memory more but was afraid. If she told him about the silver star hiding in her flour bin, would he remember he was a lawman? Or an outlaw masquerading as one? She wasn't ready to ask that question yet.

True, she helped him when he was hurt, but would that be enough if he were wanted by the law? Would he hurt her? Or worse? What if he'd double-crossed

Cletus and his bunch and that was why they'd wanted him dead? What if they came back, looking for him again?

"I have an idea." She handed him his trousers. "Put these on and then we'll go see your horse."

~

SHE LEFT THE ROOM, not wanting to watch him struggle doing something that came so naturally to men every morning. She closed the door and sat in her rocker, waiting for him to make an appearance.

Alena realized her mistake almost immediately but she froze, not knowing how to correct it. She'd left John to his own privacy but she hadn't given him any type of directions. In a strange place, he obviously had no idea how to get out of the room he was in. She knew because of the bumps and curses emitted from behind the closed door once he'd had time to dress. His language was decidedly more colorful than Jeb's, who usually muttered oaths under his breath. John's words rang loud and clear.

Despite her misgivings, she held back a giggle as he finally opened the door slowly, combing his hands through his hair self-consciously, a sheepish look on his face. Behind him, Alena could see furniture askew.

"I'm probably a mess," he apologized.

"You don't look half bad for someone who's been shot twice," she teased. "When we get back, I'll shave you. I'm sure you've probably worked up an appetite, too."

He smiled. Her heart almost stopped. His smile was a thing of beauty. She wanted to throw him down in a chair and capture it with her charcoals. Maybe later. If he'd let her. She hoped that would be the case. Suddenly, she wanted something to remember him by.

Alena moved toward him. "I'm coming over to you. Listen to the sound of my voice."

He stilled, his head cocked slightly to one side. He reached a hand out. She took his arm and stood close by his side.

"I'll lead you out. We'll go as fast as you feel comfortable walking."

"All right." He took a few hesitant steps and stumbled slightly on the rug.

She swore softly under her breath.

"I heard that," he said, grinning sideways at her.

"I meant 'dang it,'" she proclaimed. "That was my fault. I should've told you it was coming. I'm sorry. I'm new at this."

He grinned. "Me, too."

Alena laughed and shook her head. Here she was, leading a blind stranger, a possible thief and murderer, and she was laughing. The only thing more preposterous would be for Jeb to come home now, riding a camel.

She talked him through going down the three steps from the porch and then across the yard. All the while, she watched him carefully as they walked. He took in all the sounds around him, from the two squabbling hens to the wind blowing in the trees.

"Wind's coming from the northwest. Smells like rain."

"I think you're right."

He was downright conversational this morning. After his long silences, it was almost comical. She herself had spoken more the past few days than she normally did in a month. Jeb would think she'd gotten all liquored up and was out of her head to be so chatty.

They reached the barn door. "Stay right here. Don't move. I'm going to open the door."

A loud nicker sounded from the other side.

As Alena threw open the barn door, the horse went right up to John and nudged his shoulder playfully. He held on to her mane and ruffled it lovingly.

"Why, I can't believe she came to greet you. You have one smart horse, John Harper."

He smiled again, a sunny smile lighting up his sun-darkened face. "She is indeed." He cooed softly to the horse, nuzzling her muzzle with his face. "Hello, Cicero, my sweet. How's my favorite girl in the world?"

He looked around, as if he could see and were searching for something. Seeing the affection he had for the horse, Alena guessed what he wanted.

"Would you like a brush?"

He nodded. "She loves that. Actually, she's pretty spoiled."

Alena retrieved the brush from his saddle and lifted one of John's hands. A funny spark passed between them as she opened his palm and placed the brush in it. He looked at her, at least in her direction, and his muddy brown eyes seemed puzzled.

"I found it in your saddlebags, along with the lumps of sugar."

He ran the brush along Cicero's length. "She gets one a day. Two if she's been extra good."

"At least you remember that." Alena patted the horse. "I'm sure the rest of your memory will come back to you soon, John."

A pregnant silence filled the air. "And my sight, too?"

Alena let the awkward moment pass. "And your sight, too."

She let him spend some time with the horse. He groomed her and then insisted on feeding her himself. She guided him through filling the buckets with oats and water from the trough just inside the barn.

He looked exhausted by the time he'd finished. She

held him a little more tightly as they walked back across the yard.

"At least you didn't make me draw water from the well," he quipped.

"Well, I've got some butter to be churned and some beans to be stripped. You just might earn your keep after all today, mister."

She made him a breakfast of cold ham, biscuits, and coffee, and sat and chatted to him about various chores she had to do that day.

"I think I'll wait on the shave, but I will help churn that butter."

"No, I was teasing. Besides, you're a guest."

He grinned. "I'm not a man that thinks that kind of chore is demeaning. In fact, I have churned quite a bit of butter in my day. My grandparents lived on a farm about twenty miles from our town. I'd spend weeks there in the summer. Granny would have me doing all kinds of things. Work might be simple, but the results can be awfully good."

He helped her with several small tasks before tiring. She insisted he nap after that. She decided to paint while he slept.

Alena lost track of time. The first thing she realized was when he bumped into her rocker.

"Rocker," she called out. "Move to your left. I mean your right. It's my left."

"Great directions, Alena. Keep it up."

"About ten more paces and you'll be at the table. Pull the chair out. Good."

John sat. He wrinkled his nose and reached out.

"Don't move, or else we'll have a disaster in the making. I don't want you to knock any jars over."

He slipped his hands into his lap but his nose crinkled as he sniffed the air about him. "What's that smell? It's not an everyday scent, but I'm familiar with it."

"It's my oil paints."

John nodded. "That's it. You paint?"

"I've drawn and painted since I was a little girl. Jeb sells some of my paintings in San Francisco. You ever been there?"

"I live there!" he exclaimed. His excitement was catching. She smiled.

"I may go there someday. Not anytime soon, but someday."

Actually, she'd been longing more and more to get away from their homestead. She'd grown increasingly curious about life outside her small world. And though she hated to admit it, she found Jeb controlling nowadays.

"There's a great art community in the city," John told her. "Mostly painters, but some sculptors, musicians, writers. It's becoming a cosmopolitan place. People from all over. Businesses are thriving."

"Do you own a business?"

John frowned. "No, I don't think so. But I do own a few paintings. In fact, I remember I finally saved up enough and bought an *A McClaine* landscape. He's the most popular artist around now. He's been my favorite for a few years but I never could afford anything before. This one was a real bargain. If I didn't love it so much, I could probably sell it for twice what I paid for it in a year."

Alena grew still. John Harper owned one of *her* paintings.

If John had paid a pretty penny for the painting— if it was true that her work had become so popular— then why hadn't Jeb ever said anything to her? Why did she have to ration her peppermints in order to make them last?

Mistrust filled her. Jeb had been her savior. Her everything since she was a little girl. Now, John's words shook her to her core. The implicit trust she had always held regarding Jeb seemed to crumble instantly into dust.

Alena knew the time had come to have a serious conversation with Jeb.

One which might decide her entire future.

CHAPTER 10

*A*nnabelle's mood was somber as the New York skyline came into view from their cabin's window. She had slept very little since Henry Smith informed her of Braden and Johnny's kidnapping— and even less since she'd received a cable from Monroe Feldman, her husband's business agent.

She had accompanied Smith into the largest nearby town and wired Feldman her permission to draw the necessary funds in order to set her loved ones free. Feldman's return cable had been vague and full of bloated concern for her. In the end, it recommended that she return to New York immediately and meet with him at her earliest convenience to discuss paying the ransom. She and Olivia packed and left Italy that same day. Feldman chose not to respond to further wires that implored him to pay the men with haste.

The rest became a blur. Smith assured her he would contact both Feldman and their attorney, Bryce Mitchell, as to their arrival date. Annabelle expected both men to meet them at the docks. While Bryce's original office had been established in Pennsylvania, where Braden originally retained the attorney, Bryce's various business dealings had led him to set up another branch in New York. He and his wife now made New York their home, while Bryce's younger brother handled the Pennsylvania office. Braden wouldn't allow anyone but Bryce Mitchell to handle his affairs.

She and Olivia went up on deck for the short time until they landed. The captain told her they could disembark before any other passengers. He would have his personal steward handle their luggage. Annabelle gave him Mitchell's law office address. Their baggage would be sent there upon landing.

Late fall hung in the air. A cold wind snapped off the waves as they steamed closer to the city. Annabelle once thought their return would be one of joy. Instead, heartache filled her. She squeezed Olivia's hand, more to comfort herself than anything she could do for her stepdaughter. The girl had been withdrawn on the return trip. Where Annabelle had been restless and awake, Olivia escaped into sleep.

As they entered the harbor, she searched the crowds gathered on the docks.

"Mark." It surprised her to spy Johnny's tutor in the masses.

Olivia quickly skimmed the crowd. "I knew he'd come," she said fervently.

Of all the things Annabelle didn't want to deal with now, at the top of the list was Olivia's crush on Mark Gandelson. One of the reasons Annabelle had been so enthused about their European sojourn was to keep Olivia from pining away her days mooning over Mark. Especially when Johnny's tutor could barely hide his own infatuation with his employer's wife.

Standing next to Mark was Bryce. Thank God he was here. Bryce Mitchell was level-headed and one of the most intelligent men Annabelle knew. He could be diplomatic when called upon but a person always knew where he stood with Bryce Mitchell. Braden often remarked how lucky they were to have Bryce as their attorney. Annabelle was thankful to call him her friend. He had been a father figure to her when she married Braden a decade ago but she had come to know Bryce and his wife, Liddy, well in the ensuing years.

Bryce greeted her warmly when they reached the end of the gangplank, his graying hair mussed by the wind. Annabelle noted how he seemed to have aged considerably since she'd last seen him on the night before they sailed for England. His strength was still obvious, though, as he took her hand firmly in his. Only then did Annabelle sense how much she was trembling. She gave him a tentative smile. No words were necessary.

Mark Gandelson stepped forward, gazing at her with worshipful eyes full of concern. "Glad to see you back, Mrs. Reynolds. I am sorry it is under such troubling circumstances."

Bryce smoothly stepped in. "Mr. Gandelson witnessed the incident on the train, Annabelle. Perhaps we can allow him to accompany us to my office and you can hear the details."

The attorney smiled at her and placed a fatherly arm around Olivia. "Well, my dear, you look all grown up. You remember my wife?"

Olivia nodded even as she stared adoringly at Mark.

"She's to meet us at my office and take you out for a spot of lunch and some shopping. It isn't often a young lady can shop the stores of New York."

The girl returned her attention to the lawyer and smiled shyly. "That would be nice, Mr. Mitchell."

Bryce led them to a waiting carriage, and they arrived at his office inside twenty minutes. Liddy Mitchell swept Olivia away with reassurances to Annabelle that her stepdaughter would be well cared for. Annabelle knew she couldn't place Olivia in better hands. Liddy was by far one of the most delightful women Annabelle knew. Her crinkling blue eyes and easy smile betrayed Liddy's sense of fun.

Finally, they settled in a small conference room, gathered around an oak table, with hot coffee served in delicate china cups. Annabelle knew such social proprieties must be observed but she was chomping at the bit for matters to proceed. Her years of being a proper Washington wife helped her hide her impatience, though. She knew better than to outwardly display her feelings.

Bryce's assistant closed the door. Annabelle sat up, eager to hear Mark's version of the events. The tutor looked overjoyed to have her full attention. He selfconsciously brushed back his dark hair and cleared his throat.

"We had gone out to California by train. The senator insisted on everything being first class. I feel terrible that I encouraged him to take Johnny, but you do remember how you wanted them to spend more time together while you were away."

Annabelle nodded, guilt flooding her. Braden spent so many long hours in session and committee meetings. Johnny was rarely awake when his father came home after a long day involved in Washington politics. She had encouraged Mark to throw father and son together whenever possible during her time in Europe.

"The senator had pressing business in California. Something about railroad investments. I suggested that we accompany him and Johnny could easily continue his lessons along the way. We could include the geography of the land we passed through as well as his regular studies."

"Go on, Mark." she encouraged the tutor, wishing he would speed up his version of the events. She knew, however, he had a meticulous nature. Mark would leave no stone unturned in his tale. And as much as she needed to hear what had happened, her stomach tightened and twisted all the same, knowing the crux of his story had almost arrived.

"We had just crossed into California. Couldn't have been there more than a few minutes when I was thrown into the aisle of our car. Papers went flying. The senator's cigar was lost for a moment and then set a cushion on fire. It was very upsetting, a sudden stop like that."

"Mark. Please?"

"All right." He took off his wire-rimmed glasses and polished them with a handkerchief as he continued.

"We were alone in a private luxury car, but I could still hear raised voices and a few ladies' screams from the cars in front of us. I knew something was dreadfully wrong. Suddenly, the door flew back and in walked some fairly despicable characters."

"Did they have guns?" Annabelle was trying to get a picture in her mind as he spoke.

"Guns? Good God, they were train robbers. Of course, they had guns! They brandished them about like toys." An odd look crossed his face and Annabelle realized Mark was barely holding on to his composure. "One… one held a knife to my throat."

"Oh, Mark. I'm so sorry." Annabelle longed to pat his hand reassuringly but she didn't want even her slightest gesture misinterpreted. Besides, if she made the time to comfort him, it would only delay what Mark could tell her about Braden and Johnny.

The tutor pulled himself together. "They demanded our wallets and valuables. I gave them my grandfather's gold pocket watch." A look of sorrow crossed his face. "He presented it to me on my sixteenth birthday."

She saw him visibly shaking as he added, "Another one rifled through all our papers. He was the one who first recognized the importance of stumbling across the senator."

"Did he hurt Braden?" Annabelle knew the question had to be asked.

"He asked the senator if he was the man referred to in the various papers, and your husband refused to answer. The outlaw slapped the senator hard enough to knock him from his seat to the ground. The senator kept his composure, though. He took a handkerchief out and wiped his brow, and then returned to his seat as if nothing had happened."

Annabelle swallowed. "And then?"

"The outlaw asked him again if he was Senator Reynolds. He couldn't deny it. Papers all over screamed his identity. Then the robber said he had a good idea. Three of them huddled together for a minute or so and then pounced on the senator. Wrestled him to the ground and bound him hand and foot."

A sob broke through despite her best effort to keep it inside. Bryce came to stand behind her and put a hand on her shoulder. He gave her an encouraging squeeze.

Annabelle brushed away her tears. "The rest?" she asked. "I have to know it all."

Mark hesitated. "Well... Johnny ran from where he'd tumbled onto the floor and tried to save his daddy. When the men figured out he was the senator's son, they took him along, too."

She expelled the breath she'd held. Gone. Just like that. She listened to the rest of Mark's account with half a mind. The passengers that were robbed. Several sacks of money taken from the baggage car. And her two loved ones put upon horses and whisked away.

Bryce held out a hand. "That will be all, Mr. Gandelson. Thank you for your valuable report." He paused.

"If you will wait outside, we must speak to Senator Reynolds' business manager now."

Annabelle was glad to see the tutor go. She was angry with him. It was silly, but a part of her wanted him to have fought back against these criminals. To have gone in place of Braden or Johnny. Then again, what would thieves want with a poor but well-educated private tutor when they could ransom a wealthy government representative and his son?

She nodded, dimly aware that Mark had left the room. She found herself drifting, as if the story Mark had related had nothing to do with her or her family. She thought of the art books and train set they had purchased for Johnny in France. The set of china she had ordered that would look so lovely when entertaining Braden's colleagues. The Savile Row suit she'd chosen the material for, having secretly obtained Braden's measurements from his Washington tailor. This was reality. Not some fantastic tale Mark Gandelson had invented. Surely she would awaken from this nightmare. Johnny would eagerly greet her. She and Braden would go to the opera while in New York. Olivia could accompany them.

"Annabelle?"

Bryce looked at her sympathetically. "You need to speak to Feldman now."

She nodded, her eyes closed, trying to muster more courage. She was angry at Feldman, as well. He had ignored her request to allocate the funds necessary to free her family. Annabelle could not imagine why their business manager would stall in such a drastic situation. She would be discreet and hold the tongue-lashing she longed to give him until she heard what he had to say. She doubted any excuse would be acceptable.

Monroe Feldman slithered into the room.

Annabelle always thought him oily and couldn't understand why Braden placed such faith in the man.
Feldman avoided meeting her gaze.

She decided a direct course of action was necessary
when dealing with a man lacking character and said, "I
will dispense with the niceties, Mr. Feldman, and get to
my only concern. Why have you not released the funds
these outlaws demanded? Why aren't my husband and
son free?"

Feldman shrugged, a frown on his face. "To be honest, Mrs. Reynolds, I'd like nothing better. Funds are a
bit... tied up, though."

"What do you mean, 'tied up'? Explain yourself
clearly."

Feldman shifted in his seat. "The senator has investments in numerous places, ma'am. Both here and in
Europe. Capital tied up in one venture or another. Outstanding loans here and there. Even—"

"You can't lay your hands on the cash?" Annabelle
heard the rising hysteria in her voice but did nothing to
quell it. "Then sell, Mr. Feldman. Sell! Yank the money
from every investment. Sell Windowmere. Any prop-
erty. My jewels. Whatever it takes. I want my family
back!"

"You know I've been the senator's business manager
for many years."

"Too many, if you ask me." Annabelle glared at him.

He finally met her gaze. His Tidewater accent
dropped. In its place was a lower-class dialect from
New York. "You need to understand. The truth is that
we've mortgaged most everything to the hilt. The senator owes a lot of people, some of them a bit shady. I've
juggled the best I can for the last eighteen months. He
authorized too many bad investments. Gambled away
too much on cards and the horses."

Feldman shook his head. "He's broke, Mrs.

Reynolds. Flat broke. I might be able to raise a tenth of what's being asked."

"What?" Annabelle could scarcely believe her ears. They had a fine house. Servants. She had fashionable clothes and expensive jewelry. She and Olivia spent money hand over fist in Europe. "What are you talking about?"

"When this hits the papers, ma'am, the scandal will only be the tip of the iceberg. Lives will be ruined, Mrs. Reynolds. I can't authorize money to pay kidnappers when there's no money to be had."

Feldman stood and wordlessly left the room. Annabelle was too stunned to demand he stay. Nausea washed over her, much worse than what she experienced during her confinement. She tightened her jaw, refusing to be sick on Bryce's fine Oriental rug.

No, Feldman was wrong. He had to be. The nausea subsided, only to be replaced by feelings of anger. It was impossible. She had been so upset that she misunderstood him. She had never had her hand in any form of business, other than dealing with the household accounts every month. Bryce would explain things to her so that she would understand. He would make certain that Braden and Johnny returned safely.

She turned to Bryce. Open-mouthed. Not sure how to begin. One look at him, and her world came crashing down. She knew without a doubt that what Monroe Feldman spoke was the truth.

"Did you know anything of this?" Annabelle carefully kept her tone neutral, not wanting to accuse her friend of complicity in this disastrous situation.

Bryce looked at her sympathetically. "Braden has limited what I've handled and what I could know for several years now. I heard a few rumors along the way, especially about his mounting gambling debts, but I had no idea how bad things were until Feldman briefed me."

Numbness filled her. "So you are saying I cannot pay these men. Even with the inheritance I received upon my father's death last year."

Bryce shook his head sadly. "I only stayed long enough to speak to you in person regarding this matter, Annabelle. I owed you that much. I will be leaving in the morning. The authorities in California have asked me to take the first train out. I will work with them closely to see that Braden and Johnny are freed."

"Then I'm coming with you."

Bryce looked shocked. "Now, my dear, I can see—"

"Don't patronize me, Bryce," she snapped. "I will go to California, whether you see fit to escort me or not. I want to speak to the men in charge. I want every available lawman on this case. No one, least of all me, will rest until my family is safe in my arms again."

Determination flowed through Annabelle's veins. Nothing would keep her from her son. Or husband.

Bryce shook his head, a wry smile on his face. She read the look of resignation in the slope of his shoulders.

"You can rest assured they have a dozen marshals on the case now, all trying to locate Braden and Johnny. Had, at least."

Annabelle narrowed her eyes. "What do you mean?"

He sighed. "They know of two who've tangled with the men who supposedly took Braden and Johnny. Both are dead. Another has gone missing."

A dull roar began in her head. "Who? Who's missing?"

"A marshal out of San Francisco. Name of John Harper."

Annabelle fainted.

CHAPTER 11

J ohn sat up quickly, the blinding pain almost unbearable. He pushed his fingers into his hair, pressing down hard upon his scalp. Flashes of light exploded inside his head. With each burst, he winced, not knowing how much more he could take.

Then it abruptly stopped. The pattern of the last two days held true. Fortunately, he had experienced these incidents alone. He was already in Alena's debt as it was. He didn't want her to think him even more of a burden than he already was.

Little aftershocks of sharp tingles hit as he relaxed. These had never happened before. He sucked in his breath. Clamped his jaw. Willed the pain to go away.

"John?"

Damn, he hadn't heard her. He was already so attuned to her step. Her scent. The ache in his head, though, pushed his remaining senses into uselessness.

He lifted his head to face the direction of her voice. "What?" he growled, irritated that she'd caught him in a vulnerable moment. As an afterthought, he casually lowered his hands from his head.

"How bad is it?"

She was near now, nearer than he would have liked. He wanted to make like a wounded animal and crawl into a hole, far away from prying eyes.

"I'm fine." He hoped his curt tone would push her away.

"Fine as in excellent— or fine as in delicate?"

He heard the humor in her voice and wished he could see the smile he knew played upon her lips. Then another pain hit, searing him in agony.

"Fine as in leave me the hell alone," he snapped. The stinging dominated each breath he took.

"How long has this gone on?" The humor faded quickly, replaced by an edge. Her tone indicated she wouldn't stand for any messing around.

"A while," he said begrudgingly.

"That's a start."

The faint scent of jasmine came closer. John scooted back on the mattress.

He held up a hand in front of him. "I don't need you playing nursemaid to me."

"Who said I would?"

He fell silent. Neither spoke for some minutes.

Another jolt of lightning tore through him unexpectedly. He gasped, hands flying to his head again.

"Get out! Now!"

He rode the wave of pain, oblivious to all else. As it subsided, he broke out in a cold sweat and shivered. He'd been to hell and back in the war.

This was far worse.

"John." Alena's voice was soft but it sounded like a trumpet blaring in his ear. That one word, coupled with the next spasm of pain, sent him over the edge.

He threw off the hand she had placed on his shoulder and turned in the direction she sat.

"You don't know what it's like," he said hoarsely. "To be... helpless. Unable to do for myself. Not to know

93

ALEXA ASTON

who I am or why I'm here. Banging into furniture left
and right. Making a fool of myself each minute of every
day."

John let go of the bitterness that had built within
him. "I'm not a man anymore. I'm powerless. Trapped
in a world where I have no control, with a slip of a girl
caring for me out of pity. Hell, you should boot me out
your door and shoot me if I try to come back."

He raked his hands through his hair. "I'd shoot myself if I could find a gun, but you'd probably just go save
me all over again." He laughed bitterly, clamping down
the hysteria that rose within him. "If I'm lucky the next
time, I'll just shoot my ears off. That way I won't be
able to see or hear you."

He heard her sharp intake of breath and knew she
would start to protest, as the next wave of pain struck
without warning. John rode it out with gritted teeth.
Into his darkness crept flashes of light. With each burst
of light came a fresh bloom of unbearable burning that
raced through his head, buzzing as angry bees. When it
ended, his strength was spent. He trembled as much
with fear as cold.

"Lie down," Alena commanded.

He meekly obeyed her, exhausted from the intense
bout. Tears formed in his eyes and he quickly wiped
them away. He turned his face from her as he felt the
weight of a quilt covering him.

She left the room and returned a few minutes later.
John heard the sound of water. A cool cloth bathed his
face. The pain subsided to a dull throb.

She moved again, somewhere behind him, and then
gentle fingers began to rub his temples. He lifted his
head to protest but fell back weakly. The incident took
more out of him than the others beforehand. And as
much as he wanted to push her away, he craved the
comfort she brought.

94

Alena began to hum softly, her fingers brushing him in light circles. A peacefulness came over him, like nothing he had ever experienced. It was as if her fingers absorbed the hurt and lifted it from him. He floated along, the melody cushioning him.

He slept.

~

JOHN AWOKE, refreshed and full of energy. His shoulder throbbed some. Even itched a little. He took that as a good sign. Men in the war told him when they needed to scratch, they knew they were on the road to recovery.

He stretched, not bothering to open his eyes. What good would that do anyway? This world of darkness seemed almost normal to him now. Not that he enjoyed it. His legs alone had enough bruises to prove otherwise. Despite Alena's best directions, he had bumped into more furniture the past few days than he thought possible. Only her amused laughter mingled with words of regret for his mishaps made him overlook his shortcomings. Frustration simply became his new way of life.

He heard the rocker in the other room and so he knew she had probably finished her chores outside. He had grown to appreciate her wit and sense of humor over the last few days spent together. He also liked that she didn't view him as totally helpless. She gave him several tasks to do. It relieved his boredom and gave him a chance to think. He knew the key to unlocking his memories lay around the corner.

John removed the heavy quilt that covered him and slowly rose to his feet. He took three slow steps, his hands stretched in front of him. He actually had a good sense of the room's layout now. He imagined the type of wood the dresser was made from and the colors of the curtains. Lord, he was getting as fancy as Annabelle.

As any time an image of his lost sweetheart came, his heart grew heavy. In his gut, he knew he oftentimes had pushed thoughts of her away. But since he'd awakened in this dark world, she filled his mind. He wondered why her memory was so pressing.

He reached out and touched the dresser. The door would be to the left. He searched for its handle and turned it, stepping back to swing it open. Sounds sprang to life. The rocker squeaked more loudly. Alena's humming was more distinct. He could hear the pot boiling in the fireplace and smell the stew within it. Outside, he heard the song of a bird and a gentle wind whistling softly. It amazed him how much he had taken for granted when he had his sight. The mundane took on a new life since he'd gone blind.

"I'm sorry." He offered a simple apology to Alena and headed in her direction. To the left of the rocker was a chair and he went and sat in it. John had become pretty astute at reading her moods but he didn't have a clue about her current state of mind.

"I don't remember much from before, but I know I hurt your feelings. I never meant to do that."

The rocker stopped. He sensed she was studying him.

"Why didn't you tell me about the headaches?"

He shrugged. "I don't know."

"Maybe you think you've become too dependent on me? Or did you hide them so I wouldn't think you weak?"

She took his hand. "It wouldn't make me think less of you, John. I wish you trusted me more."

"It has nothing to do with trust," he said, a little too quickly

96

She tightened her grip. "It has everything to do with trust." She released his hand.

He took a deep breath. "Maybe you're right." He grinned. "My nanny used to say, *'John Harper, you must always agree with a woman, for she's always right. Even when she's not.'*"

Alena's laughter permeated the air. "Your nanny was wise beyond her years."

"I suppose. I haven't had much experience with women."

Her disbelief radiated between them. "A fine, strapping man like you? I'd sooner believe the pope was a New Yorker than to believe such tales, John Harper."

"I'm not saying I'm a monk, Alena. I've just been unlucky in love. That's all."

She sighed, a wistful sound that made him wonder about her own love life.

"How long have you and Jeb been in love? When were you married?" he asked.

Blood rushed quickly to Alena's cheeks, and her hands flew to them. She was glad John Harper could not see her discomfort. She knew the way of the world from watching animals mate in the woods all these years. She could never see herself doing something like that with Jeb.

"We... we've known each other for years. Jeb's farm was next to the one my parents owned." She stalled for time, not sure how far to go.

"Did you play together growing up?" Alena watched a mischievous smile cross John's face. "Maybe hide-and-seek in the woods?"

"No," she stammered. "It wasn't like that. Jeb... Jeb is much older than I am. When... when my parents died, he took me in. Things... just happened after that. We've only been married a short while."

Her confidence grew in her story. "That's why I'm so eager for him to return from his trip."

"I see."

Alena wished she could read John's thoughts. She wished even more that she could understand her own. Just gazing at his strong, tanned face made her go breathless. It brought that funny feeling to her belly, too.

"Well, if he's going to be home soon, I hope he won't mind that you've taken in a complete stranger."

"Oh, no," Alena assured him. "We always show kindness to travelers. In fact, Jeb will probably be glad I've helped a human, for once."

She enjoyed his puzzled expression.

"What do you mean?"

She chuckled. "I seem to have a habit of attracting wounded animals. Rabbits. Squirrels. Birds. Deer. They come to me for help. Jeb teases that I spend more time with my furry friends than caring for him."

John smiled. Alena wanted desperately to paint that smile.

"I know I mentioned it to you earlier, but could I draw you, John? It wouldn't take long."

He ran a hand through his wavy brown locks. "I don't know if I'm presentable, Alena." He reached up and touched his chin. "I probably would need a shave."

"Oh, I can do that," she said quickly.

He cocked his head. "You just don't want me to nick myself all up and ruin your pretty picture." He grinned at her and butterflies erupted in her stomach.

"Oh! No, that's not what I meant. I—"

"Sure, pretend you don't have ulterior motives."

"I… I don't know what you mean."

She saw the flicker of some emotion run across his face, too quickly for her to guess at it. "That's fine. Let me fetch my razor. It's in my saddlebag."

She stood at the same time he did and they brushed against each other. She started to fall backwards, but somehow he knew. Strong fingers tightened around her arms and righted her.

"I'm sorry," he apologized. "I should have stayed in place until you had moved away. I'll know better next time."

Alena waited for him to let go, but he remained rooted to the spot. She finally stepped back and his hands fell to his sides.

"I'll go get your razor from the barn. I'll be right back."

She fled the cabin, which had become overheated, making her almost dizzy. The cool wind that greeted her in the yard forced her to hurry. She unlatched the barn door and slipped inside. John's saddlebags sat on the floor, where she'd put them while first tending to Cicero.

Alena bent and opened the left pouch that contained his personal items in it. She had gone through his saddlebags after Cletus and his men visited. Filled with suspicions and aware how vulnerable she was with Jeb gone, Alena found nothing in the bags that gave her a clue as to her visitor's identity. She withdrew his razor, soap, a mirror, a comb, and a silver pocket watch. She wondered why he hadn't worn the watch until she noticed the second hand didn't move. Still, he'd kept it, probably for sentimental reasons.

When she'd first seen it, Alena hadn't wanted to invade John's privacy and so she'd left the watch where she'd found it. Now, she ventured it might help him in regaining his memory. She looked at the polished case again and turned it in her hand.

On the back was an inscription she had missed the first time. She fingered the tiny script.

To J— who owns my heart for all time. A

The words brought a swift ache to Alena's heart. She had denied that she had feelings for John, simply telling herself that she would have cared for anyone in his position. Yet as the days passed, Alena had prayed for Jeb to be delayed, for she savored every waking moment with John. In an incredibly short amount of time, he had become her whole world.

She couldn't keep the watch from him. Somewhere, a woman worried about him. Wondered where he was. If he was safe. This watch held the key to John's memory. She had to give it to him, no matter how much her heart would break when he left.

She decided to gather his items up in the poncho that was in his other saddlebag. She lifted his tin cup and plate and removed a set of matches and gloves. Alena took out the poncho and was surprised to find an extra shirt underneath. She'd missed that before, having left the poncho in the bag. Alena discarded the mirror and wrapped the remaining things inside the poncho and returned to the house.

John waited docilely at the table, his hands neatly folded in his lap. Ever since he had almost tipped over her paints, he was very careful around the table. She knew how self-conscious he must be.

She, too, was self-conscious as she looked at him. In no way did Jeb's old shirt fit him. He was much broader in the chest, and so he had to leave it unbuttoned. The gap revealed a muscled torso. Thoughts of this alone kept Alena awake for long hours several nights in a row.

"I found what we needed," she told him. "Let me put some water on to heat." She placed the razor, soap, and comb on the table in front of him and hung the shirt on the back of a chair. The watch she slipped into her pocket. She would wait until she approached John about it. Maybe when his sight returned, she would give it to him and let him read the inscription.

Alena pushed aside her guilt for hiding the watch and put fresh water in a pot and gathered a bowl and some towels. As she did this, she watched John reach out and touch the items in front of him. He handled them with care, running his fingers over each one, turning them back and forth. A lump formed in her throat as she watched him. Her art was such a large part of her life. If an accident claimed her sight and she could never sketch or paint again, she would be lost. Alena wondered if John's work depended upon sight.

She went and placed a hand upon his shoulder. "I bet the water's ready." She poured the heated water into the bowl and guided his hand to it. He familiarized himself with where things were positioned.

"I can help you along," he said and she knew he needed to. His pride demanded it.

John rinsed his face and then worked the soap up into a lather, coating the beard that had grown in since his arrival. Patches of water dribbled down onto his shirt.

"Here, let's take this shirt off," she told him. "I found you had an extra one in your saddlebags."

Alena eased Jeb's shirt from his shoulders and pulled it from his arms, taking care not to disturb his shoulder. She noticed a tear under one arm and dropped it on the floor, thinking she'd wash and mend it later.

"Why don't we finish the shave before you put it on? That way it'll stay dry."

He sighed. "I'm afraid Jeb fits into that shirt better than I do. I'm sorry. I could feel it starting to split. It'll be nice to have on my own shirt."

Alena took the razor and began humming as she

dipped it into the steaming water. "Just relax and hold still. I'm very good at this."

"You're good at a lot of things," he said. The admiring tone made her tingle as she stepped between his legs and tilted his chin up.

"That's not being still. No talking."

"You're a hard taskmaster, Alena. I promise I'll be quiet."

Good to his word, John remained motionless. His razor was sharp. Alena concentrated, not wanting to cut him. As the stubble melted away, she found he was even better-looking than she'd imagined. A strong jaw and sensual lips complemented high cheekbones. His eyes, staring vacantly ahead, were a warm brown. He matched Alena's vision of what Alexander the Great must have been like— handsome, tall, and confident. She had read where the ruler conquered much of the known world in his time, and she'd spent many hours daydreaming about his exploits. Alena could see John Harper conquering the hearts of women wherever he went.

She finished, but relished having an excuse to stand so close to him. He gave off a mix of heat and masculinity that made her mouth go dry, especially now that she wasn't concentrating on her task. The pounding of her heart told her she better move away or she might give in to her impulse to kiss him.

"There," she said, hoping he would miss the slight tremble in her voice. "I think you can rinse now." She stepped away from him, but still enjoyed his profile and bare chest.

John located the bowl in front of him and washed the soap from his face. She sat in a nearby chair and handed him a towel, and he patted himself dry. He reached a hand up and ran it along his jaw.

"At least you're now seeing who I usually am," he quipped. "I wish I could see you."

Alena laughed, glad that he could aim to be light-hearted despite his troubles.

"Well, I'm not much to look at now," she told him. "I'm wearing an old flannel shirt of Jeb's and a pair of pants that must be at least a hundred years old." Alena stood. "They're wet, too, from your shave." She laughed and John joined in the laughter.

"Maybe they need to be washed?" he asked.

His hand found the bowl in front of him and he playfully flicked water in her direction.

Alena squealed and did the same to him. John cupped a hand of water and held it up.

"You wouldn't," she dared.

John smiled. "Oh, I do love a challenge." He flung the handful at her before she could react. Alena sprang away from the table. John picked up the bowl and held it to his bare chest.

"Now, where could she have gone?" he mused.

Alena giggled, giving her direction away. John moved lightning fast, tossing another handful at her.

She gasped, trying to hold in the laughter. "You're too good at this," she told him. "I give up."

"Winner and still champion," he proclaimed.

"We'll see about that," she told him. "Put the bowl down and I promise to give you your own shirt."

"I can't pass that up."

John reached out, searching for the table, but he was too far away. Alena took his elbow and guided him in the proper direction. Just before he set the bowl down, he flicked his wrist and drenched her.

Alena burst out laughing. She couldn't remember the last time she had laughed, much less laughed so much.

"Who would've thought a grown man could be so mischievous?"

She lifted his shirt from the back of the chair and snapped it in the air for effect.

John tilted his head and listened. "You've got my shirt."

"Yes, I do."

"Give it over."

"No."

He dived toward her. Alena sidestepped him, whipping the shirt behind her.

"Come and get it," she said coyly.

John stood still for a few seconds and then leaped in her direction. Alena was caught in a tight bear hug, close to his chest.

Her pulse began to race. Her knees grew weak. "You win," she whispered. "Let go."

"And have you take off with my shirt?"

His face was just inches from hers. Alena couldn't breathe, couldn't think. The room spun around her.

"Let her go," a voice said, anger simmering in it.

CHAPTER 12

Jeb was tired. It had been a lengthy trip. He couldn't wait to get home. He'd been away too long this time. He would make it up to Alena. He knew he was being selfish. He shouldn't keep her away from the world as he did, but she was the only good and clean and pure thing in his life.

She gave him back a bit of Margarita, whom he'd lost so long ago. When he looked at Alena, he saw Margarita all over again in the bloom of her youth. And since he hadn't been able to save her, a fierce protectiveness came to the surface just glancing at Alena.

He had never married. Never been a father. And yet, he knew in his heart of hearts he was Alena's father. Kevin McClaine hadn't been her daddy. The man had never deserved to be a father, much less a husband.

So he took Alena and spun a world as best he could without Margarita. Alena was his pride and joy. His everything. Jeb didn't know how much longer he could keep her isolated from the world. He saw signs of her wanting to widen her narrow experience. She was more curious about the visitors that passed by. Though shy by nature, she had started to interact more with them. He knew the day might come when she would break the invisible bonds he had cast about her, and spread her wings to fly into the world.

Every time he came home from a trip, he was scared to think that she might actually be gone. Plenty of money was hidden under the floorboards. To be honest, it all belonged to Alena. The quilts she made brought in a tidy sum but it was her paintings that made the real money. If she only knew how much, she would hate him for keeping it from her.

He had a bank account in both their names in San Francisco. But all he ever did was add to it. He liked to think of it as her nest egg. Income for her once he was dead and gone. Almost all of her art sold in San Francisco, making the transactions easier. The last couple of years, she had gained quite a reputation in the community. Most of the swells thought themselves fortunate to possess a work by A McClaine, he was learning. Even some of her immature, earlier efforts now fetched a pretty price.

Should they quit the life they now had? Venture into the city?

Alena might not enjoy it at first, but San Francisco was a growing city with people of all ages and races gathered together. He knew her beauty, a combination of raw earthiness and naïve innocence, would take away the breath of any man on the street. Would he be willing to let her have a life, the kind of life her mother deserved and never got? The kind he had kept from Alena?

He didn't know.

All he knew now was a weariness in both his body and soul. The events of the last several days had worn him to a nub. He needed to be with Alena, to share in the comfort of her spirit.

He opened the barn door and fought to keep it from slamming shut again. A fierce wind kicked today. He led the horse and wagon inside, not bothering to light a lantern. The light from outside would suffice as he unhitched the wagon and proceeded to rub the horse down. He poured a fresh load of oats in the bin and was startled to hear another horse nicker. He smiled to himself, wondering how Alena had attracted a horse this time.

Jeb looked over, only to have his jaw drop sharply. Standing in an empty stall was one of the most magnificent horses he'd ever seen. The bay's head was cocked, her ears perked up with keen intelligence. He wondered whose horse she could be. This wasn't one of Alena's injured animals that came to her for refuge. Jeb didn't know how the creatures found her, unless animals could talk. If that was the case, then word had spread all throughout the forest that Alena would forever take in the sick, the injured, even those too weary to fight their own battles.

But this horse did not fall into any of those categories. And where there was a horse, there would be a man. Jeb could imagine the kind of man that would ride a horse of this stature. A thousand thoughts rushed through his mind. He had to get to Alena. He had to get there now.

He unholstered his gun. No need to check. It was always loaded. He cocked it— and the gun became one with his hand. Ready to shoot on sight whoever had invaded his house and his Alena.

He'd never become a hothead like his stepfather. Sure, he'd scrapped some as a kid, but watching his stepfather's explosive temper, he knew that wasn't the way to go. That's why his stepfather lay in an unmarked grave. Jeb's brother, dead these many years in a barroom brawl, had not mastered that lesson. He hated that a quick temper had cost Anthony his life.

Jeb was no fool, though. He learned from mistakes.

He maintained a calm façade even as he fought to control his temper. He never rushed into any situation blindly. Silence and surprise had sometimes been his biggest allies in a tense situation. With that in mind, Jeb crept toward the house. A chicken ran across his path, squawking her dismay. As he moved closer, he heard the sound of... *laughter*?

Alena had always been a solemn child. There hadn't been much to laugh about in the McClaine household, even when Kevin went away on one of his benders. Alena and Margarita had been quiet individuals, and Jeb always teased Alena that still waters ran deep. Her smiles were rare, and Jeb would pay a bag of gold to see one of them. He couldn't remember the last time she smiled— much less laughed aloud.

He paused outside the door and listened. He regretted that he hadn't heard more of that musical tinkling in their years together. Then he heard a man's voice. His blood ran cold. A voice of a leader. A voice of command. No, he wasn't commanding people now, but Jeb knew away from this cabin, maybe in another lifetime, this man held a position of authority. This man was used to getting things done.

This man was the biggest threat that had ever entered Jeb's life.

Laughter erupted again. He could stand it no longer.

Without further consideration, he moved to open the door. It might not be the right move but he felt compelled to do so. He threw open the door.

In a million years, the scene that met him would have been the furthest from his imagination. A tall, good-looking, shirtless stranger had himself wrapped around Alena, a flirty smile on his face. He looked ready to kiss her.

"Let her go," Jeb commanded.

~

ALENA'S BODY TENSED. John reacted to it at the same time he heard the man's voice. Instinctively, he knew the voice belonged to Jeb, Alena's husband. John wasn't a foolish man. He didn't know everything about himself. He didn't even know what he did for a living.

But he knew his arms shouldn't be wound around another man's woman.

He wasn't even sure how it had happened. It was the first time since the blindness and amnesia hit that he felt lighthearted. Just touching his razor and comb, handling those familiar objects, gave him a little hope. He had seen a few flashes, bits and pieces of memories. Standing in front of a mirror. Shaving himself.

It assured him he would regain all his memory. It was only a matter of time now. The blindness still had him worried. But just for a few minutes, Alena's laughter banished all his fears. It freed him from the bonds of darkness. He had enjoyed the sound of her laughter and simply being with her.

He remembered Maureen laughing at his pranks as a child, scolding him, although her eyes danced merrily with amusement as she rebuked him.

With Alena, John felt right. Ever since she'd told him about her husband, he sensed things were not as they should be between the two. When Alena revealed that Jeb was much older than she was and had taken her in after her parents had died, John wondered as to their relationship. Maybe Jeb's sense of honor tied him to this obligation.

He pictured an old, crotchety bachelor in his head, one who liked living in this isolated area and used Alena more as a housekeeper and cook. He couldn't— wouldn't— see his new friend as a bedmate to a much older man. Alena deserved a better life, sharing her sweet spirit and sense of fun with people. She needed friends to talk with, not simply wounded animals and an irritable loner who left her by herself more often than not.

And as a woman, she needed pleasure.

John remembered pleasure. At least the physical part. Love he had experienced with Annabelle, a love that had never been consummated. Their relationship remained chaste, with only hand-holding and stolen kisses. When he lost his first love, desolation filled him. The war came then and he hadn't time to think about women much. But after the war, John knew he'd turned to other women to fill a need within him.

A picture rose in his mind of a redhead, with creamy skin, beautiful green eyes, and a figure that would pop the braces off any man. He knew in an instant this woman now served as his mistress. He felt no love for her, but they had an easy companionship that he enjoyed.

Maybe that's what had started his growing attraction to Alena. John hadn't known it had been present before this moment. It simmered under the surface as they got to know each other. He recognized her step. Her jasmine scent. He knew the way she would pause and reflect before she answered a serious question. He listened to the beautiful music she made. How she made the rocker squeak. He appreciated the strong hands that cared for his wounds, and had experienced the tender heart that also ministered to him so well.

He didn't think he was in love with her but experience had taught him that love was a feeling that grew with time. Alena had shown a kindness to him. She could have turned him out that first night, or even after a day or two. She could have cleaned his wounds and sent him on his way, not the least bit guilty, only having done her duty to a stranger passing by— one who hadn't a clue to his identity.

She had taken an enormous risk. Not only by bringing him into her home, but keeping him close to her heart. He remembered how fast he had reached for the guns at his sides when she had him down in that hole. The thought flew through his mind again. Was he a lawman, or a gunslinger? He hadn't even remembered that moment until now.

And yet, she had cared for him. Was it her nursing and healing touch that brought about the initial attraction? John didn't think so. Alena simply possessed a kind soul. She was enjoyable to be with. Interesting. He guessed her to be very talented, the way she cared for her paints and the time she used in pursuing her art. Without having seen one brushstroke on a canvas, he was certain of her ability. He heard the careful brushstrokes. He sat by the fire, not even rocking, because he wanted to listen to the subtle scratching. A brushstroke against a page had come to mean Alena to him.

She had become John's entire world. And now that world had come crashing down.

～

"Jeb!"

Alena untangled herself awkwardly from John's arms. She wouldn't think about how good it had been to be in them for a brief moment.

Jeb was home.

She looked in his eyes, seeing a flash of anger absent for many years. He wore the same look he had when Kevin McClaine had wronged them. Jeb had despised her father. Alena barely remembered the man, but nothing could make her forget the cold look in Jeb's eyes on the day her father ran away. The day he killed her mother. Jeb's look now was strong enough to kill.

Her eyes fell to the cocked revolver in Jeb's steady hand. The gun was aimed at John. She broke from John and moved toward Jeb.

Her priority was to protect John. This need consumed her. The shock of seeing Jeb after so long a time was nothing compared to the need to see to John's safety.

If Jeb attacked John in any way, he'd be helpless. He would never see Jeb coming.

Alena stepped closer to Jeb so she was between both of her friends. Her treasured friend from her past, who had done everything for her, and her new friend who, despite not knowing who he was, showed her very much the kind of man he was. John Harper was a good man. She sensed it in her soul. And now she must calm Jeb. Divert his attention.

As Jeb glared past her at John, Alena stumbled toward him.

"Jeb, it's so good to see you. I've missed you so much."

He stared at her a moment without speaking. His silence enveloped the room with its anger.

"I see you've taken in another wounded bird," he growled, his voice low and gravelly.

"Yes. Oh, Jeb, he was hurt badly. I wish you'd been here. I hope I did the right thing."

Before Jeb could reply, John spoke up. "Jeb, I'm... sorry I don't know your last name, else I'd address you more formally. My name is Harper. John Harper."

Alena looked over her shoulder. John took an awkward step or two, holding out his hand. She turned and looked at Jeb's eyes and saw surprise flicker across his face. She knew Jeb realized in that moment that John was blind.

CHAPTER 13

$\mathcal{J}$eb extended his hand and took Harper's firmly in his own. He looked the stranger over warily. Despite the man's blindness and obvious shoulder injury, Jeb smelled trouble. Trouble had been a constant companion in his youth and it dogged him to this day. It rarely followed him home, but it greeted him now as easily as rain fell from a storm cloud.

He didn't like surprises, and Harper's presence was a bolt out of the blue. He glanced over at Alena, concern written across her brow. This man had wormed his way into Alena's heart. That could prove to be a bigger menace than anything he'd faced before.

He had to get rid of John Harper.

The man interrupted his thoughts. "I know you and Alena must have lots to talk about. If you don't mind, I'll excuse myself."

He turned his body slightly to the left, his head up, searching for the right direction. Jeb watched as Alena called out directions.

"Turn slightly to your left, John," she said softly.

When he had, she continued. "The bedroom door is straight ahead. Eight paces."

113

John started toward it, as confident as Jeb thought a blind man could be in a strange place. He walked slowly and carefully, his posture straight and proud, until he reached the doorframe. His hands went out on both sides as he ran them along its edge before he stepped through and closed the door.

Jeb marched to the cabinet and opened its door. He stood on tiptoe to grab the bottle on the top shelf. Once in his hand, he opened it and took a long swig. The amber liquid burned his throat and pooled in his belly.

He turned and caught Alena's disapproving stare, her lips pursed, her mouth set. Kevin had been a drinker. Alena still associated alcohol with her long-gone father.

He glared at her and stormed across the room and out the door, letting it slam behind him.

Jeb scrambled down the steps, kicking at the chickens, cursing under his breath. Alena followed closely on his heels. He turned to face her, deliberately drawing another long pull from the bottle, defiant as a child caught with his hand in the cookie jar.

"You know I don't approve of you drinking."

"And I don't approve of strange men staying in my home, pawing my daughter like she's a common whore."

She flushed darkly, her embarrassment evident. "That... we were... oh, I don't give a goat! You wouldn't understand."

Jeb capped the bottle and tossed it aside. Lightning quick, he grabbed her shoulders, his grip tight. "What don't I understand? That you broke every rule we have while I was gone? You aren't supposed to speak to strangers when I'm away, much less invite 'em to stay as long as they like and play hanky-panky like a strumpet would."

Alena's tempered flared to match his own. "And

what was I supposed to do? Let a man bleed to death in a raging storm?" She crossed her arms. "I gather it would've been all right to bury his dead body the next day, once the rain cleared up."

Jeb shook her once for emphasis. He didn't approve of her new, rebellious attitude. "You could've been in danger, Alena. You might've put both of us in danger. We don't know this man from the President. Once inside, he could've robbed us blind and stolen your virtue, too."

He pushed her aside and turned his back. Jeb thrust his hands into his pockets, not wanting her to see how they trembled.

"Jeb, he was unconscious. He was shot. He wasn't a threat. In fact, he was so far gone, I doubted I could save him at first. I thought I had a better chance patching up his injured horse. I'd already begun to think of places to bury him before he came around."

She sniffed. "And if you haven't noticed, he's blind. I doubt he could've caused much trouble."

Jeb faced her. Alena's jaw was set in determination. This was a new girl, much different from the one he had left weeks earlier. She had always been protective about each wounded bird or animal that she cared for, but this new Alena seemed like a fierce mother bear guarding a beloved cub.

And as she shielded John Harper from his wrath, Jeb saw that the stranger had awakened things in her that she might not be aware of yet. Before him stood not a girl, but a woman. He thought of Alena gathered in Harper's arms, the picture that greeted him upon his return. He wasn't even supposed to stop off here. He had too much to do but he'd wanted to ease Alena's worries since he'd been away longer than usual. The sight of his Sweetie Pie frolicking with a half-naked man did not sit well with him.

"Not so blind that he couldn't find you."

Alena looked at him in confusion. "Jeb, his horse brought him here. He was barely in the saddle, half-alive."

"Well, he's the picture of good health now, judging how he was romping around with you. Didn't I raise you better?" Jeb shook his head. "I suppose not, since I found you snuggling with a strange man who's stripped to the waist."

She gasped. "Jeb! That's not fair. John's been so down. He was feeling better today. I shaved him and was helping him get cleaned up. We just were fooling around—"

"'Fooling around' is right. Silly games have gotten many girls into trouble. I know. I've seen it happen—and I've seen those same girls have to grow up fast. A baby on their hip and no man around to support them."

Her mouth fell open. Jeb read the shock that crossed her face. He sighed inwardly, glad that he had read the situation wrong. Alena might have some budding feelings for this fellow, but he doubted that kind of fooling around had been on her mind. She was still too naïve, he decided. Harper, on the other hand— blind or not— knew better. He wouldn't trust the man sooner than he'd trust Satan.

"Jeb, really. I mean... I mean... you can't think... why, I've never even kissed a man!" she proclaimed, color flooding her cheeks.

His knees went weak at her announcement. He thanked his lucky stars. She was still his little girl.

And he would keep it that way.

"He's got to go, Alena. You need to tell him to pack up and be out tomorrow morning at first light."

"I will not!"

Jeb examined the dirt under his fingernails, not wanting to make eye contact with her. "I understand that you helped him. Probably did more than most. But the time's come when Mr. Harper needs to get on his way."

"He can't. He doesn't know what that way is."

Jeb's head flew up "What do you mean?"

Alena sighed. "He doesn't know who he is. Whenever he was shot, he fell hard. He had the biggest goose egg on the back of his head that I've ever seen. It's played tricks with his memory. He didn't even know his own name when he first came to."

She rubbed her hands up and down her arms as if she were cold. "He's started remembering bits and pieces. His name. Things about his family. Growing up. He remembers as far as fighting in the war, but he doesn't know why he came West after the fighting finished. He doesn't know where he lives or what he even does for a living.

"And," she concluded, "he's blind. He wasn't before his accident. Since he's begun to recollect things, we're hoping his eyesight will return, too."

Alena came and placed a hand on his arm. "I can't turn him out. He couldn't see where to go even if he did know his way. We've got to let him stay. Please?"

Jeb knew she was telling the truth. Alena never lied to him. He'd also been with Anthony after a particularly vicious barroom brawl. His brother fell and smacked his head so hard on the floor, the board cracked in two. Anthony hadn't known who he was for three days, and after that, he didn't remember the fight at all.

Still, he didn't like leaving again with a stranger in his house. Maybe Alena should come with him, at least for part of his trip. He had to get her away from the attractive stranger because he was afraid he'd lose her.

"Well, Sweetie Pie, if you feel so strongly, I guess he can stay."

"Oh, thank you, Jeb." She threw her arms around his neck and kissed his cheek. He felt once again like the champion of her youth. Her father. Her protector. Her friend. Having her in his arms again reassured him they were family and would always be together.

"Now you, on the other hand, might need to come with me."

"Come where?" Curiosity sparked in her eyes.

"San Francisco."

A gambit of emotions rushed through Alena. Excitement first, at something new and wonderful and forbidden. Jeb wanted to escort her on one of his frequent trips. She wondered so many times what life was like outside the small niche they had carved into the world. Her books helped. They told her what the world could be like.

Oh, she knew she was naïve. She knew it couldn't be as good as her books said. Make believe was always better. But just once, wouldn't it be fun to go and explore and see and do? And yet, memories from long ago edged their way to the surface. She remembered Rio Vista. The people. The stares and whispers. A sick feeling washed over her. No, she couldn't do it. Wouldn't do it.

Then she thought of John. He had a calming influence on her, a steadiness, and she thought if John were by her side, she wouldn't hesitate going for an instant. Guilt flooded her. Here was Jeb, whom she'd known practically her entire life, offering her a forbidden fruit. A trip to somewhere she had dreamed of. And yet she preferred to go with a man who was little more than a stranger.

Or was he?

Alena shook her head. "I can't leave John here by himself, Jeb. As much as I would like to travel with you,

I need to make sure he recovers. So he can be on his way."

She saw disappointment flicker in his eyes. She couldn't help it. How could he ask her to abandon John? Jeb was so protective. It wasn't as if John were a stranger to her anymore. In fact, there were days when she believed she knew him better than she did Jeb. Jeb was one for silence. He rarely opened up about his feelings. John, despite his memory loss, seemed like an open book to her. He had shared so much with her. She felt comfortable in his presence.

She shoved her hands into her pockets. Her fingers touched the pocket watch. Remorse at having kept it from John swept through her. Alena had told herself she would share it with him when he was ready, when he could see and was remembering more about his current situation.

But would she ever be ready to let him go?

CHAPTER 14

Alena looked at Jeb, hoping that he was over his spell. He had never been angry with her. Not once in all the years she had known him. She realized how upsetting it must have been for him to come home after weeks on the road and find a blind stranger in his home, especially after all the warnings he'd issued in the past.

She smiled brightly at him, glad he would allow John to stay. Why, in two days' time, they'd be the best of friends. John had a way with words that put people at ease. Alena looked forward to the days ahead, as the three of them sat around sipping coffee after dinner. Maybe she could convince Jeb to play his harmonica for John. Jeb knew all kinds of songs and even made up a few of his own.

That made her wonder if he had gotten the coffee beans and other needed provisions. Jeb's trip had lasted much longer than usual, and now that he was home, it roused her curiosity.

"Did you sell all the paintings? Get the supplies we needed?"

"Supplies are out in the barn," Jeb told her. "I'll unload them later. As for your paintings…"

His voice trailed off and Alena's throat grew thick. She always worried that her work wouldn't sell.

Jeb guffawed loudly. "Can't tease you, Sweetie Pie. You've got about as much color as a dead fish's belly." He ruffled her hair affectionately.

"We did good. The paintings— you know— the one you had trouble parting with?"

"Oh," she said, as a vision of the doe and her fawn came to mind. That had been a particularly hard one to let go. She thought it was her best effort to date.

Jeb nodded. "It went to a good person."

"How do you know? What's involved when you sell one?" she asked. Though she had never inquired about the process, she wanted to know what it consisted of. It was as if John coming into her life made her more curious about the workings of the world beyond.

"Let's go inside and I'll tell you about it."

Jeb swung an arm around her shoulders as they climbed the steps to the cabin.

Inside, the fire warmed the room, chasing away the chill of the day. The door to her bedroom was closed so Alena assumed John was still in there.

Jeb shuffled over and took a seat at the table. He slipped a hand into his top pocket, and from the well-worn flannel he removed a small bag of peppermints.

Alena's mouth watered at the sight of it and he tossed it to her. Catching it, she immediately opened it and dropped a single candy into her mouth, the rich sweetness flooding her taste buds. Lord, she had missed the taste of peppermints.

But she wasn't going to be put off by a treat. She gave Jeb her most determined look and said, "I'll put on some coffee. If you're hungry, I'll make something to eat. While I'm working, you can tell me about selling the paintings. All of them."

Jeb shook his head, almost in resignation. He put his

ALEXA ASTON

elbows on the table and steepled his fingers in front of him.

"It's worked one way or another in the past," he began, as she busied herself with the coffee fixings.

Jeb leaned his chair back on two legs. "Well," he drawled, "I go to several places nowadays. They have picture stores. Actually, I guess you call it an art store."

"A gallery?" she prompted. She knew the term from one of her books.

Slowly, he nodded. "A gallery," he agreed. "I've stopped by for so long now that they know me. Or they know," and he winked at her, "A McClaine, that is."

A warm feeling filled her. It had been Jeb's idea to go by her first initial. He told her there might be some prejudice against a woman artist. Every time she finished a landscape or nature scene, the last thing she did was scrawl her signature on it. A McClaine. It filled her with a sense of accomplishment.

"Once I go in," he continued, "depending upon how many you've placed in the wagon, I go to two, maybe three galleries. I try to trade off so that a different one is first each time. "Oh, Sweetie Pie, you'd be pleased. Most try to talk me into offering them an exclusive deal, but I don't want you tied to one place. So I move around and visit a few."

Alena nodded, eager for him to continue, trying to picture it all in her mind.

"I go in and we sit, have a drink. Two, sometimes. And we talk. I tell them what A McClaine has been up to. I tell them, 'This time, I have four A McClaines that the artist is willing to part with.' Darling, you should see their eyes light up. They try to hide it, but I can see the excitement tingling just under the surface.

"They ask exactly what I brought and I'll tell them what I'm offering. Got a few nice ones, I'll say. A still pond. A swan. An Appaloosa. Rolling hills with a sunset

122

or a mama and her baby deer. I tell them just enough to whet their appetite and then I get up to go."

Jeb chuckled. "Each time, it's the same. They insist I sit back down. Talk a while longer. But I play it close to the vest. I tell them to think about it and I'll be back. I do that two, three times with a day or two between my visits. I want to make sure they are itching to buy and will give us a good price."

"What about the doe and her fawn? If you sell directly to these galleries, how do you know who bought that one?"

It hurt to let go of that particular painting. The mother came to her with a broken leg, barely able to walk, heavily pregnant. Alena cared for her close to a week before her time to give birth arrived. It had been a hard labor. When she held the newborn deer in her arms, she experienced such a contentment and sense of peace, it made her wonder if she would ever hold a child of her own in a similar fashion.

Just seeing the mama and baby together made her happy. She painted them when the doe was about three weeks old. Eventually, the mother's leg healed and Alena released the pair back into the wild. She thought she had seen a glimpse of them once, and so she painted them, once again, from memory. She wasn't ready to give up that painting yet. It hung above the fireplace. In time she would become attached to another effort, and this painting would be let go.

"I go back and we haggle a bit. Eventually, the owner of that gallery accepts one or two of your paintings. I never let a place have more than two. As we closed the deal, a gentleman was in there. Very well dressed. Like a guy from one of your books. Immaculate suit. Brushed hair. An air of money about him.

"He stepped up to us and says, 'I couldn't help but

overhear you had a new A McClaine. I heard the part about the doe.'"

Jeb placed a hand over Alena's and gave it a squeeze. "Despite his fancy air, he looked like a good man, Alena. He said he wanted to give the painting to his bride. They were to be married in less than a month. He motioned over his shoulder and I saw a young girl about your age, looking at paintings displayed upon the wall. She turned and her eyes looked like the eyes of your mama doe. And I knew that painting would hang in a fine home. As I left, he and the gallery owner sealed the deal."

He gave her hand another squeeze and then sat back in his chair again. Alena got up and poured the coffee. As she handed him the steaming mug, she also took out a couple of slices of cold ham and cut a piece of the peach pie she had made yesterday.

Jeb didn't have a hearty appetite but he lit into the pie before he ever touched the ham. The sounds he made let Alena know he enjoyed it. Of course, John also made the same appreciative noises yesterday when the pie was fresh.

Alena wondered what John was doing. He wasn't the type to listen at the door to their conversation. She could see him sitting on his mattress cross-legged, a contemplative air about him. She'd found him like that several times now. Alena wondered what he thought about and what he remembered.

JOHN WANTED TO KICK HIMSELF. He was surprised Jeb hadn't done it first. He pictured the scene that greeted the farmer when he came in after a long trip away from home. Hell, the man should've shot him, the way John had been wrapped around Jeb's wife.

That he hadn't proved just how pitiful John was. Nothing but a blind, helpless fool who'd taken his playful teasing too far. Alena did that to him. She made him comfortable and frisky at the same time. Part of him didn't want his memory to return because that meant he'd have to leave and get back to wherever and whatever came before her.

He'd just been funning with her but their play swiftly turned to something else. If Jeb had walked in his door five seconds later, he would have seen his wife being kissed senseless. Alena felt right in his arms, like no one before. Just being close to her made his pulse race. When she'd been in his arms that brief time, he wanted nothing more than to taste her. Run his fingers through her silky hair. Smell the jasmine behind her ears.

John wondered what Alena looked like. He had a fair vision of her size after being around her. Her hands were small but strong. She came just past his shoulder in height. But how to picture her? He never really had before. His overall impression was hazy. Did those silky tresses reflect the sun much as Annabelle's blonde ones had? Were her eyes blue or green or brown? Did she blush as easily as Annabelle, where the rosiness painted her cheeks?

Disgust at his thoughts filled him. She was married. He had to stop these fantasies. Alena had showed him nothing but kindness. He didn't want to cause trouble between her and Jeb, not after everything she had done for him.

John blocked out the voices in the next room, but the aroma of coffee and the lure of peach pie did him in. Besides, he was curious about Jeb and needed to scratch that itch.

He rose and counted the steps to the door. He took a deep breath and turned the handle.

"Mind if I join you?" he called out. "I'm a sucker for that peach pie."

He heard Alena's musical laugh. "You could smell it with the door closed?"

John grinned sheepishly and headed for the sound of her voice. "Can't say I ever paid much attention to smells before."

He reached the table and put a hand out to touch the chair back before sliding it out and slipping into the seat.

"The good ones I took for granted. The bad ones are best left forgotten."

The tinny smell of blood flooded his memories, along with the smell of death and decay. If the odors of war bothered him that much with his eyesight, he couldn't imagine what it would be like now.

He heard the knife on the pie plate and the scraping sound as Alena pushed it across the table.

"Coffee?" she asked.

"No better way to eat pie than with a cup of black coffee," he replied.

He was amazed at the difference Jeb's presence made in the room. From their handshake, John knew he was taller, broader, and much stronger than Jeb, yet the man's essence filled the room. He wanted to know why. How did a country farmer have so commanding a presence?

John tilted his head to the left. "Did you have a successful trip, Jeb? Alena tells me you went to sell her quilts and paintings."

Jeb's fork clicked on his plate. "You could say so."

Tight-lipped. John knew Jeb was studying him intensely. It was as if his sight had miraculously returned and John could actually see Jeb doing so. This would be a man who gave little away. He would try his best to sound affable, hoping to ease the guard Jeb kept about him.

"I do appreciate your hospitality, Jeb. If not for your wife, I would be dead by now."

A pregnant silence filled the air. John knew in that minute that Alena had lied to him.

She wasn't married to Jeb.

SOUNDFAITH

against attacks, hoping to save the pace, jeb kept about 20m.

I do appreciate your hospitality, jeb, if not for your care I would be dead...

prepared self and called the mr. John Kaley told that known that Alena and that had been

She when man...

CHAPTER 15

eb cut his eyes quickly to Alena. Even though Harper was blind, Jeb knew the man sensed he did so. Alena gave him an apologetic shrug. He realized she had told their visitor this tale for protection. Had the man gotten fresh with her before? Was this her way to warn him off?

And yet, they had seemed so comfortable together when he arrived an hour ago. Alena was a serious child who'd grown into a quieter woman. Her rare smiles rained down like a gift from God. He cherished each one of them. That she'd given them to John Harper, along with her lyrical laughter, ate at his craw.

She was smart, though. She'd probably told him she was married from the beginning. Jeb heard her do it once before when a shady-looking character stopped by for a drink from their well. Jeb caught a part of their conversation as he rounded the barn door and played his part, putting an arm around Alena's waist as he eyeballed the passerby. The man understood possession when he saw it and made haste to drink his cup of water and move on.

Jeb expelled a loud rush of air. "To tell you the truth, John, it's kinda hard thinking of Alena as my wife." He banked on the fact that Alena would have shared she grew up here.

"I took Alena in when she was nigh-high." He gestured with his hand and then let it fall, realizing his guest couldn't see. Flustered, he added, "We just fell into an easy relationship and then... love bloomed."

"Sounds poetic, Jeb. Now remind me how long you've been married?"

It sounded like a trap. Jeb looked to Alena quickly but she only shook her head, a frown creasing her brow.

"Well, I'm no good at dates. Sweetie Pie, was it—"

"Last July," Alena interrupted.

"This past July?" Harper asked with interest. He turned his head from side to side, first looking in the direction of Jeb and then Alena. Jeb knew their guest couldn't see their shaken expressions, but it spooked him all the same.

"No. Not a few months ago," Jeb added. "Summer before this past one."

Harper nodded. "I see." He found his coffee mug and took a long drink from it. "Guess it must be hard to leave for so long a spell and leave a pretty wife behind."

Alena blushed. *John thought she was pretty?*

He didn't even know what she looked like. She pictured herself in her mother's comb and mantilla, the silk shawl draped around her. When John regained his eyesight, that's how she wanted him to first see her, the way she looked when she dressed up when Jeb was gone. She suddenly felt embarrassed for the way she ran around the rest of the time, in loose trousers and Jeb's shirts, her hair tied back in an unflattering fashion.

Frustration filled her. Why did she even care about John seeing her? Once he did regain his sight, he would soon be gone from their lives, never to return.

"I don't mind Jeb's trips," she said evenly. "I have my chores to do and my animals to care for. I have my paintings and quilts to work on. I don't get lonely, John."

But even she heard the wistfulness in her voice. She never realized it before John Harper had arrived, but she lived a lonely life— and remained lonely when Jeb returned. She longed to be around people her own age. Walk down a city street in a pretty dress. Attend mass in a real church like her mother had told her about. Alena realized that despite her fears, she was done with living so far away from society.

More importantly, she yearned to put her lips next to John's. She would have if Jeb hadn't interrupted them. Now, she was glad he had. If he'd come through the door five minutes later, Alena would have been doing much more than merely kissing John Harper.

And that would have signaled his death.

Jeb would have shot first and asked questions later. Alena said a small prayer of thanks to the Virgin for protecting John from Jeb's wrath.

Alena sensed something in the air between the two men. She was grateful for a moment that John couldn't see. She pictured the pair like two wolves circling each other, sniffing out their opponent.

She broke the tension with the only thing that came to her mind.

"We had visitors come looking for an outlaw."

Jeb jerked his head to her, demanding, "What kind of visitors?"

Alena had his full attention now. "Three men. They said they were lawmen but I think the only place they'd graced inside a sheriff's office might've been the jail."

He frowned but she could see the worry in his eyes. "What did they look like?"

She shrugged. "Two were ordinary enough. Rough-looking. Dressed in clothes they'd probably slept in for a few days. Said they rode through the night looking for a man who was a bank robber and murderer."

Jeb took in her words and then asked, "And the third?"

"They called him Cletus but he never introduced himself properly. He had a mean streak in him, though. I could tell by his eyes."

"They haven't been back?"

"No. They probably found their man else they would've returned," she replied, worried the trio still might make their way here again.

"Did you see them?" Jeb looked to John.

Instead of reminding Jeb to use John's name when he spoke to him, she quickly added, "John wasn't here then. He came a couple of days later."

Jeb looked back at her and slowly nodded. He scratched his chin and then stood up. "Might as well unload the supplies. I'll be in the barn for a while." He slapped John on the back. "Don't go eating all my peach pie."

John laughed. "How about we talk Alena into making another one?"

"I'll make one for each of you next time so you won't have to share," she said. "Maybe apple?"

"Sounds good, Sweetie Pie." Jeb squeezed her shoulder and headed out the door.

Alena cleared the dishes and set them in her wash basin. She would wait and add the supper dishes before she boiled water to clean them. She turned to offer John a peppermint and was startled to find he was standing right behind her, a scowl on his face. She hadn't heard him approach.

Nervous, she said, "I'm sure glad Jeb's home. I've already had one peppermint. I might celebrate and have another tonight."

Her attempt at conversation died in her throat as she picked up on the cold anger emanating from John.

"I want to know why you lied just now."

Alena tried to control her breathing to answer him but it was hard with all the fluttering in her belly as they stood only inches apart.

She tugged on the cuff of her sleeve and said, "I know I told you we were married," she confessed, deciding she had to be honest and tell him the truth. "I've done that when strangers come by. It just seems safer—"

"I don't mean that. We'll get into that lie later." He drew closer to her. "What I want to know is why you lied to Jeb."

Panic filled her. "About what?" She was certain John could hear her heart hammering.

"About why I arrived a few days after those men came around. They were looking for me, weren't they?"

Alena nodded her head and John must have sensed the gesture.

"Why?" His blank eyes looked down at her. "I'm... I'm not a murderer. Am I?" He gripped her shoulders. She could feel the imprint from each heated finger. "Tell me what you know, Alena."

"I don't think you're a murderer," she stammered. "You're too much a gentleman."

He laughed harshly. "That's what Bluebeard's wives all thought."

Clueless, she asked, "Who's Bluebeard?"

"A man who murdered half a dozen wives. Maybe more."

She shivered. "You're no Bluebeard. But... they were looking for the man who rode the bay horse they found in our barn. They knew Cicero, John. I told them she arrived here riderless, and I tended her."

Alena touched her palm to John's cheek. "They *were* looking for you, John. They were up to no good."

"But why didn't you tell me about this while I've been struggling to remember things?"

She swallowed. "I don't know. You were sick. I didn't know what you could handle. I wanted you to get well first. I didn't even realize that you knew they had been here."

"I remember bits and pieces of it. Their voices. Being in the dark, far away. That's about it."

He released her and turned away. She should show him the badge now, the one she'd buried in the flour. Her heart told her those men were responsible for John's condition. Either they were telling the truth and John was an outlaw they pursued, or Alena realized he must be the lawman who pursued them. They had tried to kill him and when they hadn't, they tracked him here, lying about their identities and his.

John Harper was a sheriff or marshal or some other authority figure. She'd buried any thought of who he might be when she'd hidden his badge in the flour. Alena understood how she'd fooled herself for far too long now. She had grown fond of John, more than she'd realized. She hadn't wanted him to remember who he was. She wanted to keep him all to herself, away from the world and the danger that lay in it for him.

Jeb's arrival changed everything. She must give up her girlish fantasies. She must give him the badge. The time had come.

Alena stood. "I have something to show you, John. Something important. I think it will help you remember who you are."

The door opened. Jeb walked in and threw the flour sack slung over his shoulder onto the table.

"Here's the first of things for inside, Alena. Want me to fill your flour bin?"

CHAPTER 16

*A*lena froze. She couldn't remember how low the flour had gotten. She wanted to talk to John about the badge in her own way. Jeb discovering it while he poured flour in the bin would ruin everything.

Not that everything wasn't already ruined. Alena imagined John's reaction to her keeping the badge from him. It brought a sick feeling that overwhelmed her.

"No. Just leave the sack on the floor. I trust you pouring sugar a lot more than I do flour."

Jeb chuckled. "I do seem to make a mess at times."

She forced a smile. "Just bring in the sacks. I'll make sure things get where they belong."

He nodded and went back out. She heard his footsteps taking him away and waited for John to speak.

"What is it, Alena? What do you have to show me?"

"Not now, John. It can wait."

"Wait?" he hissed through clenched teeth. "What's so Gol-darned important that I have to wait?"

She flinched at his tone. It let her know what would come when she handed him the silver star. When he regained his memory.

"Go lie down," she ordered. "You've had a lot of excitement today. I need to focus on putting up the provisions Jeb brought home."

A startled look crossed his face, his jaw dropping in disbelief. Then he squared his shoulders.

"Fine," he snapped. "I'll go sit on the porch."

Alena watched him stand and start toward the door. Automatically, she said, "Take another—"

"I don't need your help." John cut her off and kept walking.

He bumped into a chair and swore under his breath but made it to the doorknob. Alena turned away, her throat swelling with hurt. She opened the flour bin and reached in, burying her hand and searching until she found the tin star. She pulled it out and slid it into her pocket, next to John's pocket watch. Remorse filled her, but she would deal with that later. She wanted privacy when she gave John his two possessions.

And she didn't want Jeb to know what a fool she'd been.

THEY SPENT most of the evening meal in silence. John was sullen. Jeb was tired and quieter than usual. Alena put on a bright face for Jeb. She didn't want to ruin his homecoming but she was shaky at best.

After dinner, Jeb retreated to the porch to smoke. Alena hated the smell of tobacco and always made him smoke outside the cabin. Tonight, however, she joined him, not comfortable for the first time in John's company.

They sat on the steps, longtime companions enjoying the peace of a cool fall night.

Jeb broke the silence. "I'll be heading out tomorrow."

Alena couldn't believe he would leave again so soon. "You just got here. Why do you have to go?"

He blew out a long cloud of smoke. "I just made a quick detour here to bring home the supplies and see you. I knew we'd be getting low on things." He winked at her. "Especially peppermints."

Alena sucked hard on the one in her mouth, guilty he had taken time out to bring the sweets to her.

"Besides, if'n I'm going to go and set us up in San Francisco, I better get started."

His words startled her. "Set us up?" Excitement rippled through her, thinking of so many possibilities that lay ahead if this truly came to pass.

He nodded. "I think it's time we had a change."

"You actually want to leave your home?" She shook her head. "I don't see you in a city, Jeb. You belong here."

He patted her hand. "But you don't. I've been selfish. Keeping you all to myself. It's time you had new experiences. Mingled with people."

Panic seized her. "You won't leave me alone in San Francisco, will you?"

Jeb chortled. "No, missy, you are stuck with me. I think it's high time we had a few new adventures. We can always keep this place. If we ever feel too cooped up in the city, why, we'll come out here for a few days."

Relief filled Alena. She drew strength from the nearby lake and forest, from being around the animals that were drawn to her doorstep. "It sounds like the best of both worlds. But you don't need to do that right away."

He rubbed his temples and sighed. "No, I won't. Got a little more business to take care of before I can find us a new place."

"What?" She'd never questioned him about much of anything, but Alena wondered now why he had to take off. Locating a new home for them in San Francisco was one thing, but she couldn't fathom what else would take him away, especially since the most recent batch of paintings and quilts had already been sold.

"I don't understand. What's so important that you have to leave after less than a day at home?"

He took another drag on the cigar. "One thing that'll make us a pretty penny."

She eyed him suspiciously. "What are you talking about?"

"I came home to get the painting."

Alena was confused. "What painting? I sent all the completed canvasses with you this last trip. I've started a couple but they won't be finished anytime soon."

"The doe and baby, Alena. That's the one I need."

"No!" She found it hard enough to part with the first painting of the two deer. The other one hung above the fireplace and she gazed upon it lovingly every day. "You know I'm not ready to give that one up yet."

Jeb gave her a hard look. "I know that's how you feel, but that nice man I told you about that bought the other one wants it."

She stood, fisted hands going to her waist. "And why on earth did you tell him about it?"

He glared at her. "You know how it hurts me that I can't provide for you like I should. Your paintings are what keep us going. This city slicker wants it for his bride and is willing to pay a good price. We can't afford to say no."

"Yes, we will." Alena stared at Jeb as twilight descended. She didn't like what she saw. She looked into the face of a stranger, cold and hard, nothing like the man who had loved her and read to her and taught her to hunt and fish and shoot. Steely determination lit his eyes.

"You can't have it." Her chin lifted in defiance. "I won't give it up."

Jeb stood. "It's a done deal. I gave him my word." He started up the stairs.

"That's it? Your word is law? You'll take my painting because you feel like it?"

He scratched his jaw. "Don't let things get ugly, Alena. It's just a painting."

"It's mine." She wanted to say more but the words died on her lips. The man in front of her was no longer Jeb. The subtle transformation showed that a stranger had taken his place. Ruthlessness flickered in his eyes.

"It's my house. You're my responsibility. I'm taking the painting. I'll leave at first light. No need to see me off."

Jeb clomped down the porch stairs and walked in the direction of the lake. He went there when he was troubled.

Alena had no intention of following him.

JOHN ROCKED in the chair he thought of as Alena's. Tonight, he needed the soothing motion it brought. Her earlier words troubled him. That she had something to show him that might bring his memory back.

Why had she not brought it out earlier? Was it because of the blindness? Was it an object that he would need his sight to recognize? Frustration gnawed at him as he mulled over things.

Then he heard their argument. He didn't mean to eavesdrop but he couldn't help it. Neither of them seemed the type to raise their voices but both were plenty angry and plenty loud. John understood why Alena could be so attached to a painting. He'd sat at the table while she worked and could hear the love in the brushstrokes as she worked on a canvas. Before he had lost his sight, he would have thought that notion silly, but his hearing was attuned to his surroundings now.

Especially if it included Alena.

It bothered him that Jeb thought to leave again so quickly. It surprised him, too. He wouldn't have thought Jeb the kind of man to leave Alena behind with a stranger. Especially the way he'd found them when he arrived. It almost sounded like Jeb was deliberately picking a fight with her, trying to make her mad enough to let him go. If Alena was so reluctant to part with this painting, why did Jeb make such an issue of it? Wouldn't the same buyer be there at a later date?

Alena stormed in without a word. He heard an unusual group of noises. Clinking cans. Rustling. A match being struck. He smelled a lit oil lantern. Where would she go with a lantern at this time of night?

She opened and then slammed the door and was gone for a couple of minutes. She returned and he heard the click of a rifle being opened and loaded. He stiffened, hoping she didn't intend to shoot Jeb, especially over a painting.

She left again. John decided to follow. He didn't know what he thought he might prevent, but he headed for the door and slipped out onto the porch. A cool breeze ruffled his hair. The night was filled with noises he had always disregarded before but now was keenly aware of.

He caught a hint of jasmine and turned his head in that direction.

At that moment, he heard the rifle cocked. Before he could react, the sound of a gunshot broke through the night.

Ping.

What was that? Alena had shot something. Thank God it wasn't Jeb.

The same pattern again. A cock of the gun and something hit. A tin can! He recognized the noise now. He listened carefully. Each time was the same. The noise of the rifle being readied and then the hollow ring from the can.

It had to be Alena. She'd set up cans somewhere, probably along a fence and was picking them off one at a time.

And she hadn't missed once.

Not a single time. John couldn't figure out how far she was shooting from but he'd bet she was a ways back. Firing by the light of a single lantern, surrounded by darkness.

He didn't know anyone who was that accurate, not even one of his fellow marshals.

John returned to the porch and sat. Alena fired another ten or so shots before silence filled the yard. He heard her trudging through the grass and from the noise she made, she must be setting the cans back up.

Again, each discharge met tin. Her precision amazed him. If he ever needed a good shot by his side, he would take Alena over any man he'd fought next to in the war.

Finally, she grew tired. Or bored. Or her anger had subsided. He heard the noises associated with collecting the cans. Her scent arrived at the porch before she did.

"Enjoy the show?"

"Where did you learn to shoot like that?"

"Jeb." She sat next to him on the porch, and he sensed waves of anger emanating from her. "I only shoot when I'm mad. I'm a much better shot the madder I am."

"Then remind me never to make you angry."

Alena sighed. John wanted to put an arm around her but resisted, thinking better of it. Then he heard a sob escape and his good intentions went out the window. He pulled her to him. Her face burrowed into his chest. He felt hot tears soak through his shirt. Instinctively, he pulled her closer.

She cried quietly, her body shaking. Whether she was still mad at Jeb or cried tears of frustration or hurt over losing her painting, he couldn't say.

"I'm sorry," she whispered, drawing slightly away from him.

John felt as if he were losing her in that moment. The person who had cared for him when he was injured. The woman who brought sunshine into his world of darkness and made him safe.

"I'm sorry, too," he said as he brought his lips down to hers.

CHAPTER 17

 John's mouth gently touched Alena's as he pulled her toward him. His lips slowly brushed against hers. Her heart beat rapidly, fluttering wildly, as he ran his hands along her back and encircled her waist. She sighed at his touch. Then he ran his tongue lightly along her bottom lip.

Alena gasped at the electric feel of John's tongue. It brought a pleasant tingling that accompanied the mass of butterflies flying about her belly. She tried to ask him what was happening, but as she opened her mouth, his tongue slid between her lips, touching her own.

Sparks flew as her mouth caught on fire. His tongue explored her mouth, heating her blood and causing sensations to ripple through her. She responded to him, answering him kiss for kiss. Her flesh grew hot, as if the summer sun showered its heat on her, searing her. The warmth spread from her mouth to her breasts, which began to ache and throb. She wound her hands around his neck, pulling him closer, drinking in his kisses as a parched stranger spying a well would consume its clear, sweet water.

John's hands pushed into her hair, threading through, loosening her braid. Fiery kisses touched her brow, her cheek, and trailed along her jaw. His lips moved even lower, touching her throat. Alena mewled like a kitten, her head falling back.

A sense of urgency swept over her as the throbbing increased, spreading down her body, pulsating in some ancient rhythm she didn't understand. Alena clung to John, desperate to ask what was happening, yet afraid to break the magic spell.

He moved back to her mouth, his kisses no longer tender but fierce in nature. Possessive. Leaving her breathless. Spinning out of control.

And then they stopped.

Alena's eyes flew open as John's warmth withdrew from her, releasing her, leaving her spent. He stood, his toe reaching out to feel for the stair, and he descended the three remaining steps to the bottom. He turned and faced her, his face a mask.

She stood and reached for him, threading her arms about his neck, eye-level with him. Hesitantly, she moved her mouth to his, planting a soft kiss on his lips. John stiffened and pulled away, removing her hands.

"I told you I was sorry before I started. I'm still sorry. I regret taking advantage of you."

Confusion filled her. "Why? That was beautiful, John. The most wonderful thing that's ever happened to me. Why are you sorry?"

He scowled. "I just am. A man doesn't have to go explaining everything." He took a step back, creating space between them. "I'll sleep in the barn tonight."

The finality in his voice surprised Alena. She wondered if she'd done something wrong, something to drive him away.

"No. Sleep by the hearth. You'd freeze to death in the barn." She tried her hardest to sound calm. She feared he could still hear her racing heart thumping

143

wildly. "I'll leave a few quilts for you. I'm sure you'll be more comfortable there."

She hurried inside the cabin before he could reply. She closed the door and leaned against it for support, her fingertips touching the lips that still tingled from John Harper's kisses.

What on earth was going on?

～

JOHN LAY in front of the fire and feigned sleep as he heard the door open. Jeb's step echoed across the floor. He paused and John knew the older man looked down upon him. He maintained his steady breathing.

Finally, Jeb turned and went to Alena's door. John wasn't mistaken about that. He knew the exact number of steps it took to reach it. They weren't married. Alena had admitted to that ruse, one he believed to be smart, especially as much as Jeb seemed to leave her alone.

So why was Jeb at her door? Did he wish to apologize for the harsh words spoken earlier? Or did he want to make Alena his own while John stood by helplessly? The thought sickened him, more so because of the kisses they'd shared only hours ago.

Jeb lingered another minute at Alena's door and then trudged to his own room. He closed the door, leaving John to his own thoughts.

He'd apologized to Alena before kissing her. He had only wanted to comfort her, as she had him. But once he started, it was like a wildfire burning out of control. No other kisses ever tasted as sweet as the ones he shared with Alena. Her silky hair. The smooth, satin feel of her cheek. The slender column of her throat.

He ached for them all again.

Once his lips touched hers, all thoughts of consolation fled. He wanted her— no, needed her— more than any woman he'd ever touched. He wanted to hold her. Possess her. Make sweet love to her all night.

Two things stopped him. One was Jeb. The man was just this side of blowing off John's head with a shotgun as it was. There was no need to push him over the edge.

The other stemmed from doubt. He still didn't know who he was. The kind of man he was. Where he came from. How could he make promises to Alena with his kisses when he didn't know if he could fulfill those promises? It wasn't fair to use her and then leave her. He might not know much, but honor meant something to him. He would not dishonor her like that again.

Yet those kisses played havoc with him now. He burned with their memory. He'd never kissed Annabelle like that. He couldn't recollect kissing any woman like that.

Guilt sat heavily on him. He didn't know how old Alena was, but she was still childlike in many ways. She was untouched by the world. At least he told himself that while remembering the feel of her full breasts crushed to his chest, her little moans and sighs as she enjoyed their kisses.

Damn, he'd never get to sleep. Maybe he should sleep in the barn. A little cold might be just the cure for what ailed him. He rose to go and thought better of it. Though Alena had lived with Jeb for many years, John didn't trust the man. He wouldn't leave her alone and asleep, unprotected.

He lay back down, hands pillowed behind his head. If sleep came, so be it. Until then, he might as well enjoy himself.

John's thought returned to Alena. He smiled.

~

JEB SUPPOSED he might as well get up. Sleep eluded him. He couldn't shut off all the conflicting emotions crowding his mind. The faint scent of jasmine on his pillow didn't help. With every breath he inhaled, he received a reminder of Alena. She must have slept in his bed while tending to Harper.

He hated leaving in the middle of the night with things cross between them. She had never known him to be anything other than easygoing. She was a sweet child who'd never seen his harsh side and short temper.

That was the real Jeb Foster.

It was because of the mess he'd created that he had to leave now. He couldn't explain it and bear the disappointment and anger that would follow if he tried. Better to hurt her a little now and get his business taken care of. He'd make it up to her. When he returned, things would be different. The Harper fellow would be gone. Jeb's difficulties would be over. He would have found them a pretty little place in San Francisco and they'd start a new life. Cut all ties with the past.

If his situation worked out, they would never worry about money again. If it were meant to be, it would all fall into place. It was just taking longer than he'd first anticipated.

Jeb gathered up a knapsack and stuffed a clean shirt and a few personal items inside, along with his pistol and a box of shot. He crept from his room, boots in hand. Darkness filled the cabin. Only the embers from the dying fire allowed him to see John Harper's outline. Sitting in a chair.

Waiting for him.

He walked over to the man who had invaded his home and stolen a bit of his Alena. "I expect you to be gone when I get back. Hospitality only goes so far."

"Why are you leaving?"

The man's tone was quiet but Jeb caught a hint of danger about it. It made him question his plan to leave Alena alone with this stranger but he had no choice. The die had been cast. He must follow through.

"None of your damned business. I come and go as I please. And it'd please me mightily to see you gone."

Harper sat still, yet Jeb knew he took stock of the man in front of him. Blind or not, John Harper was smart. It was as if he saw the real Jeb— not the one Alena knew and loved. He shivered, dread washing over him. Somehow, his fate was tied to this man. But how? What harm could a blind, helpless stranger bring?

"You tell me when you'll be back and I'll accommodate you." Harper smiled. "Alena won't like it, though."

"You leave my girl out of it," Jeb hissed. "She doesn't know what's good for her."

"And you do."

Jeb moved within inches of the man's face. "I've been caring for her since she was six years old. Fifteen years is a long time. Push comes to shove, her loyalties lie with me, John Harper. Not you."

He leaned back and added, "You're no charity case. You need to be gone. Understand?"

Harper nodded.

Jeb crossed to the mantel and lifted the painting from the wall. This was the excuse he had used in order to leave today. Yet he didn't have time to go through his usual routine and actually try to sell the work. Besides, the picture meant too much to Alena. He decided to hide it in the barn's loft. She never went up there. Once he returned, he would tell her that he'd had a change of heart. Everything would be different.

And if he found John Harper still here, he'd kill him.

CHAPTER 18

$\mathcal{J}$ ohn awoke. Every morning, he tested his memory. He recalled boyhood friends and that he loved pumpkin pie with a dollop of cream on top. He reminisced about his beloved dog Shep, and fishing with his father. Sometimes, he thought about the ugliness of the war. Two mornings when he'd awakened, an anguished wail almost escaped his lips but he bit it back, not wanting to worry Alena.

This morning, he ended with his usual questions— who am I and why am I here? Better yet, what did Alena have that might cause him to remember? Why hadn't she given it to him? He vowed to ask her about it today. With Jeb gone, she wouldn't be able to use that as an excuse.

Alena said this was northern California though he continually drew a blank as to his purpose for being here. Almost more than wishing his eyesight would return, he wanted to know who John Harper truly was. What he did for a living. How he spent his time.

He stretched and sat up. After Jeb left in the middle of the night, John finally got some sleep. He knew the fire was low, so he reached to put on another log to burn. His hand came in contact with wood. He gasped.

148

Not only did he feel the wood— he saw it. Well, see wasn't quite the right word. It was a blur in front of him but, by God, he *saw* a blur. He almost shouted in joy.

If his eyesight returned, surely his memory would. John added the log to the fire and saw bits of color spark for a moment. Once again, the fire was hazy but he not only felt its heat...

He saw it.

As the wood caught, the fire began to burn a little brighter. He lay back and laced his fingers behind his head, a smile on his face. Maybe this would be the day he would finally see Alena's features.

She would be beautiful because everything else about her was. Her voice was like a song, her step a beautiful rhythm all unto itself. Her healing hands touched him not only physically but in his heart. Alena was beautiful on the inside. John realized that no matter what she looked like, he would have strong feelings for her.

But he wouldn't use the word love.

He associated that with Annabelle yet he wondered if he even knew what love was. Was it based upon the ardor of his youth? What had he really felt for Annabelle? He grew up assuming she would always be by his side. John realized only too late the mistakes he had made.

He pined for Annabelle for longer than he dared admit. He'd seen her the one time during the dedication at Gettysburg. She, her husband, and her child. He knew from his mother that Annabelle had named the boy John and that he was called Johnny. It caused him pain and yet brought an immense sense of pride.

Yet something nagged at him about the boy. What? He'd only seen the child the one time, years ago. Why did little Johnny Reynolds weigh on his heart? An image came to mind of a frightened young boy. It flashed so fleetingly that John couldn't be sure where it came from.

His thoughts returned to Alena. In the time spent together, they had built a strong friendship. He knew from his relationship with Annabelle that friendship must be the basis for love. Passions flared out. Sizzling moments turned cold. Pictures of different women flittered across his mind. He knew there had been no love between him and these women. They only met a physical need. He still had an aching gap in his soul. Alena filled it.

Their kisses last night proved it.

The power and longing behind their embrace rocked him to his core. He longed to do more than merely kiss her. That would have to wait until he learned his identity and purpose. Only with the knowledge of who he was could he commit to her with a clear conscience.

John rose and dressed. Alena had hung his shirt over a chair at the table as she always did. He could see it was a dark color. He slipped his arms into it, blinking several times, willing himself to see more.

He put water on to boil for coffee. Alena was an early riser and she liked hers strong and black. It was one of a hundred things he had come to learn about his savior.

Shadows danced before his eyes, teasing him, so he took a turn about the room. He touched the rocker, gliding his hands over its arched back, wondering at the kind of wood it was carved from.

Everything seemed familiar. He walked back to the table and sat. No sooner had he done so when Alena's door opened. She was a giant shadow as she trod softly toward him.

"I see you have the water on for coffee, John. Thank you."

He heard the warm approval in her voice. It was funny how much more he knew about her, just by her tone. He didn't think he had been a shallow man, yet the blindness touched him in ways he couldn't have imagined. She seemed in a better mood than last night. Maybe Jeb leaving had been good for them all.

Alena bustled about. He knew each step of her routine. She mixed together biscuits and put them on to bake. She turned and said, "I'll go collect a few eggs. I'll be right back."

John stood and held out his hand. "No, let me. I've done it before."

"All right."

He turned and took a few steps to the door. Panic seized him. Without thinking, he closed his eyes to return to his familiar world of darkness. He felt safe there. He knew who he was and where he was in that darkness.

He reached the door and opened it and stepped out onto the porch. He gingerly negotiated the steps before he opened his eyes. The sun was just shooting up over the horizon. He longed not only for its warmth on his face, but to see the orb blazing in the sky.

Treading a little unsurely, he gathered several eggs in his hands, the chickens squawking about him. He returned to the porch, determined to keep his eyes open.

Alena heard John's step and smiled. He had become so dear to her in such a short time. She liked his easy laughter and rich baritone that would join her sometimes in song. She loved his strong fingers and wry sense of humor and devastatingly handsome smile.

And Lord Almighty, how she loved his kisses. She'd dreamed of them last night. Being in his arms. His mouth on hers, hot and searching. She awoke with a smile on her lips because of those sweet dreams.

John opened the door and because she knew him so well, Alena instantly caught the difference about him. She wasn't sure at first what it was. The way he held his head? The ghost of a smile that played about his lips? The look in his...

"Oh, my God," she said aloud. The vacant stare that had been John Harper was no longer. In an instant, Alena realized he could see.

She rushed to him as he stumbled. He held the eggs close to his chest. She put her hands over his and looked into his sparkling brown eyes.

"You can see," she said simply. "You can see."

John grinned boyishly and nodded. "A little," he admitted. "It's not much. I see a faint outline of things. No offense, Alena, but you're one giant blur. A pretty one, I'm sure, but a blur all the same."

"When did this happen?" she asked eagerly as she took the eggs from him.

"This morning."

She set down the eggs, her excitement building. Alena had no idea how John felt, but she was thrilled for him.

He came to the table and carefully pulled out a chair to sit. Alena sat next to him and took his hands in hers.

"I knew this would happen. I had faith."

It seemed as though he looked her in the eyes. Alena knew he was only looking at what he thought was her face, but still, he had an animation about him in a way she had never seen before.

"I had faith because you did," he said quietly.

A tear slid down her cheek, a tear of joy. "John, do you..." She hesitated, not sure how to ask him.

"No. I still don't remember everything. Yet."

It was amazing how in tune they were to each other, how he anticipated her question.

"I'm sure that will come. You said earlier…" He hesitated and she thought of the badge. With Jeb gone and John's eyesight returning, Alena could keep it from him no longer.

"Do you know what? We need to bathe those eyes. I'll bet they're matted with sleep. That may be half of why you can't see," she proclaimed. "Then I have something to share with you."

She rose and filled a bowl with water and soaked a clean rag, wringing it out. She brought it to the table and placed it in front of him.

"Would you like me to…" Her voice trailed off. She'd done for him in the past while allowing him to do what he could on his own. If she had learned one thing, it was that John Harper was a proud man.

He smiled shyly. "I wouldn't mind a little help."

Alena leaned down and gently ran the damp cloth over one eyelid and brushed the outside corner. "Open up."

He did, holding his eyes wide, and she brought it underneath, as well. "You have a little sleep right on the inside corner." She put the cloth down and moved to remove it, but her hands collided with his.

Her breath caught in her throat. A sudden awareness of how close she stood made her take a step back.

"Why don't you get that corner?" she said shakily. "I don't want to poke you."

John looked up at her, his eyes squinting as if he were trying to bring her into sharper focus. He turned back to the table and touched the bowl before taking both hands and plunging them in, splashing water onto his face and eyes. He grabbed the towel and roughly wiped at his face.

"I think your biscuits are burning," he growled.

ALEXA ASTON

"Oh!" Alena ran and grabbed a cloth to pull them out. She looked down at the singed bread and said, "There's not much to salvage here."

"Don't throw them away. I ate worse in the war. Weevils got into most everything. I'll take a burned biscuit without weevils any day."

She placed the pan on the table. "The honey—"

"— is to the right. Butter to the left. I know."

Alena quickly set the table so John could prepare the biscuits the way he liked. She cracked open several eggs to fry and poured them coffee. She took a swig, the hot liquid burning as it went down, but she didn't care. She needed something to calm her nerves.

She couldn't breathe around the man this morning. Couldn't even stand next to him without turning into a puddle of mush. If she didn't know better, she'd think she was coming down with something. Instead, she realized this is what she had read about before. Being lovesick. She still didn't know why John stopped kissing her last night, much less why he apologized for kissing her. She wouldn't ask, either. Let him tell her in his own sweet time.

Alena picked at her breakfast, her stomach too nervous to get down much. Not only did sitting near John make her heart pound with excitement, but she also knew the time had come to share with him his past. Or his present, she supposed.

"Let me clear the dishes. Stay here." She removed everything and decided that she could wash up later. More important things needed to be said and done.

She reached into her pocket and placed the silver star and broken pocket watch on the table before him. Alena took John's hands and guided them to the objects.

"Your eyesight will back before you know it. Let's see if these can trigger your memory."

154

CHAPTER 19

nnabelle gave her hand to Bryce and stepped from the train. A cool breeze greeted her as she looked anxiously around the station. People met those exiting the train, many with looks of hope and joy and tender smiles upon their faces.

She felt dead inside. The entire trip west gave her time to think, looking for clues Braden might have dropped in the months before she and Olivia embarked upon their European tour. Why had he sent them on such an expensive journey? She hadn't encountered any credit problems, but being a senator's wife often opened doors closed to others.

Monroe Feldman stole a few moments with her before she and Bryce boarded their train in New York. He indicated to her that Braden desperately needed to make the trip to San Francisco because of some financial venture. Feldman hadn't revealed its nature, but it left Annabelle with a bad taste in her mouth. Braden's judgment was suspect at this point. If he planned on some wild hare scheme to save them, it had failed when he hadn't been able to show up to pull it off.

Fear for her child's safety lingered. Anger also bubbled inside her— at the savage kidnappers and toward

155

Braden. Frustration followed not far behind. Now, they had arrived in San Francisco, a city she had always wanted to visit, under the worst circumstances possible. Her husband and son were missing. She possessed enough money for a moderately priced hotel if she only stayed a few days.

To add to her other worries, she knew John was missing. Her childhood sweetheart, in his capacity as a U. S. Marshal, had gone in search of her loved ones, and now he might have given his life for them.

It was more than she could bear.

"Mr. Mitchell?"

A man headed their way, wearing a deputy marshal badge on his black wool suit coat. He looked to be in his late twenties.

"Yes," Bryce replied. "And you are?"

"Price, sir. Deputy Marshal Andy Price. I'm to escort you to headquarters. Let's see to your bags."

"Mrs. Reynolds only has the one trunk and I have my valise here. I know what the trunk looks like. I'll take care of it. Do you know where we are staying, Deputy? I can have the luggage sent directly there."

Price frowned. "I don't believe any arrangements have been made, sir. Might I recommend Baldwin House?"

Annabelle winced. The hotel was known as one of the finest in the city. She placed a hand on Bryce's arm.

"Do you think—"

But he knew. She could see the pity in his eyes.

"Don't worry, Annabelle. The firm will take care of everything."

"Not a suite," she said quickly. "A room." She might have to take him up on his generosity, but she refused to be more indebted than necessary.

"All right. I'll see to the bags." He strode off, his confident air raising her hopes.

That left her with the young deputy. He had a look of John about him, years ago, before the war. Annabelle had been shocked when she'd last seen John at the dedication of the cemetery at Gettysburg. She had heard the phrase *'war was hell.'* Looking at John Harper on that cold November day proved it. All his boyishness and easy charm had been replaced by a hard edge. He had a wary air about him, almost one of danger.

But it was the look on his face when their eyes met that caused Annabelle several sleepless nights. She regretted succumbing to her father's relentless pressure to marry Braden, a man he deemed more suitable for his only daughter. Why did she think John forgot her while away at university, simply because it had been a month since his last letter? She rushed into a marriage with the charming and eligible Braden Reynolds because she didn't want to disappoint her father.

And look where that one mistake had taken her.

She didn't regret becoming Olivia's stepmother—and wouldn't trade anything for her Johnny— but her marriage was a sham. She was window dressing on Braden's arm and knew it. She played the role of a dutiful senator's wife, the pleasant hostess, the perfect ornament. She had an easy life, one of her own making. Yet she had wished a thousand times over the years that she was Mrs. John Harper instead.

"How was your trip?"

Annabelle looked at the deputy. "It is a long time to spend on a train."

Price laughed. "Be glad it was a train. A dozen years ago you'd have come all those miles on horseback or in a wagon."

She looked around restlessly. "I wondered if you had any news about my family. Are you working on the case?"

The lawman shook his head. "No, ma'am. I'm not

assigned to it. I don't have any knowledge of how the investigation is proceeding. My job now is to collect you and Mr. Mitchell and take you straight to Marshal Johnson. He's in charge of the San Francisco office. He'll brief you on everything you need to know."

Bryce returned. "The luggage is taken care of. Shall we?" He offered his arm to Annabelle and the trio proceeded to hail a cab.

They arrived at the bureau twenty minutes later. Price escorted them to an office on the first floor. A secretary ushered them inside.

A gaunt, tall man rose from behind the desk. His mustache was as white as his thick hair and stood out from his tanned, weathered face. He offered a hand to them both and said, "I'm Will Johnson. Greetings aside, let's get down to business."

Annabelle liked his no-nonsense approach. She took the seat that he indicated.

"I won't pretty things up, Mrs. Reynolds. A kidnapping is a serious situation. I've already had two men on this case that were shot and killed, good men, mind you, but that lets us know what kind of criminals we're dealing with."

"We were told in New York that another marshal working the case hasn't reported in. Is that unusual?" she asked, clutching her hands in her lap.

Johnson held up a cigar. "Mind if I smoke?"

"Please. Go ahead."

The marshal lit the cigar and puffed on it several times. "Thank you. Helps me to think." He took a long drag and stared out across the room.

"Let me put it this way. John Harper is my best man, hands down. He's never failed to check in before. Sometimes, John does things a bit unorthodox but he gets the job done. He's pretty much a loner. Has lots of contacts. He could be just about anywhere in the state.

No one's talking. If they've seen him, they're not saying.

"If John found your husband and son, he'd already be here. If he found the men responsible, we'd know." Johnson scratched his chin. "I'm a-hoping he'll turn up but I ain't sure it'll happen now. Just being realistic."

Annabelle froze. She couldn't lose Johnny and Braden and John, too. Even though they hadn't spoken in years, she always contented herself that John was somewhere out there, alive and well. She dug her nails into the palms of her hands.

"So what progress has been made, Mr. Johnson?" She tried to keep her voice from trembling and was pleased at the effort.

"Not much, but we had a bit of luck the other day. A passenger on the train came forward. He identified two of the men responsible for the robbery and kidnapping."

Johnson snorted. "Believe it or not, the same passenger was on another train held up by the same men, right after the war ended. We know now it's the Marker brothers behind the kidnapping. Or what's left of them."

"The Marker brothers?" Bryce interjected. "Exactly who are they?"

Johnson leaned back in his chair and took another puff. "About the most ornery gang in these parts. They've been operating nigh on thirty years. Most of the original family is gone. Some died off, got shot, landed in prison. It's a fringe effort now."

"So, this passenger identified some of the men responsible for taking my family?"

"Yes, ma'am. Cletus Malloy, for one. He has a long, checkered past. The man's wanted for cattle rustling. Horse thieving. Train and bank robberies. He hooked up with the Markers 'bout fifteen, eighteen years ago."

Marshal Johnson opened a folder and took out a piece of paper. He pushed it across the desk.

"So this is Mr. Malloy," Annabelle said, studying the sketch.

Johnson nodded. "The very same."

Bryce leaned forward to look at the wanted poster. "Does this Malloy fellow run the gang?"

Johnson shook his head. "He's not smart enough. The passenger also recognized another outlaw from the previous robbery, but we don't have a wanted poster on him. Our witness heard one of the gang call the man Dingus. That's who we believe is in charge."

The lawman reached for another paper and passed it over. "This here is a picture one of my boys who's handy with a pencil drew. Took him awhile but it's the best he could piece together from our passenger's description."

Annabelle inspected the sketch. The man was ordinary, nothing outstanding about him. He certainly didn't resemble a criminal. She pictured him more as a farmer or blacksmith, with his solemn, weathered face and dark eyes.

"What do you know of this Dingus?" she asked.

The marshal blew out a long drag of smoke. "Not much. He's been sighted off and on with the Markers from time to time over the years. Doesn't seem to run with them always. There's no evidence he pulls any jobs on his own, though."

Johnson waved his cigar in the air. "Who knows? He might get his jollies playing criminal every now and then. Still, our witness insists Dingus was the outlaw in charge of the gang. Maybe since so many of the Markers are gone now, Dingus inherited the mantle of leadership. We know someone had to be wily enough to figure out who Senator Reynolds was and take him and your boy. They couldn't have known they were on the train beforehand."

"You're saying it was a stroke of luck that this gang chose to rob a train and hit the jackpot instead?"

Marshal Johnson nodded. "That's how we figure it. We'll know more this time tomorrow."

"Why?" Annabelle wondered aloud.

"One of the gang got shot in the robbery. Mind you, none of the passengers will own up to it, but someone took matters into his own hands. Wounded the man in the back. Was touch and go, but I had word not ten minutes before you folks arrived that it looks like he'll pull through. Doc Filmore said he's conscious and that we can talk to him first thing tomorrow morning. I'm hoping he'll shed some light on things."

"That's wonderful news," Bryce said. "But what of the ransom demand?" he asked. "Have you heard any more about how much they want for the senator's return?"

"And Johnny," Annabelle added quietly. She would not let them forget her son.

"Of course, Mrs. Reynolds," said Marshal Johnson. "The note we received asked for a hundred grand for the return of both."

Annabelle gasped. She couldn't raise a hundred dollars at this point, let alone a hundred thousand.

"Annabelle?" Bryce looked at her sympathetically. "Perhaps you'd like to step out for some fresh air while we finish our discussion."

She wouldn't be pushed aside. "No, Bryce. I'd like to hear everything Marshal Johnson has to say."

For the first time, the attorney looked uncomfortable. "All right." He turned to Johnson. "What I need to share with you need not leave this office."

The marshal nodded. "I understand."

Bryce hesitated a moment and then said, "Without

going into the particulars, I will tell you there aren't sufficient funds to cover whatever ransom demand has been made. Senator Reynolds' affairs are of a private nature. Unfortunately, all his capital is tied up in such long-range investments that it would be impossible to withdraw them at this time."

Johnson slammed his palm down on the cluttered desk. "You mean even if a man's life is on the line? And that of his son? You're a lawyer, man. Surely you know how to get around these things?"

Bryce gave a steady look at the lawman, trying to convey to the man without words what he wasn't saying.

Annabelle's humiliation burned but she decided to take matters into her own hands. "Excuse me for interrupting." She focused on Marshal Johnson's face, knowing if she glanced in Bryce's direction, her courage would falter.

"What Mr. Mitchell is trying to say so delicately is that my husband is bankrupt. He has made some very unwise financial choices recently. We have nothing."

"Flat broke, you say." Johnson whistled low. His look of pity almost did her in.

Annabelle's voice wavered as she said, "I'm sure you can understand that's why we can't have word of this spread. Because if it did..." Her voice faltered. Tears sprang to her eyes.

"Then the Markers might not have need..." Johnson's words hung in the air as he stopped, aware of what he voiced aloud. He stood and came around from behind the desk, offering Annabelle his hand.

"I'm sorry about your circumstances, Mrs. Reynolds, but I guarantee you we will do everything in our power to see your family safely returned. I give you my word as a United States Marshal."

Johnson's ramrod posture gave steel to the promise he made.

"Thank you." Annabelle's words were but a whisper.

She thought of her only son. Kind, bookish Johnny, in the hands of killers. How they had already murdered two lawmen. Possibly three, if she included John. She swore to herself that no sacrifice would be too great to save her child. She would give anything for his return.

But would she have an opportunity to save him?

CHAPTER 20

*A*lmost reluctantly, John picked up the badge. Alena watched as he fingered it carefully, feeling its shape, moving it from the table to his palm. He brought it close to his face and squinted, focusing intently.

"Describe it to me. My sight's still fuzzy."

"You're holding a silver badge in the shape of a shield. Inside a circle within the shield is a five-point star. It's lettered *United States Marshal* in the rim of the circle."

He ran a thumb over the letters, then slowly traced the shape of the star. He brought it closer to his eyes again, a deep frown creasing his brow. He set the badge down and reached for the watch.

"This is a blur, too."

"It's a pocket watch," Alena said quietly.

The moment she had been dreading had arrived. He would remember everything from the inscription it bore. She could hold him no longer. Some other woman, somewhere, wanted him back. Alena's dreams of loving John would be forever lost.

John closed his fingers around it. A wistful look crossed his face.

He had remembered.

"The watch doesn't work," she added. "You must have kept it for the sentimental value."

He looked at her. "Why do you say that?"

She shrugged. "I don't think many men would carry around a broken watch. Besides," she added, "it has a message inscribed on the back."

"I know what it says," he snarled. *"To J— who owns my heart for all time. A."*

Alena flinched at the bitterness of his words as he repeated the inscription, word for word. A dark scowl changed his features from handsome to dangerous in an instant. She had seen him in pain before, upset, frustrated— but this look frightened her beyond words.

Without thinking, she asked, "Who is A?"

John laughed harshly. "You mean the woman who promised her heart and then betrayed me? Gave me up without a word, spoken or written. That's who A is. Annabelle. I remember everything about her. She's someone from long ago. The reason I've never trusted a woman since."

She flinched but pressed him. "You kept it all these years. Surely, it means something to you."

"It's a reminder. That I could be a lovestruck fool." His jaw tightened. "I'll never leap like that again."

He placed the watch back onto the table and picked up the shield again. "This doesn't ring any bells." He raked a hand through his hair and sighed. "Tell me everything, Alena. About when I showed up. Any clue you can give me. And about the men you told Jeb about. I vaguely remember them being here."

Her nerves jittered like a stalked mouse sensing the cat about to pounce on it. "You came in the middle of the night. Unconscious. Slumped over your saddle horn. Cicero brought you. Both of you had been shot.

Cicero's wound wasn't bad. You were covered in blood."

"The head wound," John said.

"Yes, that and your shoulder. Scalp wounds bleed a lot so I dragged you inside to get a better look. You had a large goose egg on the back of your head."

"Amnesia and blindness. Courtesy of that, I'm sure."

"You wore the badge pinned to what was left of your shirt. I took it and hid it."

"Why? You had nothing to hide from a lawman."

"No, but I had a lawman to hide." Alena hesitated. "If you were a true marshal and had been shot, I knew the men who'd done it would come looking for you. If they did, I didn't need your badge sitting out on the table to announce your presence."

"That was smart."

She shrugged off the compliment. "Practical. I got you fixed up and sure enough, three riders appeared soon afterward."

"Describe them. Everything you can remember."

Alena leaned back, closing her eyes, trying to see the men she had wanted to forget. "Unkempt. Rude. Rough-looking. Just the way they rode gave me a funny feeling. I met them at the door with my shotgun."

"And we all know how good you are with a gun."

She smiled. "I never answer the door without it when I'm alone. The leader was tall. Swaggered around the other two, but confident talking to me, even with a gun pointed at his chest. Small scar that ran across his cheek. Black eyes so mean, you wouldn't trust turning your back on him.

"He did all the talking. The other two were quiet. Both burly. That's all I remember about them, other than one found Cicero in the barn."

"How did you talk your way out of that? And where was I?"

"The leader— they called him Cletus— acted friendly. He wanted to come inside. I knew he wanted to check things over. I threw you in the hidey hole the minute I spotted riders."

"The what?"

Alena laughed. "It's where we keep our little bit of money on hand." She explained how it was hidden by the trap door, the rug, and the broken chair.

John whistled. "No wonder you never let me sit in that chair." He shook his head. "You put me in a hole? I remember bits and pieces now. The smell of earth. The tight, cramped feeling. Like I'd been buried alive." He shuddered. "I'd thought it was all a bad dream."

"It saved your skin, John Harper. You should be grateful."

He looked contrite. "I am. Go on. About Cicero."

"I told them the horse arrived with no rider, blood all over her, which was true. I said that she'd probably been spooked if the rider had been killed and thrown him. I made a big deal about taking care of her wounds and that I planned to keep her.

"Then I turned the conversation around to why they'd come."

"And they said they were looking for me?"

Alena nodded. "They never gave me a name. I don't think they had one. Said you were an outlaw on the run, passing yourself off as a sheriff. If nothing before did it, them calling you a sheriff alerted me. Your badge said marshal. If they were the real law, they would've known more about you."

"What was I supposed to have done, other than impersonate a sheriff?"

"They said you were a bank robber and murderer."

He grew silent. Alena could see him tossing the information about, trying to make sense of what she'd said.

"And then they left?"

"Yes. I shooed them out the door since they had such a big task ahead. Made them believe Jeb was down at the lake and that we'd keep our eyes out for you. They rode out and that was that."

It was eerie how still John sat. Alena longed to comfort him, especially since she now knew the woman from the watch wouldn't take him away from her. His words, though, had been harsh regarding women. It hurt her to realize that John probably didn't see her as a woman, just a caretaker nursing him back to good health.

Yet he'd kissed her.

"Dammit!" He slammed both hands down on the table. "Damn it all to hell and back."

Alena shrank against the chair back. John's face darkened with fury. He no longer looked like the man she had come to know. In his place was one that frightened her. For a moment, she questioned whether he'd gone mad.

He stood quickly, the chair flying to the floor. "Why doesn't any of this trigger my memory? Why can't I recall anything about my job and these men?"

He wore his frustration like a coat. She pushed her chair back, wanting to put some distance between them. Instead, his hand shot out like lightning, fastening on her wrist. He stared at her, his brown eyes dark with rage.

"Why the hell did you keep all this from me for so long?" He pulled her toward him roughly. "Did you pity me? Think I couldn't handle it? Or did you believe them and think me a murderer?"

Alena couldn't fathom the depth of his wrath. The quickness of its arrival. Its rapid eruption. His fingers tore into her flesh, tightening so that she was afraid he would crush her bones.

John had known blindness for a couple of weeks, but anger blinded him now. He could remember Annabelle giving him the pocket watch as if it were yesterday. It was a graduation gift. She wanted him to have it at college and carry it so she would always be with him. The fact that he dragged it around for years like a fool only brought out more frustration. Annabelle was a married woman and had left memories of him far behind.

He found he couldn't trust her then— and he couldn't trust Alena now. He grabbed the watch from the table and threw it against the wall.

"That's one memory I don't need," he growled. "Annabelle didn't do right by me and neither have you."

She tried to wriggle from his grasp, but he dug his fingers into her shoulders. "I was just one of your playthings. A hurt animal to tend. You didn't see me as a man. You didn't think about my feelings. You saw me as a cripple in mind and body. You didn't trust me to remember. If I'd seen the badge, felt it, known about it early on, I might have remembered everything right away. Instead, you either felt sorry for me or were scared of who I might be."

"No!" she cried. "It wasn't like that. Maybe I was a little scared of you in the beginning, but who wouldn't be? You came to me all shot up. Three men came looking for you. I was frantic that you were going to die on me and I'd never know who you were or why you'd come.

"I buried the badge in the flour for both our safety and honestly forgot about it. I was too busy caring for you. The watch I found in your saddlebags yesterday when I gave you a shave. I was going to show you then, but Jeb came home and all went to hell in a handbasket."

She choked back a sob. "Maybe I didn't want you to

remember. That would mean losing you. I know it was selfish to keep it from you."

Alena threw off his hands from her. "Just get it through your thick skull that I care for you, John Harper. You've made me see life in a new way— and not through sight. You've made me feel alive for the first time in my life. Made me feel like a woman despite the pants I wear.

"I don't pity you. I value you as a person, John."

Her words cut him to the quick. Scared him beyond reason. He stormed out blindly, kicking furniture over as he hurried to the door. He ran down the porch steps and even swung his leg at squawking chickens. He headed for the barn. He had to think. Get away from everything.

At least he knew his way there. His vision was still blurry, but he could focus for a second or two and see clearly. He would go groom Cicero and feel sorry for himself.

John threw open the barn doors and stomped inside, his blood racing, his heart pounding. Alena's words rang in his head. He had to get rid of them.

He moved to the stall Cicero stood in. She nickered hello and nudged his shoulder, wanting a sugar cube.

"No treats today, girl," he said softly, reining in his anger. The horse had been his friend through thick and thin. No sense in alienating her. She was probably the only woman that would remain a constant in his life. As he took out the brush and stroked her in long, even motions, he spoke aloud.

"Damnation. Alena betrayed me. She's no better than Annabelle. She kept things from me. Things that might've made a difference." He sighed as he pushed the brush through the horse's coat. "But I can't help think if the shoe were on the other foot, would I have done the same?"

Cicero tossed her head. John didn't know if she agreed or disagreed with him.

"Truth is, I've got strong feelings for her." His head hurt from the warring emotions inside him. "I'm captivated by her, Cic. By her gentle touch and laughing ways. By how smart she is and how she completes me."

He stroked the horse's muzzle. "I don't think I can live without her. Now, how in tarnation did that happen?"

Cicero nudged him under his chin. He laughed. His temper now cooled, he tried to think straight.

"I need to leave, but I don't know where to go or how to get where I'm supposed to be. Even if I do recollect who I am, would Alena fit into the life I have?"

The horse stared at him solemnly, letting him answer his own question.

"Does that even matter? If I love her— and I think I just may— can I rearrange whatever I am to be with her?"

John pushed the brush along the bay's firm sides and then stopped. "Would I throw away the chance of a lifetime if I leave her?" He sighed. "I wish you could talk, Cic. I wish you could tell me what to do."

He continued currying the horse in silence, his thoughts jumbled. Brushing Cicero usually eased his mind, but he remained agitated, the anger building again.

"I'm so mad I can't see straight," he proclaimed, and laughed as he said it. He was blind, or partially so. Cicero snorted as if she understood the joke. He hugged her neck, wishing relationships could be as simple as the one he had with his horse.

He ran through all that had happened the last few days. The feelings he experienced kissing Alena. His sight starting to come back. Alena keeping things from him. Confronting Jeb before he left. Would it be better to leave all his new memories of Alena behind once the old ones returned?

Indecision plagued him as he put the brush aside. He wasn't ready to go back to the cabin. Alena was a woman, and women liked to talk. Sometimes, they talked things to death. He wished he could go shoot cans like she had. If she were spitting nails like he felt like doing, she might take his head off if he showed his face anyway.

Might as well stay in the barn and sleep. He was emotionally and physically spent. Cicero was a spoiled girl and wouldn't want to share her space. He knew the barn also had a plow horse and a cow. The smell of hay hit him. He decided if he could find the ladder, he'd go up to the loft and sleep off his problems.

He gave Cicero a final pat and, fighting the shadows and hazy images around him, located the ladder. Climbing to the loft proved awkward, but the hay was deep and inviting once he arrived at the top. Thoughts of him rolling around in it with Alena in his arms brought a new wave of anger.

"That's the last thing I need," he muttered.

John burrowed into the hay and fell asleep more quickly than he would have imagined, pictures of Alena whirling through his mind.

HE AWOKE, wondering how long he had slept. As he opened his eyes, it surprised him that things were in focus. Not much light poured through the cracks but he could see clearly. Pure joy swept through him. His sight had returned. Most of his memory had. When it did completely, he would have a sense of purpose.

He stood and brushed off the hay that clung to him,

picking out stray pieces from his hair. As he moved toward the ladder, his confidence grew.

Then his boot hit something. John bent and brushed the hay away. In the dim light, he recognized a painting of a doe and its babe.

Jeb and Alena had fought over this and Jeb taking it to sell in San Francisco.

Why would Jeb make such a to-do over selling the canvas— only to hide it where Alena wouldn't find it?

John knew one thing for sure. He had to tell Alena about the painting. Right now.

nnabelle adjusted her hat and gazed at herself in the mirror. Her pale cheeks and shadowed eyes spoke of the sleepless night she had suffered.

She had a thousand worries now, assuming Johnny and Braden would be rescued. How would they pay Mark Gandelson? Would they place Johnny in public school? Could they afford to send him to a university? She had never thought it necessary for him to work in the future, his health being delicate, but now it would be expected.

And what of Olivia? She had beauty and charm, but if she could not be brought out properly, she would have little chance of making a good marriage. Braden always granted Olivia's every whim. Annabelle dreaded what would happen if Olivia were told they couldn't afford to purchase her a new hat, much less the pins to hold it in place.

And this was *if* she got them back. Alive.

Annabelle decided to quit avoiding the real issue. Who cared if Johnny didn't get into Harvard or Olivia failed to marry a prominent member of society? She must face the possibility that she might never see Johnny or Braden again.

She couldn't bear the thought of losing her son. Johnny was the light of her life. She could see his eager face, telling her about some adventure he had read about in a book, excitement shining in his eyes. What if these men hurt him? He was only a boy, sick much of the time.

A sob of frustration erupted. If she never saw her child again, it would destroy her. Annabelle imagined the horror of not only being forced to live with their deaths but she would also be faced with society's stares as the scandal erupted about Braden's foolishness. She could imagine returning to her invalid mother's home, Olivia in tow, living the quiet life of a widow touched by disgrace.

All that and knowing John was dead, too.

Annabelle brushed her tears aside. She refused to think about a future without her son and husband. Instead, she must concentrate on what could be done to save them. She retrieved her reticule and left to meet Bryce in the hotel's lobby. He had stopped by earlier to take her to breakfast, but the thought of food nauseated her. She had agreed to meet him downstairs since Marshal Johnson would arrive at nine.

As she descended the stairs, a thought came to her. They might be far into debt, but she still had the jewels with her that she'd taken on the European trip. Those, along with what other pieces she had in Washington and Pennsylvania, would surely add up to more than enough to satisfy the kidnappers.

Her heart, lighter than it had been in days, brought a spring to her step. She would be able to make a difference. Relief flooded her as she reached the bottom of the staircase and scanned the lobby. She spied Bryce and Marshal Johnson, despite their backs turned from her, and hurried toward them.

As she reached them, she overheard Johnson say in

quiet tones, "All the clues have petered out. The Marker brothers have operated in this area for years, and yet we've never found their hideout before. I didn't want to give Mrs. Reynolds false hope yesterday, but unless we get some solid information from this prisoner, the situation doesn't look promising. Especially now that I know the ransom demands can't be met."

"But they can!" Annabelle exclaimed.

Both men turned and she smiled broadly. "Braden may have lost his fortune and the house will need to be sold to cover his debts but, I thought of my jewelry."

She fingered the bracelet on her wrist. "Look at this, for instance. It's a tastefully done piece, suitable for daytime wear, and yet it has several nice stones in it. Just what I brought on our European trip alone includes bracelets, necklaces, and earbobs. I have more jewelry back home that we can send for. In the meantime, we can have these appraised and—"

"No, Annabelle."

She stared at Bryce in astonishment. "Don't you think I would part with my jewelry to save my son? My husband? Surely you couldn't think me so shallow, Bryce. I will do whatever it takes to—"

"They're all fake." Bryce's flat tone caused a sick feeling to build inside her.

"Monroe Feldman told me Braden replaced all your jewels. Paste for the most part." Bryce looked at her with compassion. "When Braden was forced to raise capital, the first place he turned to was your jewels. They are all copies, Annabelle. Imitations that won't bring much."

She was stunned. How could all this have gone on around her and she be so unaware? A cold fury built inside her, anger toward Braden and what he had done. How could she save Johnny?

Then it occurred to her that she never took her

wedding band and engagement ring off. Neither had left her finger since the day she'd promised to stay by Braden in sickness and in health, for better or for worse. The band was studded with diamonds and sapphires. The solitaire was three carats alone. They would be worth a great deal of money.

Annabelle decided not to share this with Bryce. She would find a shop and have them appraised. It was time she started thinking for herself.

"It was an idea." Annabelle stiffened her back. "Shall we go see this outlaw?"

Little was said on the cab ride. Annabelle stared listlessly at the passing scenery. They arrived and entered a small clinic, where a man barely five feet tall greeted them, a broad smile on his face.

"So good to see you, Marshal. I'm Phineas Filmore, folks. And you would be?"

Johnson introduced them to the physician. "How's the prisoner today, Doc?"

"Sullen. He hasn't made much sense thanks to his high fever. Still, he's turned the corner now and will live."

"May we see him?"

"Of course, Marshal. His name's Jimbo Simon. That's all we've gotten from him. Come this way."

Doctor Filmore led them down a long corridor and into an airy room awash in sunlight.

"You have guests, Mr. Simon."

Annabelle studied the outlaw in the bed, pillows propped behind him. He was well over three hundred pounds, with thick black hair and thicker lips. Mean was the word that came to mind.

Simon's eyes met hers then dragged down the length of her body and back up again. Annabelle flushed a bright red at his perusal. She was glad for the two men who accompanied her.

Marshal Johnson said, "I won't mince words, son. You're in a heap of trouble, so let's get to business."

"We ain't got no business." Simon spat upon the ground, just missing Johnson's boot.

The lawman moved like lightning, so close that his nose almost rested next to the bedridden patient.

"Let's get this straight, you piece of rat filth. You're gonna spill your guts for me. I want to know all about the Markers. The kidnapping. Where the hideout is. If you do that, you'll keep from hanging. We'll find some lesser charge and let you do time."

Johnson moved back and studied the prisoner. "What's it gonna be?"

Simon scowled at the group assembled in front of him. "I never heard of the Markers. Can't tell you where their hideout is. I got shot in the back, Marshal. Why ain't you out there finding out who did that?"

Johnson hissed between clenched teeth. He glared at the prisoner a full minute, never blinking. Annabelle never saw such concentration before. Then he turned abruptly.

"Folks, if you'll excuse us? I figure Mr. Simon might be a little shy in front of company. He might find it more comfortable to talk without a crowd."

"Of course." Bryce took her arm and escorted Annabelle from the room. Dr. Filmore followed closely behind.

"You can pass the time in my waiting room," Doctor Filmore suggested.

Johnson appeared an hour later, running a hand through his hair. "Jimbo Simon lacks in manners and brains. I'm convinced he's just shy of a full load of bricks."

"What does that mean, Marshal?" Annabelle's heart beat rapidly.

"That he's mostly muscle and very little brain, Mrs.

Reynolds. He admitted he's a part of the Markers. He confirmed that the gang meant to rob the train. It was only after they discovered your husband was on board that they decided to up the stakes to kidnapping."

"Where are they holding my family?"

"He doesn't know. He follows instructions, but doesn't understand where the hideout is. Seems he's always ridden along and never gone out on his own. He has a vague idea, but I doubt we'll get much more out of him."

"So we're back to square one?" Bryce asked.

"'Fraid so. We'll keep at him, of course. See if we can squeeze anything new from him but I wouldn't count on it."

Annabelle knew the time had come to take matters into her own hands. "May we return to the hotel, Bryce? I'm not feeling well."

"Of course." Bryce helped her to the waiting carriage. When they reached the hotel, he told her, "I think I'll return to headquarters with Marshal Johnson, Annabelle. Do you need me to accompany you to your room?"

"No, thank you. I'll be fine. I'd just like to lie down for a while."

She allowed him to escort her into the hotel. "Please go ahead, Bryce. I think I'll stop for a bite to eat before heading upstairs. I didn't eat this morning, you know. I'm sure I'll be fine once I get something in me."

"Then I'll see you later, my dear." He brushed a quick, fatherly kiss upon her brow and walked back through the lobby while Annabelle stepped inside the hotel's restaurant.

"Are you dining alone today, madam?" the maître d' asked.

"I'm sorry. I've changed my mind." She left the restaurant and crossed the lobby.

Bryce was nowhere in sight. Annabelle waited another two minutes and then stepped outside. The cab they had returned in was gone.

She looked down at the rings on her finger before she squared her shoulders and began to walk down the street in search of a jeweler's shop.

CHAPTER 22

John hurried down the loft's ladder, ready to confront Alena about Jeb's deceptiveness. It amazed him how quickly his sight had improved. As Cicero nickered, he walked to her, his steps sure.

"Hello, Cic." He stroked her velvet nose as she nudged his hands. "No treats on me, but I'll find where Alena keeps her sugar cubes." He was glad to gaze upon the beautiful bay once again.

Then it hit him. Had Jeb recognized him? Did he know John Harper as a U.S. Marshal?

He bid Cicero goodbye. Besides discussing the painting with Alena, he needed to apologize to her. She had offered him nothing but kindness, and he had behaved like a spoiled child, throwing the watch and accusing her of being untrustworthy. If anything, she had proved her trust in him over and over. She'd saved his life when Cletus and his men came looking to finish the job they had started. She'd hidden him at great personal risk. Alena had protected him from Jeb, too, when he'd arrived home and stumbled upon them horsing around.

And she cared for him. Alena admitted that to him before he stormed off. The truth was, her words scared him. He cared for her. He could barely admit it to himself and wasn't eager to tell her. He straightened his shoulders. Apologies first, then talk about Jeb leaving the painting behind. Only then would he broach the rest.

He stepped out of the barn to much clearer images. They were slightly fuzzy, but nothing that a good pair of spectacles wouldn't cure. He laughed, thinking how his mother had recently written him about his father finally agreeing to wear eyeglasses for the first time. If it came to that, John would do so willingly. He knew he would never take his sight for granted again.

The afternoon light hurt his eyes so he brought a hand up to shield them from the sun. They were also sensitive to the slight breeze in the air. He hoped this would pass.

He walked across the open yard, seeing the cabin for the first time, the place that now seemed like home. As he climbed the porch steps, a flutter of nerves ruffled his belly. He didn't understand what caused it. If he was a marshal, he must be at least outwardly brave. He had also seen duty during the war and had vivid memories of that.

So why would he be anxious about speaking with Alena?

He shrugged it off and pushed the door open, not bothering to knock.

Alena sat at the table, totally engrossed in her painting. John watched her work, the smell of oil paints thick in the air. As he stared at her, his vision totally cleared. She took his breath away.

Alena was nothing like what he had imagined. Nothing like Annabelle, which pleased him in some way. He had never seen a woman like her before. Hair the color of the blackest midnight hung to her waist, so dark it had a blue sheen to it. Her oval face was lit with luminous violet eyes. Her skin was smooth olive, not the fashionably fair complexion of most every woman he saw in passing.

A wisp of a smile played at the corners of her mouth as she worked. Before he could speak and make his presence known, Alena frowned slightly. The smile faded. A deep concentration replaced it as she made adjustments to the canvas. The intensity of her effort rippled through the air.

John realized how fond he had grown of the smell of those oil paints. They were so much a part of Alena. In an instant, he desperately wanted to make her a part of his life, whatever it was.

Memory be damned!

He strode over. Pulled her from the chair and into his arms before he could talk himself out of it. A hundred reasons might exist why he shouldn't become involved with her.

But only one sang in his heart at this moment.

He had to have her.

Alena looked surprised to find herself in his arms. He cut off the question her lips formed with a kiss, swift and hard, one that aimed to convey passion and possession.

John kissed her over and over, like a man drowning and fighting for air. He needed his mouth on hers, his arms wrapped around her, his body pressed against hers. As he slanted his mouth over hers again and again, Alena responded passionately, matching him kiss for kiss. He grew dizzy with the buzzing in his ears. The pounding of his blood racing. The sweetness of her mouth.

He moved from her lips to her chin and down the column of her throat. Her head fell back with a sigh. That one sound caused a rush of heat to ripple through him and he held her more tightly. The jasmine scent on her skin intoxicated him, making his head spin. He pushed his fingers through her silken tresses and wrapped a bunch of it around his hand, pulling on it slightly. Alena's head tilted back and John brought his mouth down on hers, feasting again.

A hunger built inside him, gnawing, pushing him. His lips trailed along her throat again and then stopped, the material of the shirt she wore in his way. He slipped a hand to the button and worked it through the buttonhole, exposing more of her perfect skin. A new wave of jasmine floated up as he eagerly pressed his lips to her warm flesh.

Alena moaned softly and pressed nearer, her arms wrapping around his neck, bringing him close to her. His hand slipped to her breast and kneaded it gently, his thumb grazing across it. Her nipple hardened, causing his knees to almost buckle. Desire burned through him.

He unbuttoned the second button on her shirt and pushed the material aside, exposing her perfect breast. Round. Firm. Begging for his attention. He kissed it tenderly, flicking his tongue around and then across the nipple. She gasped and clutched him for support.

Though a rational man, cautious by nature, all sanity fled. Alena was everything he had ever wanted in a woman, pure and wonderful and beautiful inside and out. Who cared who he was or what he did for a living. He could stay forever in this cabin, in these woods, Alena in his arms. Jeb be damned. Nothing would keep them apart.

John lifted his mouth to look at Alena now that he could. He needed to drink in her intoxicating beauty. It surprised him that her eyes glittered with unshed tears. Her lips, already bruised from their passion, trembled.

What in God's name was he doing?

Alena was untouched, unspoiled by a man. His actions had probably frightened her into submission. He realized how far he had gone. He couldn't ask her to make a commitment with her body without a commitment of their hearts.

And somewhere out there, he had a mission to accomplish, one that he might never return from.

It had been wrong to kiss her. To want to make love to her. She was an innocent. He must put a stop to this.

John gripped her elbows and put some distance between them. His breathing sounded ragged to his ears. He fought to slow it in order to speak calmly.

"I'm sorry," he began.

"Don't go apologizing again, John Harper." Alena's eyes darkened to deep purple, anger sparking in them. "You did that the last time you kissed me and I won't have it."

She threw his arms off and stepped back, studying him with suspicion. "Is that what you say every time you kiss a girl? Get her all worked up? Make her feel like she's the only woman in the world? That she's special and adored?"

He tried to interrupt but she raised a hand. "Do you know what you do to me? Not when you kiss me, but even when you come near? Do you know how many times I thought I would die, my heart beating so fast with excitement, simply because you entered the room?"

She shook her head in disgust. "Every time I see you, hear you— taste you— I want more. I want it to never end." Alena came and stood directly in front of him, breathing hard, her chest heaving, her hair in disarray.

She poked him with her finger, hard, those violet eyes now almost black. Without hesitation she said, "I love you, John Harper. I want to be with you."

He replied by sweeping her off her feet and marching into the bedroom.

CHAPTER 23

*J*ohn placed Alena on the bed, his heart hammering wildly. It was hard to reconcile her femininity wrapped in old castoffs of Jeb's. The worn blue shirt swallowed her. She'd rolled the sleeves above her elbows. Paint spatters decorated its front. The placket had four buttons, two of which he'd already loosened, revealing a glimpse of cleavage.

She'd tucked the shirt into faded buckskin pants, held up by a rope tied about them. The legs were turned up several times, revealing moccasins covering her feet. Her hair hung loose, framing her face and draped across the pillow.

He had never seen a more tempting sight.

"I'm going to love you, slow and sweet," he whispered, despite the fact that they were alone.

Her eyes widened and a tremulous smile appeared. "All right," she whispered back.

He sat next to her and slipped his hand around her ankle, slowly pulling off a moccasin. He tossed it to the floor and removed the other one, then took her foot in his hands. Slowly, he began to rub it, his gaze locked on hers.

Alena swallowed, tingles of anticipation shooting

187

through her. John Harper was all she had thought about for days, especially since he kissed her. He had awakened something within her and she wouldn't be satisfied unless she knew all.

He leaned down and languorously ran his tongue across the top of her foot. She nearly jumped from the bed at the shock that ran through her. He playfully nibbled on her big toe and then slipped it into his mouth, sucking hard. She fisted her hands into balls, trying to control her breathing which skyrocketed out of control.

"Are you sure, Alena?" he asked.

She found her voice. "I've never been more sure."

John's smile lit up the room, catching her off guard. It was a smile from the heart, one full of promise. She returned it, joy flooding her. He took her face between his hands and pressed his lips softly to her forehead. Alena felt treasured with that one simple kiss.

He threaded his fingers through hers and pulled her up, his kisses deep and fervent. Then gently he slipped her shirt from her body. She barely noticed the coolness of the room as he continued the drugging kisses. He pushed her back into the pillow, his lips never leaving hers. Alena was conscious of his weight against her, the rough feel of his shirt against her skin as he kissed her passionately. The core running through her radiated heat, matching that of his body.

John broke the kiss and sat back, looking at her. She became self-conscious of his gaze and moved to cover herself. He caught her wrists and placed them on the bed, holding them lightly there.

"No. I want to see you." His eyes, so warm brown, glinted with golden flecks as he smiled down at her. "You are so beautiful," he said softly. "Perfect."

She sensed the blush that burned her cheeks, but she didn't concentrate on it long. He had returned to his ministrations, touching her breasts, stroking her, kissing her, loving her. The world was all John, all male, his scent everywhere, his mouth everywhere, stoking the fire inside her.

He slipped the buckskins from her slowly, sensually. The throbbing between her legs intensified. Alena felt no more embarrassment, seeing how he looked at her, touched her. It was as if he worshipped her with every glance, with every brush of his fingers, as something precious and true.

His hands were like fire as they glided up her legs. As they climbed higher, the throbbing pulsed harder. She couldn't begin to understand what it meant, only that John Harper was the answer to its call.

"Just lie there a minute, sweetheart," he said. He removed his shirt and pitched it onto the floor.

Although Alena had seen him unclothed before, his physique still took her breath away. He was Odysseus and Sir Galahad rolled into one. The broad, muscular chest tapered to a flat stomach and narrow hips. A fine matting of dark hair covered it, disappearing into his trousers.

Without thinking, Alena licked her lips like a cat hungry for a saucer of milk. John chuckled softly and took her hand. He kissed it tenderly, his lips brushing against her knuckles before he turned it over and pressed hot kisses into her palm, heating her body. He kissed it once more, softly, before releasing it and turning away to remove his trousers. She watched the muscles in his back ripple as he did so. His buttocks were firm and his long legs were as muscular as his torso. Alena's heart sped up, her fingers itching to touch him.

When he turned toward the bed, he quickly stretched out beside her, cupping her face in one hand, stroking her hair with the other. His fingers running through the strands caused her scalp to tingle. She smiled shyly at him.

"What do you want me to do?" she asked.

John slowly dragged the pad of his thumb across her lips, back and forth. "You don't need to do a thing." He kissed her, deepening the kiss, and she pushed her hands into his hair, toying with the dark waves.

Then he touched her in a way she had never been touched before. Alena caught her breath as John slowly ran a finger along her womanly parts. She found she couldn't breathe as he cupped her. She broke the kiss and looked at him questioningly, her breath coming in rapid spurts.

"Trust me. I'll take care of you."

He kissed the corner of her mouth. As he moved to her throat, his fingers started working some kind of spell. He eased one into her and she jumped. The throbbing burst into a new rhythm all its own.

"Oh!" she exclaimed.

"Good?"

Alena nodded, not trusting herself to use words. John continued his explorations. With each movement, her heart beat faster. He began a rhythm that answered the call of hers, a gentle motion that begin to grow faster. Her world spun out of control. She dug her nails into his shoulders and cried out. His soothing voice was always there, talking to her, words she could hear but couldn't begin to understand.

Then a burst of heat exploded from her. Her hips rose again and again, meeting his fingers, as she rode some golden wave of pleasure.

"That's it, sweetheart. Roll with it," his voice assured her as the wave peaked and then slowly subsided. Her breathing was shallow and fast. She looked up and saw tenderness in his face. His eyes, though, danced with an excitement she'd never seen before, causing a shiver of anticipation to run through her.

John slipped his fingers from her and then something else took their place, filling her. The fullness was foreign but not unpleasant.

"Wrap your arms and legs around me," he instructed.

Alena did as he asked just as he pushed against her. A flash of pain blurred her vision for a moment. She held in a scream as he kissed her forehead.

"It won't hurt anymore. Never again. I promise."

She nodded, unsure, but trust won out. Gradually, he began to move again. As he did, a ripple of pleasure filled her, not unlike before. Alena relaxed. It would be all right. John had told her so.

He continued moving, in and out, in and out, and the throbbing and pressure inside her built again. Her hips rose without her realizing it, meeting his thrusts. Then the spark caught on fire and the flame erupted again. Alena cried out at the same time John did, a cry of happiness and joy. He collapsed against her, his lips on her temples, on her hair, murmuring noises. The roar in her ears subsided and she breathed deeply.

John rolled from her, still breathing hard. He brushed a stray lock of hair from her face and then drew her close, his strong, muscled arms drawing her to him. Alena nestled her head against his chest, where she could feel his heart beating wildly. It gave her a womanly thrill that she excited him.

Slowly, his heart slowed and his breathing grew quieter. She realized her exhausted man had fallen asleep. Alena smiled.

So this was lovemaking. The intensity had frightened her at first, then delighted her. She never knew such feelings of physical exhilaration existed. Is this why her mother married her father? Had they experienced a grand passion for one other?

And why had it turned sour? What made two people adore each other one day and then fall apart the next? Her mother gave up everything. Position. Wealth. Even her family in order to run away and marry Kevin McClaine. Had their love been only one-sided?

Was her love for John the same way? She had told him she loved him and now wondered if she should have uttered those words so impulsively. He hadn't said the words back that she longed to hear. John certainly showed her love, but it would be nice to hear such tender words come from his lips.

Alena decided she wouldn't repeat them again until he said them to her. That would make what happened real and she would know he was committed to staying with her— though at this point, she would go anywhere in the world to be with him.

But what if he left? What would make John leave?

She feared his memory returning, the thing she had most come to dread. She calmed herself. It hadn't even been when he'd seen the badge and the pocket watch. Instead, he'd gotten angry about the watch and Annabelle, the woman who gave it to him. Who could ever be so foolish as to give up a man like John Harper? Yet this Annabelle from John's past had done just that, betraying him somehow that caused John to not trust another woman.

Alena clung to the hope that things could remain as they were at this moment. That John would stay with her at the cabin forever. He didn't need to risk his life as a marshal. She wanted him here, with her, doing exactly what they did just now. Every day for the rest of their lives.

She fell asleep, clinging to that thought as much as she did to John himself.

CHAPTER 24

*A*lena awoke, the fading afternoon light dim. Immediately, she became aware of John next to her, his breathing even and deep. She propped a hand under her head to study him better. She marveled at his perfection. He had called her perfect, but he was the flawless one. His muscular body looked as if it were sculpted from the finest stone. She shivered as she recalled their coupling, his body hard and strong against hers, bringing her pleasure beyond anything she had ever known.

A stray lock of hair had fallen across his eye. She brushed it away. John opened his eyes and grinned lazily at her, causing her heart to skip a beat. He turned and braced a hand under his head so they were facing each other, inches apart.

He ran his free hand through her hair, bringing a strand of it to his lips to kiss.

"You are so lovely. I've never seen a woman with hair as jet black as yours. So silky and fine." He brushed the lock against his cheek and sighed. "And your eyes, Alena, they're like dazzling amethysts."

She touched a hand to his cheek. "My father had the same eyes. It's the only thing I remember about him.

That— and his temper." She frowned at the unpleasant memory intruding upon their interlude.

John took her hand and kissed the palm. Tingles pricked her scalp and spine. "I don't want to talk about your father, Alena." His eyes gleamed. "Not when I want to be doing this."

He kissed her and she melted into him. His arms came around her and all thoughts of Kevin McClaine fled.

"You have the most kissable lips," he murmured against her mouth.

All other thoughts disappeared as Alena became lost in his kiss.

What followed was something totally different than before. The first time John made love to her, he was as gentle as a summer breeze, touching her everywhere. This time flew by like a whirlwind. Quick. A maelstrom of limbs and emotions. Alena found herself caught in a completely new experience, unlike what happened before.

Yet it was just as satisfying. It amazed her how varied lovemaking could be, from tenderness to urgency and back again. Both fulfilled her in different ways. She thought it like her paintings. Sometimes her art evoked strong feelings as she placed the paint upon the canvas, while other times aroused tender feelings with each brushstroke.

Every inch of her had been loved. Alena knew she was now a woman in every sense. Though John had come into her life such a short time ago, she would never see anything in the same way. Today started the rest of her life.

She only hoped it would be spent with him.

A loud gurgle disrupted her thoughts. He grinned sheepishly.

"It's my stomach."

They both laughed, comfortable with each other. He told her to stay in bed, that he would make them something to eat.

"You've spoiled me for long enough. Now that I can see, I want to pull my share of the load."

Alena agreed and allowed him out of bed, enjoying the view as he pulled on his clothes. When he had left the room, she took the pillow from her head and squeezed it against her. She couldn't imagine being happier than at this moment. She would daydream about John's kisses until he called for her to come out.

After several minutes, she already missed him. Climbing from the bed, she scrambled into her hand-me-downs from Jeb. Alena swore that tomorrow would be different. She would bring out the dresses from Mama's trunk. The ones she'd only tried on when Jeb was gone. She was a woman now. She wanted to look like one for John. Please him. Make him proud to be with her.

She left her bedroom but didn't see John. A quick burst of panic spread through her.

"Out here," he called from the porch. "I was just coming to get you."

She followed his voice and saw a plate in his hand.

"Come sit outside. The table had all your paints scattered everywhere. I didn't want to move them. Besides," he said, "we can watch the sun set from here."

Alena took the plate he offered and they seated themselves on the porch steps. They made small talk as they ate, comfortable together as if they had known each other for years. When they finished their meal, John took the plates in and washed up, insisting she do whatever she needed to do with her paints.

Since he had startled her from her work several hours ago, Alena did what she could to close up the tubes and rinse her brushes. She glanced at the canvas she had been working on. Nearly complete, it would only require a few finishing touches tomorrow. She had painted the scene in a variety of ways many times before, so she wasn't worried about leaving it undone for now.

Alena looked up to find John standing in the bedroom doorway, watching her, a smile playing upon his lips.

"Let's turn in for the night."

She nodded and walked toward him. He put his arms about her and held her close before leading her into the bedroom. She tried to stifle a yawn and he chuckled.

"I know you're exhausted." He brushed her hair back from her face. "Me, too, truth be told."

They climbed into bed. He wrapped around her so they nestled together as two spoons. His arms about her made Alena feel protected, cherished. She dropped off to sleep with a smile on her face.

JOHN WOKE IN A COLD SWEAT, images lingering. His dreams mixed pictures of the war's ugliness with something else. He stared up at the ceiling, trying to bring back fragments that hung just outside his memory. He closed his eyes again, willing the dreams to come back. Nothing.

And then he saw cabins. A cluster together that he headed toward. He peeked inside. Saw the boy— and the man who sliced off the child's finger. John swallowed, remembering his frustration because he couldn't help the boy. Then running, scrambling up a canyon, sliding back down. Whistling for Cicero. Thank God, the horse was there. Aiming his revolver over his shoulder. Being shot at. Then nothing.

Until Alena.

It pleased him so much came back, even if it was scrambled. It could only be a matter of time before he recalled the rest. He looked around in the pale morning light, happy that his vision seemed normal now. He realized Alena was curled up next to him, his arms around her as if it were the most normal thing in the world. She fit perfectly within the circle he had created, her head resting on his chest. It was a good feeling to wake up and have her there, as if she had always belonged at his side.

John decided to go put the coffee on. Getting out of bed might stir up more memories about the boy. He found it hard to believe Alena was still asleep, early riser that she was. Of course, he had worn her out pretty well. Best to let her rest.

He slipped from the bed and covered her, fighting the schoolboy grin that came as he gazed upon her. She was better than anything he had imagined. Not a fair angel like Annabelle but a dark beauty all her own. An original.

He drew water from the well in the crisp morning air and reveled in the sight of everything surrounding him. He felt on top of the world.

As he returned inside, he glanced at the table where Alena's canvas lay. The picture staring back at him caused him to drop the pail.

"My God!"

Alena shot up at John's hoarse cry. She'd been luxuriating in bed. She felt him slip from her side and knew he probably would spoil her by putting on water to boil for coffee. She had a dozen chores to do— milk the cow, feed the animals— but she stayed in bed five more minutes to enjoy the new feelings awakened inside her.

Did she look different? She remembered she wanted to dress as a lady today. She hoped John would appreciate her in something besides a flannel work shirt and trousers.

Now she stumbled from bed and ran into the outer room. He sat at the table, his jaw slack, her unfinished canvas between his hands. He shook his head, mumbling. Alena knew in an instant that he remembered everything.

And that it wasn't good.

John raised his eyes to her. "Where is this canyon? How far from here?" He stood and set the painting down. The intense look on his face caused her to take a step back.

"I was there. I need to go back. I can't remember how, though. It's... my head. It hurts." He closed his eyes and pushed against his temples as if he could force himself to remember the way.

"I'm not sure where it is."

His eyes whipped back open. "What do you mean? This painting is chock full of details. I know. I've been there. You have, too. Now, where is it?" he demanded.

Alena wrung her hands. "I don't know. I've painted it in some fashion all my life. I don't know if it's real. The image comes to me at times and I have to put it down on paper. It's as if I've been there but I don't know when."

John strode to her and grabbed her shoulders. He shook her roughly and her hair spilled everywhere. "You've got to remember. It's important. Lives are at stake. Johnny's life. I have to get to him."

His actions scared her but she had to ask. "Who's Johnny?" She hesitated and then asked, "Who are you?"

He straightened, his hands falling to his sides. "I'm U.S. Marshal John Harper, assigned to the case of Senator Braden Reynolds' kidnapping. The senator and his son, Johnny, were taken from a train destined for San Francisco. I traced them to the Marker brothers, a vicious gang who's operated in this area for years. The core gang has died off or been imprisoned, but there's still a small group active and full of mischief."

"Do you think that's who came looking for you?"

John nodded grimly. "I'm sure of it. The leader you described. Cletus. He might be the one that hurt the boy."

"How?"

Alena saw a shadow of pain cross John's face. Something bad had happened to Johnny Reynolds and John had witnessed it.

He shook his head.

"Tell me." She forced him to look at her. "What did Cletus do to the boy?"

Reluctantly, John explained the outlaw's action. Her stomach lurched, going queasy. She had no idea such people existed. What shocked her more was that the man she loved intended to go after this gang.

Alone.

"I'll do whatever I can to help you find them, John."

He ran a hand through his hair and began pacing. "I was going for help when I was wounded. There were too many of them for me to try a rescue attempt. I need to get back now. Who knows what they've done in the meantime? I can't wait for reinforcements."

Disbelief washed over Alena. "You can't go back alone. I won't let you. Your shoulder isn't totally healed. If you were no match for them whole, how can you stop them now?"

Her words halted him in his tracks. "You don't have faith in me? I can do it, Alena. I have to." His voice broke. "I can't live with myself if I don't try." He marched over and clasped her elbows in his hands. "Try to remember. Where is that canyon?"

Alena started crying in sheer frustration. "It's like you and your memory. You know you've seen it and can't remember how to get there. I suppose I've seen it, too, but it must have been years and years ago.

"I never leave here. I've only been to Rio Vista once, and even then, that was so long ago. I don't know. I just don't know!"

John's fingers dug into her. "You've got to remember. Think!"

Alena tore away from him and went to her rocker. She sat and closed her eyes, shutting out the world. She began to rock slowly, her arms wrapped about her.

When did I first paint this scene? How old was I? Did I draw it or paint it first?

She rocked and rocked. Time stood still. Alena was aware of John's presence yet, in a way, she became lost in the past. She thought back to the day her mother died. The pain rose anew. Her father, that coward, left that same day. Jeb took her in. Jeb, always there, protecting his little Magdalena, helping her, teaching her.

Jeb took her there.

She couldn't remember how long ago it had been. Probably not soon after her mother died and her father deserted her.

"It'll be a little adventure, Sweetie Pie. I've gotta do business with some men. I won't be long. I don't want you talking to them, though. They're bad men. They don't like little girls."

"Then why are you talking to them?"

"Business is business. Sometimes you have to do it and move on. Don't ever ask me about business. Understood?"

They rode there together on his horse. She had named him Peanut when Jeb told her the horse didn't have a name.

Alena saw the canyon in her mind now, more clearly than she had in years. Its stark beauty. The bright sun that summer day. The picture had stayed with her all these years. She didn't remember anything at all about why they were there, just that Jeb said don't talk, so she hadn't.

An old Mexican woman had been present. Alena sat outside with her. They didn't speak. She didn't know if the woman even knew English, but when they left, the woman came, too, walking behind Peanut. Alena couldn't remember where the women had gone. She hadn't come home with them. But the next time Jeb went on business, the woman came and stayed with her. She did that many times over the years when Jeb had to leave. She taught Alena how to nurture animals and care for the sick and injured ones.

Then one day Maria didn't come. Alena didn't know if Jeb thought her old enough to stay by herself or what. And she never did know what his business was. She never asked questions. She respected Jeb's privacy.

Nagging doubts plagued her. What did he do? Had he ever gone back to this canyon and those men?

She stopped rocking and looked up at John.

"I have an idea where the canyon is, but I'm going with you."

CHAPTER 25

$\mathcal{A}$nnabelle had no idea where to go to have her rings appraised. She hoped if she set out, she would find a reputable jeweler nearby. The Baldwin House was known as one of the finest hotels in San Francisco. Surely the neighborhood surrounding it would be comprised of respected business establishments.

Two blocks into her walk, her feet ached. She wished she had the luxury of hailing a cab and trying to spy a shop from a seated perch, but she had very little cash. She couldn't share her plans with Bryce and ask for money from him. He had proved to be a friend indeed, but she wasn't willing to push friendship over the edge of propriety. Besides, she was sure Bryce would heartily disapprove of her actions.

There!

She spied a jeweler's shop across the street, about a block down. Good thing her eyesight was sharp. Annabelle watched the passing traffic, waiting for a break in the movement of carriages. Funny, she had never had to do that before. In the past, she had always been escorted by a man and assumed it was his job to care for her. How little she had done for herself, she realized. With the boat Braden had placed them in, she would need to become more self-reliant.

That frightened her to her core. She had never been on her own nor made any real decisions of any importance. Her biggest problems consisted of what dinner guests to seat next to each other or which hat might go best with her new frock. She had gone straight from her father's house into Braden's, and they were the real powers in decision-making. She lived a petty, self-absorbed life.

Until now.

But her son's life was at stake. Annabelle got a grip on her shaky emotions and resolved she would take charge of this situation. Once Johnny was safe, she determined never to find herself so helpless or dependent upon a man again.

She entered the shop to the tinkle of a small bell. A thin man wearing pince-nez sat on a stool behind the counter, reading a newspaper. His bald pate shone under the lights of the store. He stood and greeted her.

"Good day, madam. Do you have a specific piece I might interest you in?"

The bell sounded again as she stepped up to the counter.

"No, I have no need of new jewelry, sir, but I would like your assistance."

The man nodded warily. "Very well," he said, his quiet tone matching her own. Then he looked over her shoulder and called out, "Feel free to browse a moment, sir. I'll be with you shortly."

Annabelle removed her glove and rested her palm against the counter. Her rings gleamed in the well-lit store. She pulled off her engagement ring and wedding band and handing them to him. He seemed surprised that she offered them.

"Would it be possible for you to give me an idea of

their worth?" she asked softly. She had no idea who had come into the store and hated conducting such personal business with one stranger with yet another one present in the room but she had no choice. Time was of the essence.

"I see."

The man became all business. He reached under the counter and removed a round piece, which he brought up to his eye. With this apparatus in place, he lifted the engagement ring first and studied it carefully.

"A nice cut," he murmured as he turned the stone to see it from different angles. "A little over three carats, I'd say."

"Yes," she said faintly.

Annabelle remembered the day Braden slipped it on her finger. Her parents were present and her father had called for champagne. She had only known Braden for three weeks. Even in all the excitement, she experienced a sense of panic, knowing she was being rushed along.

And an ache— for even then, she knew she had betrayed John.

She brought herself back to the present and watched as the jeweler examined her diamond-encrusted wedding band. Once again, he turned it, letting the light catch the stones in different ways. She was also aware of the other customer somewhere behind her. He moved to her left and bent to study the case in front of him. Annabelle glanced at him from the corners of her eyes but didn't dare to make eye contact. She was alone in public, without an escort, doing business with a tradesman. It wasn't the done thing but she would do whatever it took to save her family.

"Well?" she asked, impatient to find out the value of the rings.

"I can give you an estimate, madam, but I'm curious

why you would want to know. Is it for insurance pur-
poses? Surely your husband handles such
transactions?"

She knew a lie would not come naturally to her and
so she chose to remain secretive. Either the man would
help her or he wouldn't. "I'd prefer not to discuss it, sir.
Suffice it to say the rings must be sold."

"I see." The jeweler studied her carefully. "So you
intend to sell the pair?"

Annabelle nodded. "I know they are worth a great
deal. You yourself noticed the cut and beauty of the
stones."

"I don't normally buy off the streets. I can tell you
their worth and recommend somewhere to try and sell
them but I must prepare you that often one cannot get
full value at those... establishments."

"I understand." Her knees started to shake. She
forced them together and leaned upon the counter for
support. "How much would they bring?"

The jeweler named a price that fell far short of the
ransom demanded by the Marker brothers. Although
worth a great deal, the rings did not come close to the
amount it would take to free her family. Desperation
ravaged her as she replaced the rings on her finger.

"Thank you so much for your time. Good day." She
smiled shakily and exited the shop.

Blindly, she walked down the sidewalk, her composure ready to crumble if someone so much as said "boo"
to her. What to do? Where to go? She had no answers.
No hope.

Annabelle rounded the corner and spied a church.
At least here would offer some solace, some refuge. She
hurried inside.

∼

DINGUS RUSHED to keep up with the woman. He had recognized her immediately from the picture in the pocket watch he'd taken from Braden Reynolds. A golden-haired beauty, with delicate features and eyes a deep azure blue, he knew he could not be mistaken when he spied her on the street.

He had come into San Francisco to find out what was happening. It was too isolating being out in the middle of nowhere. He wanted to see if the senator's wife had arrived and what progress, if any, the U.S. Marshal's Office had made on the case. Dingus had dozens of contacts here— some reputable, some far from it— so he knew he would learn within a day or two where things stood. He wanted to wrap up this business and wash his hands of the Marker brothers for good.

He was ready to retire. This ransom, if successful, would allow that to happen.

Or so he'd thought. Why was Mrs. Reynolds trying to pawn her wedding rings to a jeweler? He'd heard bits and pieces of their conversation, enough to arouse his curiosity. Enough to believe things didn't bode well. A sick feeling lurched in his gut.

As he followed her down the street, Dingus knew whom to blame. That snake-oiled senator, Braden Reynolds. Somehow he'd wasted the family fortunes, be it cards, the ponies, or women. Whatever the vice, Dingus realized no ransom would be paid.

He didn't like the pompous senator. The man didn't give his son the time of day. In that moment, Dingus felt pity for the desperate Mrs. Reynolds. Maybe the money from the rings would be enough to give her the boy back. A pretty little thing like that could surely hook another husband, maybe a decent one this time around. It would also give the boy a chance to get out from under the shadow of his father. Johnny seemed like a good kid.

Dingus could give all that to them. Mrs. Reynolds would be better off with Braden Reynolds dead. Why shouldn't he take the money from the rings and keep it all for himself? What was left of the old gang was a joke. Maybe those who remained would blame Cletus and string him up. A world without Braden Reynolds and Cletus Malloy was looking better and better to him.

Besides, once the gang figured out the double-cross, he would be long gone. They didn't know where he lived. Didn't know how he spent his time away from them. Hell, they probably thought Dingus Doolittle was his real name.

He watched as the senator's wife scurried up the steps of a church. The last thing he wanted was to spend time in the house of the Lord. Dingus reluctantly followed the pretty blonde inside.

The church was dark with candles glowing at the back. That meant Catholic. He never saw the sense in lighting candles and shoving money into a poor box. If God bothered to hear prayers, Dingus didn't think He charged for the service. The Catholics simply had a nice racket going. Probably a relative of Jacob Marker thought that up a thousand years ago. He held in his chuckle and went and stood next to a stone pillar, keeping a close watch on Mrs. Reynolds.

She removed her gloves and lit a candle. As she knelt, she locked her fingers together. Dingus could see whitened knuckles from where he stood. Without meaning to, he took a step closer as she began to pray aloud.

Dingus made out most of what she said. She prayed for her son's good health and safe return. By the intensity in her voice, he knew Johnny meant the world to her. She asked for forgiveness for the anger in her heart. That referred to her husband. He didn't care much about Braden Reynolds so his eyes wandered about the church.

Then she said something that caught his attention. She prayed for a way to come up with the ransom money. His worst fears were justified. He needed to cut his losses before something else went wrong.

Dingus decided in that moment he had to talk to her.

CHAPTER 26

*D*ingus watched her rise unsteadily from her knees. He stepped forward to take her elbow but she turned to her left, away from him. He watched as she slipped into a pew and sat down. She placed her elbows on her thighs and locked her fingers together. Her forehead came to rest upon her hands.

He glanced around. The church was empty save for a woman near the altar, about thirty rows away. Dingus stepped into the row behind Mrs. Reynolds and sat.

He remained quiet, studying her as a shaft of light drifted through the stained-glass window and onto her, causing a myriad of colors in her hair of spun gold. He leaned near her ear.

"You seem troubled, ma'am."

She turned. A look of fear, then revulsion, crossed her face as she sprang to her feet. She recognized him. In an instant, he knew his face had finally made a wanted poster. That meant time would be of the essence now as he quickly hatched a plan.

Her mouth quivered but defiance was there, all the same. She sat back down on the pew, careful to keep her distance from him. This girl had spunk.

"Where is my son? Is he all right?"

Dingus noticed she didn't ask about her husband. He decided he'd been right about the senator. It strengthened his resolve to get rid of the man. He didn't need loose ends.

"And my husband? Is he still alive?"

"That obnoxious sumbitch?" Dingus chuckled softly. "I don't know if he'll be in one piece by the time I get back. My boys don't take kindly to his sort."

She winced and Dingus was immediately contrite. He didn't want to wound her with spiteful words. She had done nothing more than exercise bad judgment in marrying the wrong man. He hastened to reassure her.

"Your boy's fine. For the most part. A little accident, but nothing serious. I'm sure he's ready to get back to his mama."

"Accident? What do you mean?" She narrowed her eyes. "What did you do to my son?" she growled, her voice low and sounding dangerous.

Dingus had never meddled with a mama bear and her cubs, but he figured if he had, the she-bear would've worn a look similar to the one Mrs. Reynolds sported now. It also told him those in charge had kept from her that Johnny's severed finger had arrived in a tidy package at the San Francisco office. Relief washed over him, knowing he would be long gone by the time that fact became known. He wouldn't want to be the one tangling with Mrs. Reynolds then.

"I said he was fine. Better a little hurt than dead, right?"

Her eyes flashed with anger, but she controlled it. Damn, if she wasn't some woman. With new respect for her, he softened his tone.

"Now that you and me are here, we might as well do a little business. I'm sure you've been told by the Marshal's Office about the ransom?"

She flushed. Up close, he could see the dark circles

under her eyes, a sure sign she hadn't slept much. She looked frail and helpless in the muted light, despite the determination that kept her back ramrod straight. He couldn't be influenced by the fact she was a woman, and a beautiful one at that. Best to stick to business.

"My husband's attorney and I... we've spoken to his business manager. I hadn't a clue as to how to convert Braden's stocks and bonds into... money for you... and I..." Her voice trailed off. He watched her struggling with the lie she thought to tell and saw the moment she gave up on spinning fairy tales.

"I can't raise the ransom," she said flatly. Her bitterness gave him pause. "My husband lost everything. Everything. *Damn him.*"

She raised a clenched hand to her mouth and held it there, holding back the unshed tears he saw in her all too blue eyes.

"I was too foolish to know what went on. The salary he earns as a senator? I haven't an inkling what he is paid. The cost of the dress I am wearing or Johnny's tutor or the fresh flowers that are delivered three times a week to our home in Washington? I'm utterly clueless."

She slammed her fisted hand down on the pew back. Her fevered whisper gave him chills. "I deserve what has happened. I have been a puppet all these years. I married Braden Reynolds to please my father when I was in love with another man."

She looked startled that she'd uttered aloud words from her heart. "Oh, God." She angrily wiped the tears that spilled onto her cheeks. "Why am I telling you all this? Things I barely admit to myself?"

"Could you be with this sweetheart again? Is he free?" It surprised Dingus he voiced the question.

"I don't know," she answered, red-rimmed eyes searching his face. "I suppose I should ask you. He's assigned to the kidnapping and went missing. He didn't report in when he should have." She studied him a moment. "Did your gang murder John Harper?"

Anger boiled inside him. He knew of two marshals his boys had already dealt with. Had John Harper been a third who'd come calling at the canyon hideout while he was away? Why hadn't Cletus told him about this lawman's visit? What else hadn't Cletus told him?

He would take it out of the man's hide a piece at a time.

Dingus took a calming breath. He needed to focus on the matter at hand. "Let's get back to our business, pretty lady." He was more than ready to make her a widow. His soul was already damned a thousand times over. One more death at his doorstep would be nothing.

"I'll give you the boy back for your rings. That's the deal. Take it or leave it."

The first sign of hope lit her face. "Would you?" she asked softly. "I know you have asked for much more. Will that be enough to appease you?"

"I'll let you in on a little secret. What they'll fetch will be all mine. As long as we're sharing confidences, Mrs. Reynolds, I will tell you that you might not love your husband, but I've never loved my life as an outlaw."

Her eyes grew wide. He nodded. "I want to quit the life. Spend my remaining days fishing. Not a worry crossing my mind other than should I have flapjacks or eggs for breakfast." He chuckled. "Or both."

Dingus grew serious. "We didn't plan on taking your husband and boy. It happened in the course of a robbery. I can't change things now but I'll try and make it as right as I can."

He placed his weathered hand over hers. She flinched and withdrew it. He shrugged. So much for comforting her. What should he expect? He was the outlaw that stole her child. He couldn't blame her.

"I'll bring back Johnny for you. He's a sweet kid. I'm partial to girls myself, but he's a good one. You done a fine job raising him."

"You have children?" Annabelle watched as a wistfulness crossed the outlaw's face. Her first impression of a farmer seemed correct. It was hard to reconcile his lined, weathered faced with that of a desperado.

"No," he said gruffly. "I loved another once. She wasn't free. I've none of my own. Wasn't meant to be, I suppose."

Annabelle made her decision. She might be a fool for having confidence in an outlaw, but something in his eyes, especially the way he talked about children, touched her. Dingus Doolittle was her one hope of getting Johnny back. The marshals might have good intentions, but this man in front of her now knew where her son was. She staked Johnny's life on her gut feeling. She would take the bargain he offered and pray she was doing the right thing.

"I accept your terms," she told him, proud that her voice didn't waver. "When can I expect to see Johnny?"

He thought on it. "Tomorrow afternoon."

"May I come with you?" she asked boldly, not really expecting him to agree.

His eyes looked her up and down. "My boys'd gobble you up like a piece of peach pie. Ain't no way I'd take a lady near them." He paused. "We'll meet at noon a ways outside San Francisco. You'll need to hire a driver."

The outlaw gave her directions on where to have a coach waiting. "You'll be miles and miles from my hideout, so don't think about leading the law there. I'll meet you at the rendezvous point with the boy and be off. If

I sniff even a hint of trouble, you'll never see him again."

She held her head high. "I would do nothing to risk Johnny's life. The marshals haven't been able to help me. I see no reason to bring them into this."

"Agreed." Doolittle glanced down at her gloved hand. "Give me the wedding band now as a measure of good faith. We'll trade the engagement ring for the boy tomorrow."

Annabelle pulled the glove from her hand and slipped the rings from her finger. She returned one to her hand and handed him the gold band studded with diamonds. She rose from the pew, eager to be gone from his presence.

As she reached the aisle, she paused. "You never answered my question about John Harper. Do you know what happened to him?"

A funny light shone in the outlaw's eyes. For a moment, Annabelle thought Doolittle might reveal another confidence to her. She couldn't believe she had told him about her marriage and its lack of love, much less the fact he'd confessed to her about not liking his life of crime. What strange bedfellows circumstances had made of them.

He shrugged. "I haven't been at the hideaway the entire time. I've had other business to attend to. If this Harper came while I was gone, no one told me about it."

His face darkened with grim determination, a look that frightened her. Had she made a deal with the devil?

"*N*o way would I take you with me, Alena. The situation's too dangerous." John spoke firmly, hoping to convey to her the gravity of the matter.

Alena's chin lifted a notch. "You think you can shoot your way in and back out of the place, all while rescuing the senator and his son?" she asked. "John, you can't even raise your arm past your shoulder yet. I can imagine what a gun recoiling on you would do. You have to take me with you."

She took a step toward him and lay her palm against his chest. Even a simple touch caused his knees to go weak with wanting her. He kept his face a mask, though, not wanting to telegraph his thoughts to her.

"I won't risk taking you into that canyon. Just tell me your best recollection of where it lies and I'll be on my way. Every minute counts."

"John Harper, you know I'm a good shot. Better than any man in the Marker brothers' gang. You'll need someone to cover you. Distract them." Her eyes pleaded with him. "You need me."

He admitted to himself she was right. He had been going for help when one of the gang wounded him.

He'd been seriously outnumbered. But who knew what had happened while he'd healed from his injuries at the cabin? Annabelle must be out of her mind, frantic with worry over her loved ones.

John realized the hideout was so remote that he doubted any lawman had stumbled onto it since he'd been there. No one had discovered it in all the years the Markers had operated. He was certain the hostages hadn't escaped. He needed to return and rescue them. Not because he owed it to Annabelle. He didn't owe her anything. But he needed to see his mission through. He must go back, extract the hostages from the cabin, and bring them to safety.

But how could he do it? He hadn't shot a gun in what seemed like a month of Sundays. He was half-tempted to take Alena up on her offer. She was the best shot around. Of course, that had been with tin cans sitting still on a fence post. How would she react in a situation with desperadoes?

He glanced down at her. Where did she get that stubborn set to her chin? He'd always thought her tender and kind. It was probably better he'd gotten to know her before seeing her, because this kind of determination usually spelled trouble for a man when a woman was this hell-bent on something.

Defiance filled her sweet face. "When do we leave?"

Damn. The woman wasn't backing down one bit. She must've seen him wavering. He had to be crazy to consider taking a woman along.

Or desperate. Together, that was a dangerous mix.

"Let's get a meal in us and pack up. We can talk about what supplies to take as we eat."

Alena fried up some bacon and eggs while John milked the cow and fed the animals. He couldn't find a sugar cube and so sneaked one of Alena's peppermints for Cicero. She sniffed it suspiciously at first but seemed to take to it right away.

John returned and they ate quickly, with purpose.

"I have your gun," Alena told him. "I've kept it down in the hidey hole. You have some ammunition in your saddlebags but not nearly enough for what we may be up against."

"And you have?"

She went and lifted a revolver mounted on the wall. "I know how to use this and the rifle I hit the cans with. In fact, I may have something else we can use."

She returned to her bedroom and opened the chest containing her mother's clothes. With regret, she lifted out the dresses, the mantilla, and comb and set them aside. She'd never put on one of them for John. Now, he might never see her in this finery. For what might be the last time, Alena draped the mantilla about her and lifted one of the dresses up to her.

A low whistle startled her. She looked up to see him standing in the doorway. Embarrassed, she tossed the dress onto the bed.

"No, let me take a look at you." He lifted the dress back up to her and she took it while he stood and admired her.

"Of all the sights I've seen since my vision returned, you are the loveliest."

Tears formed in her eyes. John's callused thumbs brushed them away. He took the dress from her and laid it on the bed and then pulled her into an embrace. He held her close, no words necessary. Then he raised her chin and gave her a sweet kiss, tender and loving.

"So, are you going to dress up special to blast away the Marker brothers?" he teased.

Alena realized he was trying to lighten the moment. "No, these are just Mama's clothes. What I came looking for are these."

She removed the guns her father had used as a soldier in the Mexican War. Though standard Army issue, Kevin McClaine had pearl handles put on them. The rich luster gleamed in the light.

"I clean and oil them once a month. They're in good condition even if they are old." She strapped on the holster and placed both guns into it, then quickly pulled them out and aimed straight ahead.

"Can you shoot with both hands?"

Alena grinned. "Of course."

They gathered up what they needed from the cabin and went to the barn. The only horse left was the plow horse.

"You'll need more speed than Millie can provide. You can't ride with me because I hope to have two more with us when we leave. We need to go into Rio Vista and get a couple of horses."

Alena hadn't been to the town since she was a small child. It was only seven or eight miles away, but that seemed worlds apart. She and John rode in on Cicero together. This time, the glances that came their way were admiring ones. Every woman they passed seemed to be interested in John.

But the looks she received weren't judgmental as in the past. Maybe even those had only been curious ones. She was older now and realized that all the whispers she remembered may have been because of her parents and what had happened to her mother, not the fact that she looked so different from most of the townspeople.

They purchased supplies at Rio Vista's General Store. John selected ammunition, matches, some jerky, and bandages. The clerk tried to strike up a conversation but John was in no mood for chitchat. Alena insisted on paying for her share with money she brought with her from the sales of her paintings. She would also use that for a horse. The money was just as much hers as Jeb's, she reasoned.

The blacksmith had a couple of horses for sale. Alena fell in love with a large chestnut, which seemed just as smitten with her. They completed the transaction, which included a saddle, and John purchased a second horse. She figured it would carry the senator and his son when they made their escape.

If they had a chance to escape.

John packed their supplies on the spare horse with haste as she arranged for the blacksmith's boy to stay at the cabin and feed her animals for the next few days.

They set out due east since John remembered that much about the location of the hideout. He set a quick pace.

Alena had a vague idea of the direction of the canyon. Her fears calmed as she rode. The horse, which she named Chessy, responded well to direction.

They rode about twelve miles out of town. John let her take the lead. She knew instinctively a landmark would greet them, something that would jog her own memory about the canyon's whereabouts. When they came to a fork in the road, she motioned for them to go left.

A light rain started and with it came a cool breeze. John signaled for her to stop and he removed his poncho from his saddlebags.

He offered it to her. "Put this on."

She protested. "It's your poncho. I'd rather—"

"Would you take the damned thing?" His voice was edged with exasperation.

Alena nodded and he pulled Cicero beside her and pulled it over her head. "I don't mean to snap at you. It's just that we're going into a situation that I won't have any control over and I'm dragging you into it against my better judgment. I'm worried sick I won't be able to protect you and get the job done. At least let me take care of you while I can."

Her heart did a little dance at his words. She reached for his hand, entwining her fingers with his. "We'll get through this. Together."

As they rode, the rain steadily increased. Despite the oversized poncho, bits of icy water slipped down her back. A constant stream dripped from the brim of her hat. At times, she had trouble seeing but a few feet in front of her. Her fingers ached with both cold and the wetness, the rain sneaking into her gloves and pooling at her fingertips. She urged Chessy onward, encouraging the horse to keep pace with Cicero.

They continued for an hour until John halted. He studied the rock formation and said, "Over there. Jimmy Littlefoot told me about a passage. I remember now. That's the way to go."

As they rode, Alena thought he must be crazy. She couldn't see any kind of opening. As they got right upon it, it amazed her that a place to pass through the rocks did exist.

"Who's Jimmy Littlefoot?" she asked as they went through single file.

"One of my contacts. He's never let me down. Some people think Jimmy's loco, but I've always found his information reliable."

"Is he a criminal?" Alena asked timidly.

John laughed. "I don't know what you'd call Jimmy. He led me to the Marker brothers once. Let's hope we can find the way again."

It was late afternoon. Dark would fall within the next hour. The rain continued in a steady downpour, pelting their faces with sharp stings. She wondered how far a ride they had once they passed through the crevice. She wished John would share his plan with her.

Would they work under the cover of darkness? Wait for the morning light?

"Best I remember, we've got another hour's ride," he said suddenly, as if reading her thoughts. "Let's go through this opening in the rock."

John stepped Cicero in front of Alena's horse, the spare one following on the leading rein. In a way, this passage symbolized a crossroads in his life. He could turn around right now and return to a simple, uncomplicated life with Alena. He could imagine them growing old together, sitting on the porch after dinner, watching a thousand sunsets as their children played in the yard before them.

Or he could go through these rocks into his former life of danger and see his obligation through. Whatever happened, he would protect Alena at all costs. That remained foremost in his mind. How he would do that and rescue the two hostages, though, he hadn't a clue.

He'd hesitated in front of the telegraph office in Rio Vista, agonizing over whether to send a message to Will Johnson or not. The crusty marshal would send a slew of lawmen his way, but John hadn't the slightest idea how to direct them to the gang's hideout. Between Alena and him, they had only a vague hunch on where to go. It made no sense having Will and ten marshals descend when he couldn't pinpoint the hideout's location. The same held true for approaching the local sheriff in Rio Vista for help. He doubted the man would up and leave his community to wander about.

So, he took a chance now. It was the biggest risk he had ever taken. Lives were on the line. His own, Alena's, and the hostages. He wasn't the praying type. The war had torn most of his churching from him but he sent one anyway to the heavens. He had another hour before they arrived at the cluster of cabins that housed the

Marker gang. Maybe divine intervention would step in and give him the strength and a solid idea on how to put an end to this case and the anger flowing through him.

Was it possible to hate being an honorable man? He'd always been the gentleman with Annabelle, though he'd burned for her in the burst of young love. He had never cheated on an exam, and that was rampant at university. Never cruelly torn the wings off flies as other boys did. Integrity centered his every action.

Even when fate dealt him the biggest blow of his life, he remained honorable. He didn't confront Annabelle or her father, whom he knew had to be behind the sudden turn of events. John Harper had never been good enough for the man's daughter. Marrying a senator might not put David Martin on the road to certain success but John knew the man would try to ride Annabelle's coattails there.

The best he could do was complete his mission, do the right thing, and probably die trying. What hurt most is that he'd finally found love. With Alena, his blood still boiled and yet sang at the same time. He looked at her as an equal in every way— intelligent, passionate, thoughtful. She was more than a woman. She was his soulmate, his life. She'd given life back to him when he would have died. He owed her everything.

Yet how did he try to repay her? By probably getting her killed. Where was the honor in that?

He stepped Cicero through the crack in the rocks, the packhorse following behind. It took a good half-minute to maneuver through the passageway. As he emerged on the other side, he sensed a presence. He jumped from his horse and bent to the ground, flattening his palm against the mud. Even with the ground so soft, the vibrations hummed against his hand.

Riders, lots of them, headed their way. Both the

storm and wet ground muffled their hooves, but they would be here within a couple of minutes.

He looked over his shoulder as Alena passed through. She immediately stilled. Their eyes met.

"Someone's coming," he told her. "We'll have to take cover. There are too many of them. We don't have time to plan an ambush." He remounted Cicero.

They turned the horses around and went back through the crevice. The other side of the rock formation provided more places to hide. He jumped from his horse and tossed Alena the reins. She immediately took the horses behind a large set of rocks tall enough to hide their stature and looped their reins around a low branch.

John rounded the corner. "I thought I might try to cover our tracks but the rain's already washing them away. They shouldn't notice anything amiss."

Both drew a gun, preparing for what might come, as they hid. Alena's heart beat so loudly, she was glad for the rain and occasional bursts of thunder that hid the noise.

Then above the storm, they heard a man wheezing over the sound of the approaching horses in the distance. Alena leaned around and saw what looked like a madman come through the crack. His eyes were wild with fear and panic. Hair was plastered against his face, which had been beaten severely. A gaping hole existed where there were once teeth. In an instant, she knew this was the senator fleeing his captors. But where was his young son?

The man looked around and stumbled, pushed back to his feet, and fell again. He babbled incoherently as he lay in the mud, beginning to weep like a baby. The horses approached now. Alena exchanged a look with John, wondering if they should try and hide the senator.

It was too late. Alena watched as Cletus appeared on foot, coming slowly through the crack, his eyes scanning the land until he spied his hostage. She began to shake, thinking of what John had told her this outlaw did to little Johnny Reynolds, and her finger flirted with her gun's trigger.

John's hand covered hers. He shook his head and she understood that it wasn't worth killing Cletus when so much else was at stake. She relaxed the grip on her gun, forcing the finger away from firing.

Other men followed Cletus. She counted five more. Someone must be holding their horses on the other side. It probably wasn't worth the time it would take to bring them along the perilous entrance to the canyon. They must have spotted Reynolds going through the rocks and known he couldn't get far.

Alena watched as Cletus walked to the senator, who babbled irrationally when he saw the outlaw headed his way. She realized this vicious band of men had totally broken their captive.

Cletus knelt to the ground and taunted, "Lookee at you, Mister Senator Big Shot. Stripped of your manhood, behaving no better 'n a child. The kid you left behind is more a man than you are."

She heard John's quick intake of breath. At least the boy was still alive. Alena laid a hand over his and gave it a squeeze as she wondered what kind of father would leave his son behind with a band of outlaws.

Cletus stood and kicked Reynolds hard in the ribs. He screamed and clutched his side, burying his face in the mud.

"Let's see. Do you have courage? No. Honor?" The outlaw laughed. "I'd say no to that, too. Balls?" He dropped back down to the ground and grabbed the man's private parts, twisting hard as Reynolds shrieked.

"Barely." He turned to the men now surrounding the

hostage. "Boys? Seems like the senator still has his balls. Since that's all he's got left, maybe we should just peel those away, too."

The men murmured their assent. Cletus ran this show. They would do whatever he instructed.

"I say we unman him. He's stripped of his pride and his high and mighty ways. We might as well see the job through."

Alena buried her face in John's shoulder for a moment. She was thankful her life hadn't been touched by such evil.

Yet she felt a burning inside her, as if her own animal nature rose up. She watched as Cletus tied a rope around Reynolds' neck and tossed it to one of the men, who pushed the senator back through the hole in the rocks. They all laughed, shouting obscenities. Alena knew she could scratch out Cletus's eyes for what he'd done to an unseen boy, much less for the humiliation and pain he put Senator Reynolds through.

The remaining gang members started toward the crevice, joking about the ways they would remove the senator's testicles. Only Cletus stood in view. Alena saw him turn to survey things before he stepped through the passageway.

He stopped dead in his tracks. Surprise colored his face a brick red. Alena looked to where Cletus stared.

Sitting on his horse was Jeb, who'd silently ridden up in the rain.

CHAPTER 28

hy was Jeb here, in the middle of nowhere?
Confusion reigned in Alena's mind.
Jeb was in San Francisco, selling her painting, attending to whatever business he had. He couldn't be in the thick of a rainstorm, miles from any town. She turned to John, utterly bewildered.

The grim set of his mouth made her own go dry. He knew something. What had he kept hidden from her?

Alena needed to talk about it. She rose from her crouched position, a hand outstretched, but John pulled her back down.

He wrapped his arms about her like a steel band and whispered in her ear, "Too dangerous. Stay put."

She nodded mutely and he released her.

"Helluva day we're having," Cletus shouted. "And why're you creeping up like a ghost?" He laughed. "I have enough guilt and Markers haunting me. I don't need to add you to the list."

The downpour started to subside. Alena strained to hear their conversation but no voices could be heard. The rain slowed to a trickle. Still nothing was said.

"Hell's bells. I don't need your help anyway. What about that ransom, Dingus? You got any news on that?

And did you see us having to round up the senator? Bastard fled the coop, leaving that boy of his behind. Damn shame, a man turning tail like that."

Even without seeing them, Alena sensed the strain between the pair. Cletus was too chatty and uncomfortable. Her mind reeled as to the implications. He'd asked Jeb about the ransom.

It hit her hard, as if someone sucker punched her. She doubled over, collapsing to the ground. *This was Jeb's business.* This is what he was. What he'd always been. Why he left her alone for long periods.

Jeb was one of them.

She had to look upon the scene. She couldn't trust what her ears heard. Alena leaned slightly around the rock again, ignoring John motioning her.

"Quit your yapping." Jeb turned toward the crevice and spied one of the outlaws peering back through. "Go on. Git. Cletus and I have business to do. Take Reynolds back. I'll see you shortly."

Dismissed, the gang member left. Alena picked up on Jeb's tone. It wasn't one that would invite questioning. He was a man with status in this group. Nausea rose in her. It grew tenfold with the look Jeb gave Cletus. She saw a complete stranger then. A man she had no knowledge of. Where was the man who'd taught her all she knew about decency and trust? The man who had taken her in all those years ago and raised her as his own?

Alena felt a chill deeper than any the rain had brought, an incredible sense of betrayal.

"No," she whispered, clutching her stomach again. She would be sick. Jeb was a part of these cruel, despicable men. A criminal. Thief. Robber. She hated him.

Without thinking, Alena brought her gun up to shoot him. John pushed her hand back down.

"Not the way," he mouthed.

She pulled herself together. She had to think about the innocent victims here, that poor man and his boy. She and John had to get them out.

Then the bloodbath would begin.

"They want a good faith measure. They don't want the boy in any more pieces." Jeb glared at Cletus as he spoke. "I'm taking him back. I'm dealing with the wife only now. She'll give us half the ransom when her boy's returned. We'll negotiate the rest later."

"No," Cletus said. "That's not what we decided."

Alena watched as Jeb's gaze caused Cletus to pale. "*We* don't decide anything. *I* decide everything."

Her knees went weak. Jeb's statement was the final death knell. Her childhood champion, her friend, her protector— was no better than pond scum.

"I'll take the boy now. I've already got his mama waiting on me, as we speak. We'll get fifty thousand then. The other half after producing the senator. I'll arrange a place to leave him."

Cletus only grunted his dissatisfaction with the arrangement.

Jeb's lined face shone with pure evil. "I didn't promise they'd find him there alive." He took off his hat and ran his fingers through his hair. "Go ahead and have a little fun with him while you can. I'll retrieve the boy and will be gone about a day. Have Reynolds ready tomorrow morning. I'll be back then."

A new burst of thunder cracked. Lightning filled the sky as the rain started up again.

Jeb turned to mount his horse. "And Cletus, ride a sweep around to check on things before you return."

"You think you were followed, Dingus?"

"I'm never followed. But I never take chances either."

Cletus disappeared through the crevice and returned with his horse. He mounted up, sullen, and

Alena could tell he didn't want to follow through with his orders. He tossed a surly look over his shoulder, but Jeb and his horse had already vanished through the opening in the rocks.

Cletus turned and dug in his heels to the horse's sides just as Alena saw a hand appear in the rocks. A shot rang out, the sound all but melting away in the midst of the thunder. The horse reared and Cletus fell to the ground.

Jeb emerged from the shelter of the rocks and walked over to the body.

"I never take chances. Don't know why I took one on you." He shook his head. "If only you'd told me about John Harper coming through, it might've saved your hide."

He gave the body a vicious kick. Alena supposed he checked to see if Cletus was dead.

"Too bad I didn't have time to make you suffer for keeping something like that from me. Harper is trouble that I've gotta take care of now.

"I won't make you suffer, boy," he told the skittish horse before he slapped it. The animal exploded at a gallop across the land. Jeb spit on Cletus' body and then dragged it behind a boulder opposite from where she hid beside John. He returned to the opening among the rocks and disappeared through it.

Alena threw herself into John's arms.

~

JEB APPROACHED THE HIDEOUT CAREFULLY, tamping down impatience. He circled around behind the stables first and left his horse. At least the animals seemed to be in good condition. The gang members might be stupid but they knew to care for their horses.

He walked to the bunkhouse but found it empty.

Same with the next cabin. Everyone must be gathered in the third of the cabins, which functioned as a mess hall and a place to keep the hostages. Jeb glanced through the window before making his presence known. He liked to scope out the lay of the land. He did not like surprises.

It startled him how few men were present. The Marker brothers had run twenty to thirty men at a time in the old days, before so many had been arrested and hanged for their offenses, while others drifted away to rival gangs. A quick count placed their number at six. He remembered Jimbo being shot at the train and another man who'd had a heart attack right after the kidnapping. They'd buried his body out back.

That should leave ten in all, counting him and the missing Cletus in that number. What had happened to the other two men? He'd spotted no one as he rode in. Where could they be?

He put on a poker face and walked through the door. "Howdy, boys!" he proclaimed with more gusto than he felt. "What's the good word?"

Rowdy slapped him on the back. "Hey, Dingus. Glad to see you. The boys told me they'd run into you when they hunted down Reynolds."

Jeb gestured around the room. "I saw everyone here out chasing the senator down, Rowdy. Except Moe and Petey. Where are they?"

Rowdy shrugged. "Aw, somebody had to stay and look out for the boy while the others have some fun. I didn't mind hanging behind."

Jeb's stare drilled into Rowdy's eyes. "I asked where Moe and Petey are."

Rowdy shifted uncomfortably. Silence filled the cabin. Finally, Jordy spoke up.

"They done went and got themselves killed, Dingus.

They're deader 'n doornails and I say good riddance to 'em." Jordy spit on the ground for emphasis.

He surveyed the motley group before him. One by one, every man's eyes dropped to the ground.

Jordy finally broke the silence. "Cletus let 'em go into town. Frank, too. Moe and Petey got liquored up and started a fight over some whore. Frank said she wasn't even pretty but they was being bull-headed."

Jordy mopped his brow. "Their argument spilled out into the street and before you could say 'jackrabbit,' they whipped out their pistols and shot each other."

Jacob Marker would roll in his grave if he knew what had happened in the years since he'd died. Everything he'd just heard assured Jeb he was making the right decision. Only idiots and fools were left here.

He could lay claim to a pitiful sort of life, what with his mama running off, his brother dying, and Kevin McClaine killing the only woman he ever loved. He had tried to do his best for Alena and now surveying the group in front of him, he realized he'd botched even that. After this last trip home, he didn't know her anymore. Most of that was the fault of that damned marshal, John Harper.

Jeb wondered if he'd have to kill the lawman to get him out of his hair. No need for Alena to know. The girl hadn't looked like she'd pack up and leave anytime soon for San Francisco until the Harper fellow left. Jeb fooled her once as a girl when he'd gotten rid of Mc-Claine. He doubted he could do it again.

What he needed to do was move her into an unfamiliar environment. He wanted her to depend upon him again. Margarita had and he'd let her down. It was different with Alena. He never let that girl down, not since he'd rid her of that worthless father. She had depended upon him all these years. By God, Jeb needed that. Otherwise, he'd be alone, a broken-down codger with nothing to live for.

"They always were fools over women," Jeb agreed quietly. He could sense the relief of the men present when he didn't explode in violence against those left.

"Cletus is out riding the perimeter of the canyon now," he told them. "Just a precaution. We've had a slight change in plans."

"What kind of change?" Rowdy's brow creased slightly.

"The authorities say the boy's mama is mighty upset about that finger Cletus sent them. She doesn't think she'll get her family back. I've arranged to take the boy first and claim half the ransom, like an act of good faith on our part."

The gang members nodded in agreement. "Then we'll swap her the senator for the other half?" asked Jordy eagerly.

"That's right." He glanced at the senator's son, huddling on the ground in a corner. "You ready to go home and see your mama?"

The child's lips trembled. He nodded.

"Well, come on, boy, we haven't got all day. Let's head out."

"Now?" several of the men asked.

Jeb nodded. "Yup. I'd love to stay a spell and knock back some whiskey, maybe tell a few stories, but we're on a deadline now. We've got to show the Marshal's Office we'll live up to our end of the bargain. Cletus almost botched it for us with slicing that finger off, as it is."

He looked around the room. "That and letting the marshal get away."

Astonishment filled their faces. The incident had occurred when Dingus was gone. Their surprise immediately turned to guilt.

"How did you know?" asked Rowdy.

Jeb snorted. "Hell, there's nothing I don't know. Don't worry. I took care of things." He glanced at the boy again. "You ready?"

Johnny Reynolds stood and moved toward him, not a backward glance at his father.

Braden Reynolds screamed, "You can't leave me here! They'll kill me!"

Jeb stepped quickly to where the senator sat tied in a rickety chair and slapped him hard. He turned back to the gang. "Work him over some, boys. Only until Cletus gets back, though. We don't need him dead." He mouthed the word *yet*, his back toward the boy, and was rewarded with a few snickers.

He joined Johnny at the door and took once last look around at the hellhole, ignoring the senator's pleas of mercy. Jeb walked out, set never to return.

CHAPTER 29

*J*ohn held Alena close. He couldn't imagine what a crushing blow it had been for her to learn that Jeb was the mastermind behind the Marker brothers. Nothing was ever easy about this job, he decided. Especially now. He figured it would take nothing less than Jeb's death to save Reynolds and his son.

He looked down at the woman in his arms. Would Alena be numb? Withdrawn? Angry? Feel betrayed? And what plan could he concoct? If he could stop Jeb when he came back this way with the boy, half his job would be accomplished.

But what would it take to stop Jeb and keep little Johnny Reynolds alive? Would John consider using Alena as bait to throw Jeb off? He was certain Jeb loved Alena enough not to shoot her. Would she be up to participating in any plan against her father figure after what she'd learned?

Her sobs subsided. She straightened her shoulders and raised a tear-streaked face, ravaged with grief. He was struck by both her beauty and the determination in her eyes.

"What do we have to do to save the little boy and his

father from... that monster?"

Guilt swept through him for even thinking about using her in his quest to stop Jeb. "Alena—"

"Don't try to talk me out of anything. I can't think about things now or I'll fall apart. I'll deal with it all later. Right now, we have two people who desperately need our help. What's our plan?"

John realized nothing he could say would stop Alena from helping him.

"First, we'll need to set a trap for Jeb when he rides back through with the boy. If we can secure Johnny, I want you to take him and ride for help now that we know where we are. You can make it to the nearest town and cable for help or even get local law enforcement to come back with you."

"No." The sweetest lips in all the world, the ones that kissing was surely invented for, pursed firmly together. "That would take too much time. There won't be anything left of Braden Reynolds and you know it. You'd still try to ride in and stop what they're doing to him and you'll be totally outnumbered."

Her voice softened but not her resolve. "I won't leave you, John. We're in this together." She crouched on the ground and brought her knees close to her, wrapping her arms around them. "Once we reach the hideout, how do we get the senator out unharmed?"

He knelt beside her. "We can sneak right up to the windows and bust the glass. Shoot as many as we can as quickly as possible." He ran a hand through his hair. "It's risky but surprise would be on our side. Of course, some of the gang might be sleeping in the other cabins and come pouring out. I doubt all of them would be taking a turn at Reynolds."

"It's more than risky. It's downright dangerous." She paused. "I could try to lure a few out. Go right up to the

ALEXA ASTON

door and knock. Say Dingus sent me and distract them. You could sneak around and—"

"No," he said firmly. "These are animals, Alena. Not men. They'd think you a whore, sent to entertain them, courtesy of Dingus's generosity. I can't stand the thought of them looking at you, much less pawing at you."

"It wouldn't happen. I'd shoot them first. You know I'm fast."

"The answer is no. I have a better idea. It's chancy but it could be effective. Fire. We'll smoke them out and drop them after they get a few feet outside."

She nodded in agreement. "If they're all in the main cabin, we could set the entire group of cabins on fire. Even loosen their horses' reins and scatter them beforehand. In their confusion and panic, the gang might leave Senator Reynolds behind."

He looked up at the dark sky. "This will work a helluva lot better if the rain cooperates," he noted wryly. The rain had all but let up now, with only a fine drizzle misting them. "At least there's enough junk in their storage shed to get a nice blaze going. I remember that from before."

"So, now we wait for Jeb. Dingus," Alena corrected, her voice tight as she used the name Cletus had called him. "What kind of ambush do we set for him?"

JEB FIGURED the gang would have their sport with the senator and probably pass out from too much to drink tonight, especially since Cletus wouldn't be there to keep them from doing otherwise. By the time they awakened in the morning and figured out Cletus wasn't coming back, Jeb would be long gone.

He was glad the rain had finally stopped and he

could use the remaining sunlight to quicken their escape. He would make camp with Johnny Reynolds for the night and turn the boy over tomorrow to the beautiful Annabelle. He was still taken with her, unlike any woman he'd seen since Margarita. He couldn't think of two women more unalike yet both beautiful in their own way.

If things progressed as planned, he'd have the money for the rings in hand this time tomorrow. He would head back to the cabin and give Alena some of the cash, telling her it was from the painting he'd sold. He would have to find some way to slip it into town to one of the galleries he usually did business with. It wouldn't do to leave it in the barn forever. If the roof leaked any and ruined it, he couldn't live with the guilt. He'd lied to her so much over the years. He wanted a new beginning between them.

He and the boy reached the group of rocks and the crevice that formed a perfect slit, hiding the gateway to what had become the Markers' secret hideaway decades ago. Jeb remembered the first time Jacob Marker had led him up to it. If a man didn't know it was there, he'd pass right by it. No wonder the gang's base had gone undiscovered for all these years.

Until John Harper arrived.

How the marshal found it was a mystery. Jeb didn't care now if an entire force of U.S. Marshals rode through it tomorrow— as long as he made his way safely through tonight. He decided to leave an anonymous tip so the marshals could find the hideout. Better to see those boys locked up so they'd never bump into him and Alena on the streets of San Francisco. Besides, the senator would probably be dead by then. Without him or Cletus running interference, Braden Reynolds wouldn't last. Already, the senator was in ghastly shape. This way, Annabelle Reynolds would know she was free. Jeb didn't know why, but her becoming a widow was important to him.

The setting sun touched the horizon as he and Johnny rode his horse through the narrow path.

"Don't worry, Johnny Boy. We'll be through this faster'n you can say jackrabbit and then we'll camp out under the stars tonight. Now that the rain's cleared up, we can even have ourselves a nice fire. In the morning, I'll take you down to the creek that runs nearby and let you wash off some of that grime. We don't want your mama worrying too much now, do we?"

The boy remained silent. Jeb wondered how much taunting had gone on at the child's expense. Well, it was too late to remedy that. Mrs. Reynolds would have her boy back soon. She could start whatever healing process it would take to give Johnny Reynolds some confidence.

Jeb brought the horse through the narrow opening, the sun now dipping halfway from sight. Suddenly, he pulled up, not believing his eyes.

Alena.

His two worlds collided. Panic flooded through him. Alena. Here? Why? How?

He tightened his grip on the boy, who'd gone stock-still.

"Jeb?" Alena called out, raising a hand and shadowing her eyes. "Is that you?"

He held the reins tightly, not allowing the horse to take another step forward. A thousand lies crowded his mind, but his confusion in seeing Alena out of place wouldn't let any of them take root.

"Jeb? I was so worried. John said he'd regained his memory. He told me some wild tale about a kidnapping. He said you were in on it. He rode off before I could stop him."

He heard how her voice trembled. The first seeds of

her doubt in him lay entwined within her words.

Anguish filled her lovely face. "I didn't know what to do, Jeb. I sat down to paint. You know how it soothes me. I started painting this place. You know I've painted it again and again over the years, but I didn't remember it was real until now. Something called out to me. I had to prove John wrong.

"I had to get here. To you."

An ache rose in his chest. He burned with shame. All the wrongdoing of years past had finally caught up to him. Alena would discover what he really was.

"I tracked John," she continued. "I stopped him. I... I hit him on the head, Jeb." Her voice broke and she wrapped her arms tightly around herself. "I had to get here first. I had to see for myself."

Alena stopped, her eyes fastening on Johnny Reynolds.

The color drained from her face. "Is it true?" she asked softly. "Tell me no, Jeb. Please. Tell me it isn't so."

All lies died upon his lips. She knew him for what he was. Alena's moral fiber was strong. She would never, ever forgive him. With that knowledge, the last vestige of good within him died.

Tears spilled down her cheeks as she held her hands out to him. "I see a frightened little boy, Jeb. Why is he here? Tell me, Jeb. I want to hear it from you. Tell me this isn't happening." She began to sob and the sound reminded him of Margarita's cries so long ago.

"You don't understand what I came from, Alena. How I tried to escape it. Your mother was my one hope of leaving my past behind. I lost that when Kevin killed her.

"And when I killed him, I knew my soul was lost forever."

He read the look of shock on her face. "No." She shook her head violently back and forth. "My father

239

abandoned me. You told me that. You told me that!" Her rising hysteria made her words sound as if they came from the little girl she'd been the day he had murdered Kevin McClaine.

"Don't you see, Alena? I couldn't let him do to you what he did to her. Break your spirit. You are the child of my heart. I would do anything for you."

She looked at him as if he were a stranger to her. "Rob? Murder? I don't want any part of you or your blood money."

She slowly started to back away. He urged his horse forward a few steps.

"Sweetie Pie, you have plenty of money on your own. You've becoming a famous artist in San Francisco. I set up a bank account in your name at First National on California Street. They have all the money from the sales of your paintings, far beyond what I've brought home and put under the floorboards."

He wanted to reassure her. Let her see he wasn't as bad as she thought. "This was my last job. I didn't mean to kidnap anyone. But it happened and I knew I could make enough to retire on." He gestured over his shoulder. "Those people— they don't know my name or where I live." He reined in the thought that Annabelle Reynolds had recognized him, probably from a wanted poster.

"Sure they do," Alena responded through chattering teeth. Jeb wasn't sure if it was from the cold or the shock she'd been dealt. "They came looking for John. They were at our place."

Jeb shook his head. "They don't associate me with there. They don't even know my real name, Alena. We'll both take the boy back to his mama. She's promised me her rings. We'll use that as our stake and settle down. Things'll be better than before. You'll see."

He smiled beseechingly at her. "I'll show you San

Francisco. It's beautiful."

Alena shouted in fury, "You're the last person I want to be with! Can't you understand?"

She felt her face twisting into something horrible and ugly as she flung the words at him, hoping to draw him out further from the rocks. "I hate you and your ways. I never want to see you again. Give me the boy. I'll take him back and get him to his mother.

"Go far away... Dingus. Go back to your life."

She watched his face crumple and thought he might cry. Then he grew still. A steely resolve replaced what had been there only a moment ago. He wore a look that caused a wave of fear to ripple through her.

"I can't do that, Magdalena," he said calmly. "You're my life, my Sweetie Pie. I've killed for you."

"No!" shouted the child.

Alena watched little Johnny Reynolds scramble down from Jeb's horse and take off running toward her. He ignored her outstretched arms and ran behind her, locking his arms around her waist, burying his face into her back. She looked up as Jeb dismounted, his gun drawn.

"It can't end this way, Alena. I won't let it."

She froze, her gaze locked on Jeb's, even as she spotted John from the corner of one eye. As he cocked his gun, John called out to Jeb.

"Stop!"

Jeb whipped around and shot in John's direction as Alena drew her own gun and fired. John's shot echoed, as well. She didn't know which one of them hit him, but Jeb fell to the ground. She tore Johnny's fingers from her and rushed to Jeb, never more conflicted than at this moment in time. Alena cradled Jeb's head in her lap, tears freely flowing down her cheeks.

"Why?" she whispered.

Jeb gave her a last, rare smile and died.

CHAPTER 30

$\mathcal{J}$ ohn reached Alena as she lifted an anguished face to him. Pain filled her eyes, raw and bleak. Her lips moved but no words came from them. She glanced back at her lap where Jeb lay and shook her head.

Little Johnny Reynolds stepped up and placed a tentative, bandaged hand on Alena's shoulder.

"I'm sorry," he whispered.

John watched her mood shift instantly. Concern for a boy she had never seen took precedence over her own misery. She eased Jeb from her lap and enveloped the child in her arms. Johnny began to cry softly. Alena crooned to him as a mother would, giving comfort though she had none herself.

Johnny sniffed. "He... D-D-Dingus... he wa-was... nice to m-me. Scary sometimes, but he... but he t-t-t-talked to me some. And he h-h-helped with m-m-my hand. M-m-made sure it stayed cl-cl-clean and wrapped up so it wouldn't g-g-get infected."

She stroked the boy's cheek and then took his bandaged hand, inspecting it and seeing the clean linen bound about it, grateful that Jeb had taken care of this boy.

"He could be nice sometimes, couldn't he?" she said softly, and ran her hands up and down his arms. "But you're all right now, aren't you?" She squeezed his shoulders.

"I g-guess," Johnny mumbled. The boy stared at the star pinned to John's chest. "Are you a marshal? M-Mama says they h-help people."

He nodded. "I am. My name's John Harper. This is Alena. I... we've come to take you home."

Alena stood and the boy clasped her hand tightly. "We have to go get my papa, don't we?" Johnny asked, his round eyes solemn behind wire-framed glasses.

"Yes," John agreed. "We do." He wanted to leave Alena here with the boy but he realized she would have none of it.

He looked over and saw she had gone to the horses. She returned carrying a blanket, which she placed over Jeb.

"We'll bury him later." The steel in her eyes gave him pause. He couldn't imagine how she was able to function but she looked ready to carry out their mission. He saw no reason to doubt she would pull her weight, despite the traumatic events that had transpired during the last few minutes.

John said, "I need you to tell me everything you can about the gang, Johnny. Which cabin your father is being held in. How many outlaws there are. If any are gone right now. Whatever you can remember would be helpful."

"They're all with my papa, Mr. Harper." A look of revulsion crossed the boy's face. John knew what this child had seen would scar him for life.

"Six of them are l-left. They f-f-fight all the time. Cletus— he's the b-boss sometimes. He's n-n-n-not there now."

John laid a hand on Johnny's shoulder. The boy's

face had so much of Annabelle in it. "You won't have to worry about Cletus anymore."

"Good," Johnny proclaimed. He turned and spit on the ground, asserting his impending manhood. "He's m-mean." Johnny glanced down at his bandaged hand but didn't refer to the missing finger.

"What else can you tell us?" Alena encouraged.

"When D-Dingus and I left, they were all in the cabin where they've b-been keeping us. They... they were hurting Papa." A single tear slid down his cheek. "He's t-t-tied to a chair."

Johnny glanced up at him. "He's in a bad way, Mr. Harper. I... I... I don't know if he's g-gonna m-make it."

"We'll do all we can to get him out as quickly as possible. You'll have to be brave, Johnny. We'll have to ride back there."

The boy screwed up his face and nodded. "I can do that."

"Of course you can," Alena assured him. "You've already shown a lot of courage. I know your mama will be so proud of you."

"I m-miss her." Tears filled the boy's eyes.

"I miss my mama, too," she said.

Johnny looked at her. "Where is she?"

Alena sighed. "She went to heaven a long time ago. I was younger than you are now. But I know she's with me and sees me. She's here right now to help calm my fears and see us rescue your papa."

Johnny smiled shyly. "I c-can feel my mama here, too."

John dragged Jeb's body back behind the rocks, though it was doubtful anyone would come this way. They brought out the horses, and John led Johnny over to Cicero. He gave the horse a love pat.

"This here's Cicero, Johnny. She's the smartest horse in the world. She'll carry us to where your papa is and she'll protect you while we go get him. You can watch over her and the other horses until we return."

His eyes met Alena's. She nodded, agreeing with him that Johnny shouldn't have to go any closer than necessary.

They rode to the same place he had tied Cicero before. He knew she recognized the way from how her ears perked up. He bent low and whispered in her ear as he anchored her to a nearby tree.

"It'll have a happier ending this time, Cic. And at least last time wasn't a total mess. It brought us to Alena."

He swore the horse flicked her eyes toward Alena before she snorted. John laughed and stroked the velvet nose before giving her a light peck.

"Be good, my girl. Take care of Johnny."

He bent down and placed his hands on Johnny's shoulders. "Alena and I are going down to the cabins on foot. You'll be able to see everything that happens from here. This won't happen, but if— if you see both of us fall— you climb up on this rock and get on Cicero's back. Get out of here, as fast as you can. Can you do that, Johnny?"

Annabelle's eyes stared back at him as the boy nodded. "All right, Mr. Harper. Be c-c-careful." He turned and hugged Alena, and then walked over and slowly petted Cicero.

John removed one of the saddlebags and dumped out its contents, replacing it with what they would need once they reached the bottom of the canyon. He took a deep breath and caught Alena's eyes.

They were as ready as they would ever be.

As they made their way down the canyon path, he felt a trickle of sweat run down his back, despite the cool of the night. The rain had ceased, and hundreds of stars streaked across the California sky as they made their way to the faraway cluster of cabins in the valley.

Smoke came from only one cabin. A faint light glowed from the distance, again from the same cabin. His confidence grew. With only six men to deal with and all of them in one place, the odds had increased in his and Alena's favor.

They aimed for the storage shed after glimpsing into the other two cabins and finding them empty. The unlocked shed was behind the cabin the men now gathered in. He and Alena slipped inside and closed the door.

John lit a match, getting a more informed glance as he put the flame to a candle sitting on top of a barrel. The shack housed all the food supplies for the gang, as well as other necessities such as extra blankets, bandages, bottles of liquor, lamp oil, and ammunition.

"Work quickly," he told Alena. She took a knife and slit open a burlap sack, dumping flour on the floor. Within minutes all sacks had been emptied of their contents. They positioned the sacks and blankets around the room, pouring several bottles of whiskey and oil on top.

"These will make good starters," she said.

"Let's prepare the other two cabins and then light all three at the same time. I think the smokehouse can be left alone."

"Don't forget that we need to free the horses. We should do that before setting the fires. I want to be in position when they first realize a fire's broken out."

"Agreed. I'll take care of the horses," he said. "You arrange things in the empty cabins."

Alena stood, several whiskey bottles in her arms, and started out the door. John caught her elbow and pulled her close. "Be careful," he whispered, his voice

246

tight. "We don't know when they might tire of their games with Reynolds."

"I will be." She gazed up at him. "I want us both to come out of this alive and well."

He took her chin in his hand and lowered his mouth to hers. The kiss wasn't one of passion or desire, but rather he hoped to convey reassurance. More than anything, he wanted to be standing next to Alena, this whole situation resolved, and speak to her of a life together. He didn't know how receptive she'd be but he planned to marry her as soon as possible. He didn't think she'd mourn Jeb for a year. Not after what she had learned today.

"Meet me back here in ten minutes," he said.

Gun drawn, he opened the door for her and then headed over to the stable that housed the gang's horses. He wanted to scatter them so no one would have a chance to jump on one and flee. The wind had picked up and he was grateful for the howling noise, which helped mask their actions.

Alena watched John walk toward the ramshackle barn and made her way into the two empty cabins. Once there, she stripped the beds of any sheets or blankets and poured the alcohol on top, making sure several piles of mattresses with these firestarters on top were scattered around the room.

She shook her head when she found a couple of the gang members' guns. She couldn't believe they would be so careless as to leave their guns in plain sight. It either spoke to their stupidity or the fact they were confident their hideout would never be found. Alena gathered the two revolvers and checked to see if they were loaded. Since they were, she took them with her back to the rendezvous point.

John awaited her, his face all business now. "The horses are gone. I slapped one and they all followed that leader. We're fortunate the wind's strong now. I don't think the gang heard a thing."

She nodded in agreement. Loud sounds came from the occupied cabin. Voices carried in the wind, along with occasional bursts of drunken laughter. She willed her hands not to shake as she brought the guns up for John to see.

He raised his eyebrows and shook his head. "Why don't you keep them? You'll probably do more shooting than me. I can raise my arm part way up but I know I'm limited because of my shoulder. I'll start out using my right hand, but my aim will probably be off. If the recoil is bad enough, I may switch to my left. Best you have the most firepower."

Alena slipped them into the back waistband of her trousers. "Are we ready?"

"I think so. We each know our position. You set the farthest cabin on fire and then the next one while I cover you. When I see you come out, I'll set fire to this one and get into place. I'll wait until they're all ablaze and then throw a rock through the window. The noise should put them off-kilter, especially with how far gone they are."

"Shouldn't I do that? I'll be closer, and I don't know how good your aim is, left-handed. It won't do to miss."

"You're right." He cupped her cheek and gave her a kiss, hard and quick. "Let's do this."

Alena squashed the nervous butterflies aflight in her belly and hurried to the first cabin. She removed the matchbox from her pocket and struck a match. The flame danced upon the end of the tiny stick until she tossed it onto a pile of whiskey-soaked items. Immediately, the fire sprang up, consuming the heap. She scattered two more lit matches and then scurried from the cabin to the next one, repeating her actions a second time.

As she left the second building, she motioned to John. He entered the storage shed as she sneaked over to the lighted cabin. She searched the ground for a good-size rock and found one, curling her fingers around it. Alena looked over and saw John hurrying toward the water trough and slipping behind it.

It was time.

She stood about twenty feet from the cabin, a cocked gun in her left hand and the rock in her right. She waited a minute longer, allowing the fires to glow visibly. Pulling back her arm, she readied herself to run for cover the minute she released the rock.

Just as she took aim, the cabin door opened. Out stepped a member of the Marker gang.

CHAPTER 31

The man might have been drunk, but his reaction when he spied her was fast. His hand flew down his side and was lifting his gun as Alena shot him in the chest. The force drove him back inside the cabin. She heard hoarse shouts and scattered oaths as she backed away from where she stood. Reluctant to turn away from the open door, she cautiously stepped, pulling her other holstered gun free. Both hands now held the pearl-handled pistols. Her heart hammered inside her chest.

Suddenly the window shattered as one of the gang members burst through it, flying through the air toward her. Alena dropped and rolled to her right as the outlaw came up. A shot echoed in the night and the man fell, a glassy stare at once frozen upon his face. She rolled again as another man charged from the cabin, shooting. She and John fired in response and another body lay upon the ground.

"Three more," she said to herself, slipping behind a barrel for protection. "Three more."

The only exit was from the front door. John had carefully surveyed that on his last trip to the canyon. One window and one door, both facing them now. As he predicted, the strong wind lifted embers from the blaze at the next cabin onto the one holding Senator Reynolds and caused the roof to spark. The remaining gang members were unaware of this as they fired a barrage of shots from the window.

Alena and John returned their fire. The rain-freshened air quickly filled with the burning smell of cordite. Bullets whined and whizzed over her head. Suddenly, one pierced the barrel she crouched behind. Her heart lurched. She couldn't believe John did this for a living.

An explosion rang out. A continual popping noise echoed throughout the canyon. From the sky rained pieces of the storage shed. She realized the fire must have caused the reserve ammunition to ignite, blowing apart the shed.

Alena turned her attention back to the cabin. The gunfire ceased momentarily. She wondered if the remaining outlaws understood what was happening. As she watched the roof burn, she held her breath. Before long, a section caved in. A scream sounded from within. Two more men rushed from the cabin together and split off in different directions. Alena aimed and fired at the one on her right. John had told her to shoot to kill, claiming there was nothing worse than a wounded outlaw.

Her man dropped to the ground as did John's. That left only one more. He threw his gun out the door and followed it with his hands held high.

"Don't shoot," he gasped as he fell to his knees.

John raced to him, handcuffs already out. Alena trained her gun on the outlaw in case he pulled a weapon when John came into range. Just as John narrowed the gap between them, the man whipped his hand down toward his ankle. She caught a glint of steel.

She fired quickly, her shot true, killing the man before he could pull his hidden gun.

John gazed in her direction and gave a hand signal that he was going in. Alena bit her lip as he raced into the burning building. He had been strict on his instructions to her. Only he would go in for Reynolds. If he didn't come out, she was to get Johnny to the authorities.

She held her breath as flames engulfed the building and prayed to God John would emerge unscathed. Then he appeared in the doorway, dragging a chair with Senator Reynolds harnessed to it. She ran to meet him and they both pulled the chair from the burning cabin. When they were far enough away, they stopped. John took a knife and cut the ropes that bound Reynolds to the chair. He rolled from it to the ground, hacking deeply from smoke inhalation.

Alena pulled her canteen over her head. She opened it and slipped under Braden Reynolds, tilting the container to his lips as she steadied him from behind. He got a few swallows down before he started coughing again. Even through his soot-darkened face, she could tell he was in a bad way. The senator would not live through this night.

John looked down at Braden Reynolds, who was stripped to his waist, and tried to keep his face a mask. Pity washed over him as he looked at the shell of what had once been a physical, proud man. His weeks with the Marker brothers' gang had done him in. Not only had he lost considerable weight, but there wasn't a spot on him that wasn't bruised. Some were old, having turned yellow and green, while others were fresh. His battered face was almost beyond recognition, his nose a bloody pulp, not a tooth visible in his mouth.

Burn marks covered his forearms. One arm hung

uselessly by his side. His raspy breath had an odd whine to it.

"It had to be you."

John looked quizzically at the broken man. He knew Reynolds had some knowledge of his and Annabelle's previous relationship, but he didn't know Reynolds would recognize him on sight.

The senator shook his head. "I didn't think you knew." A bubble of blood came up with the words.

"Don't talk, Senator," he urged. "You're hurt badly."

"I'm going to die, dammit," he wheezed. "I can say what I want. You can't stop me… *little brother.*"

John glanced at Alena. "He's hallucinating," he said quietly.

Reynolds began to laugh, a pathetic sound that fell off as he started choking. Alena slapped him hard on the back and he inhaled a shallow breath.

"Thanks," he whispered and then looked at John again. "I knew our dear mama wouldn't tell you. They didn't tell me either."

Reynolds closed his eyes and fell silent. John thought he might be dead. He was baffled by the senator's ramblings and chalked it up to the ordeal he had been through.

Then he opened his eyes again, his stare boring into John's soul. A chill crossed through John.

"She was married before. To my daddy. I never knew him. He was years older. Investor. Went down on a ship coming home from Europe. They all assumed he was dead. Mama went out of her head, Uncle Randolph told me. The relatives all swooped in. They institutionalized her until I was born, then Randolph took me home with him.

"He told me Mama was dead." Braden laughed. "I used to daydream she would come for me but she never did." He shifted. A shadow of pain crossed his features.

253

"Later, I found the receipts for the money they used to keep her away from me."

John's mind reeled. He remembered once when he was young, opening mail that had been delivered. His mother became hysterical at what he'd done, rifling through the open envelopes until she came upon something which she tucked into her pocket. She warned him never to touch the mail again.

Reynolds sighed. "When Randolph died, I searched high and low until I found the legal papers that handed me over to my uncle. Termination of parental rights. Our dear mama could have no contact with me in return for receiving an annuity. I hired an investigator. He found her, married to Edward Harper, doing her charitable works in upstate New York. Doting on you."

A tear slid down Reynolds' cheek. "I hated you because she abandoned me and gave you all those years."

Braden Reynolds was his half-brother?

It seemed impossible. Yet why would Reynolds invent such lies as he lay dying? In that moment, John realized the senator spoke the truth.

His half-brother coughed again. Blood poured from his mouth. He must be bleeding internally. John would not be able to save him, no matter how fast he rode.

Reynolds stopped coughing and looked up at him with glassy eyes. "I never loved Annabelle. You might as well take her back. She kept all your letters. Even named the boy after you. He's nothing like me. Maybe you can make a man of him."

A wrenching gasp tore from the dying man's throat. He reached out, clutching John's hand. He shuddered once, twice, then was still. John reached down and brushed his hand over Reynolds' eyes. He looked down, their hands locked together, and fought all the swirling feelings inside.

Had Reynolds' misplaced jealousy of an unseen

brother been at the root of marrying Annabelle? Was this why Reynolds took her away from him? And had Annabelle truly named Johnny after him? It touched him that she had kept all his letters and, at the same time, it frustrated him. Why had she married this man? How different would their lives have been if she had stood up to her father and married him as they had planned?

He remembered her last letter to him, when his fever had finally broken and he was lucid enough to understand what went on around him. He had been out of his head for three weeks with the pneumonia and his recovery during the next few weeks was gradual. He hadn't worried about his parents. They had left for an extended vacation to Europe that spring. His father told him to concentrate on his studies instead of writing letters that might never reach them.

But he had worried about being out of touch with Annabelle, who devotedly wrote to him every day. He'd read the letters that had stacked up while he was ill, relishing each, hearing her voice as his eyes crossed the page. He opened them by the postmarked dates and was surprised when there was a gap of two weeks. That was unlike her, and so he'd torn open the last letter with interest, wondering what caused the interruption, hoping that she hadn't been ill as he had.

The contents of that final letter devastated him. It informed him that she could no longer continue their correspondence, as she was set to marry Congressman Braden Reynolds of Pennsylvania and become a stepmother to his young daughter. The one page was cold and off-putting, almost as if David Martin dictated its contents to his daughter, who'd dutifully recorded each word. By the time John was strong enough to make the trip home, his Annabelle Martin was now Annabelle Reynolds.

He raised his eyes to Alena. Her face was void of emotion. John thought the day's events must have taken their heavy toll upon her. He, too, was drained of all feeling.

A half-formed thought played in the back of his mind as he stood and looked down upon his dead blood kin.

Annabelle was free.

CHAPTER 32

Annabelle was free.

This thought pounded in Alena's head, like a storm beating against the roof of her cabin. She longed to be back there now, rocking, painting, taking care of an injured animal. Anything that would bring her comfort.

Instead, she faced the man she loved, a man with a dazed look upon his face. Alena thought of the pocket watch John had carried for years, a gift from Annabelle. Of the boy named after him. Of letters that Annabelle Reynolds had not been able to part with even after she became a married woman.

And she knew. Her heart might try to deny it— but her mind never could.

Annabelle Reynolds would want John back. Women like her needed protecting. She was John's first love, his true love. She was now a widow, unattached, and more than likely carried a torch for John, much as he did for her. They could be together finally, after years of separation, and raise Johnny and other children together.

Why would a man like John Harper want a castoff, backwoods girl? One raised by a criminal— the very type he brought to justice. Alena was the last person he would ever choose, in her ill-fitting men's trousers and sharpshooter ways. Annabelle Reynolds would smell like fresh flowers and wear beautiful gowns and know all the right things to do and say. Alena could never compare favorably.

Perhaps it would be best for John to have his society girl. The anger he had displayed when he threw the watch? Those weren't his true feelings. She, more than anyone after today's occurrences, understood the fine line between love and hate. Both those emotions regarding Jeb warred inside her. She would have to reconcile those feelings in the future but, for now, she resolved not to address the matter with John. Both he and Annabelle would alter the decisions from the past. They could now come together with nothing hindering them. Regrets would be swept away. They would love once more. Richly. Deeply.

Alena's heart ached, knowing she must see things through.

"We need to get Johnny back to his mother," she said quietly. "Take the senator's body back, too." She paused a moment. "And I'd like to bury Jeb out here. I... I don't want any reminders of him at the cabin."

John nodded. He rose unsteadily to his feet.

"We can camp out and bury Jeb in the morning. No use traveling at night. I'm sure Johnny's bone-tired. The boy could probably use some uninterrupted rest."

He smiled at her. "We can see you back to the cabin and then I'll take Johnny into San Francisco and be sure he's reunited with Anna... with his mother."

Tears stung her eyes. Already, he wanted to be rid of her. She took a deep breath.

"No, I think I'll come into the city with you."

"That's not necessary, Alena." He looked at her tenderly and it was as if he twisted a knife into her heart while pretending to care for her feelings. "I know you probably want to spend some time alone."

She straightened her shoulders. "Actually, I want to go in and investigate this bank account Jeb mentioned. If *A McClaine* is such a thriving artist or if that was another of his many lies."

"If you... " His voice trailed off, and then his eyes grew large with amazement. "You're *A McClaine!*" he exclaimed.

"Yes. Why?"

"I don't ever remember hearing your last name before. I have an *A McClaine*. I did tell you that, I remember I did." He looked at her with wonder. "Alena, you have a growing reputation as an artist. Jeb told the truth. You'll be able to support yourself easily."

Alena bit her lip. That should ease his conscience. He could leave her now without a backward glance. She would be able to take care of herself. She always had, she realized now. She didn't need John Harper or Jeb Foster. She was strong enough to survive.

On her own.

She would see what San Francisco was like and make up her mind whether to stay there or retreat to the cabin and lick her wounds. No matter what, she had to force herself to realize John could never be a part of her life. She pushed him from her heart and slammed the door shut. Her memories of him would fade, just as those of her mother and father had.

Or would they?

The touch of his hand gliding along her breast. The feel of his mouth against hers. His hands running through her hair, down her back, pulling her close...

No, she would survive. She would erase the line of his jaw from her mind. The feel of his stubble as he nuzzled her neck. Force away thoughts of his muscled chest and long legs.

ALEXA ASTON

She had to— else she might go mad.

Mechanically, she helped gather up the senator's body and then put one foot in front of the other as they made their way back to Johnny. John didn't notice anything amiss with her, further proof that the fragile link between them had shattered with Braden Reynolds' revelations and death.

Alena wished she had died instead.

ANNABELLE SAT IN THE COACH, absently twirling the ring on her finger. She'd already removed her gloves, preparing to hand over her engagement ring to Dingus Doolittle when he arrived with Johnny. The jewelry didn't matter anymore. The rings symbolized a love that never existed. A marriage built upon lies. She simply wanted Johnny in her arms now. She ached to hold him, hug him, ruffle his hair. She might be flat broke, but they would have each other.

They would return to her mother's house. She grimaced, knowing it was the only choice available. Braden's family consisted of distant relatives who hovered about. Once they learned the money had evaporated, they would, too.

Would Braden go to prison? She knew they were bankrupt. His business manager, Monroe Feldman, had alluded to illegal schemes. She wondered if she would ever know why Braden came West and if his financial dealings would have lifted them from ruin.

Annabelle no longer cared. She would have Johnny and Olivia. They would be safe under one roof, albeit it a modest one. She gave a nervous giggle, thinking how her father must be turning in his grave at the way things had worked out. David Martin had longed for his daughter's marriage to bring him status and wealth.

Neither materialized before his death. Now only biting gossip would follow.

She looked off into the distance. There! It had to be them. She spied riders. Would Doolittle have put Johnny on a horse? He had never ridden before. Between his asthma and weak heart, Annabelle hadn't dared jeopardize his health in such a manner. Besides, Johnny was more interested in scholarly pursuits, his reading and math formulas and scientific experiments. She said a quick prayer, hoping that her son would hang on another few minutes until he was safely in her arms. It would be the cruelest irony if he reached her, only to fall and injure himself.

Annabelle opened the coach door and climbed down awkwardly. The man she had hired with the last of her money to drive her to the middle of nowhere glanced at her disinterestedly and went back to picking his teeth. The approaching riders didn't seem to concern him in the least.

She placed a hand over her heart. It drummed against her shaking fingers. Annabelle made out a man with his hat pulled low and assumed it was Doolittle, although his posture had certainly improved from their previous meeting. In front of him was Johnny. Her heart leaped into her throat, her pulse throbbing wildly. Beside them was a smaller man with a spare horse attached behind him. Annabelle briefly wondered who this could be and prayed that Dingus would hold to his end of the bargain.

Her focus shifted back to Johnny. The horses pulled up a good twenty feet from her but her eyes never left her son. Doolittle eased an impatient Johnny to the ground. She burst into tears at the sight of her son.

"Mama! Mama!"

Johnny raced to her, his arms locking about her neck. She twirled with him in circles, laughing and crying at the same time, then covered his faces with kisses.

"Oh, my Johnny. Oh, my sweet boy. I love you, I love you, I've missed you so." Annabelle buried her face in his neck, happy her child had returned to her.

She finally pulled away, just wanting to drink him in. He was so thin, almost gaunt, but she would fill him with his favorite foods. Then she caught sight of his bandaged hand.

Lifting his forearm gently, she asked, "What happened, sweetheart?"

Johnny wouldn't meet her eyes. "It's okay, M-M-Mama."

Oh, no. The stutter was back. She thought Johnny had conquered that. Whatever he had been through had traumatized him enough for it to return. She cradled his wrapped hand in hers.

"Can you tell me what happened?"

Tears welled in his eyes, making her stomach tighten painfully, as he squeezed his eyes shut and said, "They took m-m-my finger."

For a moment, her son's words made no sense. How could someone take a finger? Then it dawned on Annabelle exactly what Johnny meant.

Those men had *cut off* his finger.

Bile rose within her. As did anger. Yet she had her boy back. She must be strong for him.

"We'll get a doctor to look at it, Johnny. Once we leave here."

"It's clean," he told her. "D-D-Dingus put whiskey on it. He ch-ch-changed the cloth on it every d-day."

That gave her pause. It was time to pay the piper. She released her precious boy and pulled the ransom off her finger.

"Mama—"

"Hush, baby," Annabelle told him. "I need to do

some business with... Mr. Doolittle." She walked steadily toward the outlaw, her eyes rooted to the ground. She would look at him only when she had to and only for a moment. His face had been prominent in her nightmares the previous evening. She would hand him the ring and be off.

"Dingus is dead," hollered Johnny.

Annabelle stopped in her tracks and looked over her shoulder. *Dead?* Slowly, she turned and raised her eyes to the man who dismounted from his saddle.

"Hello, Annabelle."

She gave a cry of pure joy and fell into John Harper's arms.

$\mathcal{W}$hat John longed for in waking and sleeping for so many years was now reality. Annabelle was in his arms. She smelled so feminine, felt so delicate, as she soaked his dusty shirtfront with grateful tears.

And he felt… nothing.

The spell had been broken, the one that had kept him in a trance for a decade. Alena had done that for him, awakening him to what true love was. He glanced over at her as Annabelle clung to him.

"Oh, John, thank God. You're alive. They said you didn't report in. They said it wasn't like you. Oh, I thought I'd never see you again. I would never have forgiven myself if something happened to you."

She hugged him tightly and then pulled away, staring into his eyes, a smile lighting her face. "Thank you, John. Thank you for finding my Johnny and bringing him back to me." She reached out and stroked his cheek fondly.

He didn't want Alena to receive the wrong impression, with Annabelle fussing over him. Alena had turned away, though. John awkwardly unwrapped

Annabelle's arms from his neck and took a step back. He needed some distance between them.

"I owe you everything. How will we ever repay you?"

Johnny came and stood next to his mother. She placed a protective arm about him. John thought how physically alike the two were.

"Son, I know you've met Marshal Harper, but I'll bet there's something you don't know about him."

Johnny looked at his mother curiously. "What, Mama?"

Annabelle stroked her boy's hair. "Marshal Harper and I were great friends growing up together in New York. We did all kinds of things together as children."

"Like w-what?"

She smiled at her son and then at him. John remembered when one of her smiles could dispel his darkest mood.

"All kinds of things, Johnny, such as walking to school together. Going on picnics. Catching fireflies on warm summer nights. John and I went fishing and exploring." Annabelle laughed at the memories. "We also devoured lots of cookies and drank a ton of lemonade. We did just about everything together.

"And you know what? I named you after John."

The boy's eyes lit up. He watched Johnny look from him to his mother and back again. "I d-didn't know that, Mama!" he cried excitedly.

"I know and now I'm telling you. I thought since the two of you had finally met, you would like to know about it."

"Jeez, I'm n-named for a real m-marshal? Maybe I'll grow up to be a marshal, too. I could k-kill all the bad guys. Hey, Alena! Alena? Did you hear Mama named me for John?"

Johnny scurried over to Alena.

Annabelle looked over at the other rider that she had assumed was a young man when they approached. Johnny was talking to her enthusiastically, gesturing with his hands, a huge grin on his face.

She now saw it was a woman, and a beautiful one, at that. Although the clothes she wore were dusty and obviously made for a man, she was quite fetching. Her long, dark hair hung in a single braid down her back. High cheekbones only drew attention to luminous, violet eyes. Her face, while dusty, was smooth olive, the skin flawless.

Annabelle wondered if she was part Indian. A guide that had helped John to find Johnny. Perhaps she, too, had been held hostage by the Marker brothers, although she doubted this young woman would have sufficient currency to pay a ransom. More than likely, she had been taken by the gang and abused. Annabelle had heard tales of such things happening. If so, she was glad John had been able to rescue this woman, as well.

But what of Braden? John had yet to speak of her husband. If he had located Johnny, surely Braden had been there, too. She turned back to him.

"Annabelle, there's something I must tell you."

He sounded so serious. She glanced around and saw the horse she thought had been riderless actually did have a rider. A body was strapped to it, wrapped in blankets. She felt the trembling start but pushed it away. She would be strong for her boy.

"It's Braden, isn't it?" she asked softly.

John nodded. "We tried our best, Annabelle. He... was too far gone."

"I understand."

Johnny returned to her side and she couldn't help but ruffle his hair, something she loved to do, although he'd long outgrown the affectionate gesture. He had come so close to being lost to her forever. Thanks to his return, her heart was light, despite the fact John had just informed her of Braden's death. She experienced only relief. Her Johnny was safe.

And she was finally free.

Annabelle wondered if it was a sin to have no remorse over her husband's death. Worse, she already wanted to be with another man. She couldn't help it. She had loved John Harper since childhood. The fact that they had been separated and she married another couldn't mask her true feelings. She longed to be with John in every sense of the word.

A small part of her worried that he wouldn't want her anymore but she knew that was foolish. They were meant to be together. She had made a tragic mistake, one she'd paid for over the last ten years. John must still love her. He risked his life to bring her son back to her. Oh, he would make such a good father to Johnny. Olivia, too. Maybe they could even have a child of their own. He'd want that. What man didn't?

The thought brought a blush to her cheeks. The act of lovemaking would be far different with John than it had been with Braden. She remembered John's kisses. The heat they brought to her so long ago. John had a passionate nature and Annabelle couldn't wait to rediscover it. Her only trouble would be how long before she could speak freely with him about what was on her mind.

"If you're ready, Annabelle, I think we should return to San Francisco."

Alena heard John's words but didn't dare look at him. It was enough that his precious Annabelle had fallen into his arms and fawned over him in her presence. She stole a glance at Annabelle Reynolds.

How could she think to compare with such a radiant beauty? Even with her eyes swollen from crying, the woman was stunning. It forced Alena to realize her romantic interlude with John Harper had come to a swift end. He had turned her world upside down from the moment Cicero brought him into her life. Now, she would be forced to go on without him, while he took up the strands of his old life. With his former love.

"Once we're back, John, we need to talk."

"Yes, we do, Annabelle."

Their words cut Alena to the quick. Already, they were eager to plan their future together. Bitterness flooded her, along with a raging jealousy of the woman who had always held John's heart, despite his words of protest.

"I'd like to have a doctor check Johnny over. And I will need to see to arrangements for Braden. John, would you... would you see Braden back? I don't think I could have him in the coach with us."

He nodded. "Of course. I'll accompany you back and report to Will Johnson. I know he'll want to ask Johnny a few questions." He smiled and patted the boy's shoulder. "He's been a brave boy. You have a lot to be proud of, Annabelle."

"Is that absolutely necessary?" she asked. "I don't want Johnny even thinking about this horrible experience. He's been through enough."

"Mama," Johnny interrupted. "I w-want to go."

Alena admired the determination she saw in Johnny Reynolds' eyes. He would become a good man someday.

His mother smoothed Johnny's hair and smiled. "Maybe you're right," she murmured. "I'm sorry. I know it's part of your job, John, but the sooner this business is behind us, the better I'll feel."

"Then we'll get things done in record time. We'll get Johnny to a doctor and give Will a brief summary of what occurred."

"You will go with us, John, won't you?"

Alena's heart caught in her throat as he offered Annabelle a smile. "You know I will take care of things, Annabelle."

John walked them over to the waiting coach and swung Johnny into the carriage. "See you when we reach the city, Johnny. Don't worry about a thing."

Johnny grinned. He looked over and waved at her and Alena waved back.

She watched as John assisted Annabelle into the coach. He closed the door and had a word with the driver. Alena assumed he told the man to follow them back into San Francisco.

As John walked back to the horses, Annabelle called out from the window. "My thanks again, John. You'll never know what this means to me."

He waved as the carriage pulled away. The emptiness that had been a part of him for so long was no more. It was replaced with some small satisfaction that at least they had been able to save Johnny from that den of vipers. That was more than Will Johnson had expected. John felt a sense of freedom, too, a burden lifted from him. He could finally reminisce fondly on the memories he had of Annabelle instead of the bitterness that had dominated his life for so long.

Now, he looked forward to creating new memories with Alena, ones that would last them a lifetime. A burst of warmth filled him, that sense of love and being loved in return. John glanced to her. She'd quietly mounted Chessy and sat patiently waiting for him.

Her weariness showed. Her face was pale. Smudges of shadows appeared under her eyes. He wished she would go back to the cabin and try to come to terms with who Jeb had been but she had announced her determination to go into San Francisco. He'd make sure they finished up their business regarding the Marker brothers as quickly as possible. Maybe then he'd take her by the art galleries that held her landscapes in their windows. A sense of pride in her and her talent washed over him.

"Are you ready?" he asked.

Alena nudged her heels against Chessy in reply, the packhorse carrying his half-brother's body following behind her. John respected her silence. Since things were coming to an end, he needed to give her time and space to heal.

THEY ARRIVED in the city and went straight to a doctor John knew. Alena remained outside with their horses as he accompanied Annabelle and Johnny inside. Once there, he quickly explained the situation and they were immediately taken to see Dr. Worth.

The physician unwound the bandage from Johnny's hand. John focused on Annabelle. He saw the brief look of horror that crossed her face and then the stoic one that immediately took its place. She squeezed Johnny's good hand encouragingly and looked to the doctor.

Worth turned the hand and observed it from several angles and then bathed it and poured alcohol over it before drying and wrapping it in clean linen.

Looking directly at Johnny, the physician said, "This must have hurt, young man."

The boy nodded solemnly.

"Looks like you received good care after you lost it, though. Someone cauterized it."

"Y-yes," Johnny said. "Dingus explained what cau-terize m-meant before he d-d-did it. He said it would help."

"Well, he did a fine job. I see no infection present. Is it your dominant hand?"

"N-no, sir."

"That's good. It has almost healed. It will be a bit in-convenient but it won't keep you from writing or play-ing. In fact, I'll bet most people won't even notice you're missing a pinky."

Johnny nodded and Dr. Worth looked to Annabelle. He gave her a few simple instructions and told her the worst had passed.

"Your boy shouldn't have any trouble in the future."

"Thank you, Doctor," she said.

They left the physician's office and went to head-quarters. A man rushed down the stairs as they rode up. He wore a satisfied look about him, like a cat who'd drunk cream straight from the jar while his mistress looked on and was happy he did so. John figured him for a lawyer.

"Annabelle! Johnny!" the man cried out as the car-riage containing them pulled in behind John's and Alena's horses. He assisted them from their coach and gave Johnny a hug as John climbed from Cicero's back.

Annabelle brought him over for an introduction. "Bryce, I'd like you to meet Marshal John Harper."

The man swept his hat from his head, revealing an abundant head of graying hair. "Bryce Mitchell, at-torney for Senator and Mrs. Reynolds." He smiled broadly. "I assume you're the man who's responsible for getting Johnny back to us. The one Will Johnson claims as his best of the best."

Mitchell shook his hand enthusiastically. "My thanks to you, Marshal Harper. Johnny is a fine boy. You've given him the chance to grow up and become a fine man."

John assessed Bryce Mitchell with new eyes. Reynolds had demonstrated little regard for his son. At least this man recognized something in the boy that his client hadn't seen. It relieved John that Annabelle had someone like Mitchell to help look after her in the days to come.

Suddenly, the attorney glanced back at the horse carrying Braden's body and shuddered. He mopped his brow delicately with a linen handkerchief as he glanced questioningly at Annabelle.

"It's Braden," she confirmed.

John saw her eyes mist over. He hoped Annabelle wouldn't dwell on how her husband died. He decided to turn the conversation.

"Johnny showed tremendous courage, Mr. Mitchell. The death of his father will certainly take its toll on him, but I trust you'll be able to lend a hand?"

Mitchell nodded. "Of course. I accompanied Mrs. Reynolds from New York. We'll take the senator's body back East for burial." The lawyer sighed. "Naturally, my firm will pay for the funeral. It wouldn't seem right for a United States Senator to be laid to rest in a pauper's grave."

John frowned at Mitchell. He looked to Annabelle and back at her lawyer. "What are you talking about?"

The older man waved a hand in front of him. "My indiscretion, son. Forgive me, Annabelle. I spoke out of turn."

She nodded. "It's all right, Bryce. I have no secrets from John. He's an old family friend. Johnny is named for him."

Mitchell studied her a moment and then looked into John's eyes before he spoke. "Braden was flat broke. Poor Annabelle had no idea until the kidnapping. That's why we tried to put off paying the ransom. There was nothing to sell to raise it."

John looked from the attorney to Annabelle. "What will Annabelle and Johnny do? Where will they go?"

Alena swallowed. She gripped the reins, her knuckles turning white as she kept her head bowed.

Not only did the lovely Annabelle no longer have a husband, but she needed rescuing, as well. John would be a sucker for coming to her aid. And why not? Alena herself had seen him as a knight on a white horse. Even hurt as badly as he was when he'd arrived, she remembered nursing him, seeing him as a god, a hero, an Odysseus for today.

Mitchell's words hammered the final nail in the coffin of her love. If Alena had harbored a secret feeling that John might feel an obligation to her because of what had passed between them, she abruptly freed it. Even if he offered for her now, she knew his heart wouldn't be in it. She loved him enough to recognize how wounded he must have been for all these years—and let him go. She would not be responsible for keeping him from a life with the woman he adored.

Besides, he had never told her he loved her. Alena agonized, wondering how many times he must have whispered those words to Annabelle, knowing he longed to say them to her again, once the tumult of this day had passed.

Alena listened to the remainder of their conversation with half an ear, Mitchell explaining the various arrangements he would see to regarding the senator's body. His words of thanks to John. Finally, the lawyer made his goodbyes and John walked over to her.

He held out a hand to help her from Chessy. Alena took it, not wanting to seem churlish.

"I need to speak briefly with Will Johnson and let him know how things have been resolved," John told her. "He'll want to speak firsthand with Johnny. Knowing Will, he'll also want to send a party out to the hideout tomorrow. I might have to return with them."

John smiled at her and motioned for Alena to walk with him. "I'm sure he'll want to speak to you, too. You played a huge role in things."

Annabelle and Johnny waited hand in hand for them at the top of the steps. As someone leaving opened the door, the new widow possessively linked an arm through John's and pulled him inside.

Alena trailed them at a distance, much as a servant would. Several people greeted John enthusiastically, slapping him on the back, telling him how glad they were he had returned safely. Others greeted Annabelle, who now clung to John like ivy embedded upon a wall, congratulating her for Johnny's return.

"Harper!"

A gravel-filled voice boomed over the well wishes. Alena saw John turn his head in its direction. A thin, tall man with a bushy white mustache and a head full of thick, white hair lumbered over. He came to a halt in front of John.

"Dagnabbit, boy," he proclaimed and wrapped John in a tight bear hug. "You had even me worried."

"I suspected as much, Will," John said. "Your hair was black as night last time I saw you."

The room burst into laughter. Alena saw John smile slyly. He and Will spoke for a moment and then she heard Will say, "Let's go back to my office. We have a few things to discuss."

Annabelle continued to hang on John. He escorted her down a narrow hallway, following his superior, Johnny bringing up the rear. Alena looked around the room as people returned to their normal activities. No one noticed her. Had John simply forgotten about her, caught up in the moment? Or was he embarrassed by her appearance in Jeb's old clothes, reluctant to introduce her?

Either way, she realized she would not be missed.

"Goodbye, John," Alena whispered to herself before she turned and walked quietly out the door.

CHAPTER 34

John needed to set the record straight. Now. He didn't want Annabelle thinking he'd be at her beck and call. The way she had latched on to him was embarrassing. The sooner he talked to her, the better.

They reached Will's office and his boss paused. "If you folks don't mind, I'd like to talk to Johnny first. Let him tell me everything in his own way."

Will knelt beside the boy. "You wouldn't mind doing that, would you, Johnny?"

Johnny's eyes were round behind his wire frames. "No, sir," he replied. "I'm g-gonna be a m-marshal someday. I suspect I'll be talking to you l-lots."

The salty lawman burst out laughing. "Then this'll be the first of our many talks about the bad guys." He looked up at Annabelle. "Is it all right if we do our talking in private, ma'am?" he asked.

She nodded. "Yes, go ahead. Johnny told me in the coach that he had lots of good information to share with you, Marshal Johnson."

The lawman stood and placed a hand on Johnny's shoulder. "Then let's get to it, son. I have more ques-

ALEXA ASTON

tions than a curious cat." He led Johnny into his office and closed the door behind them.

John knew this would be the perfect time to explain things to Annabelle. He looked to the end of the hall and saw an open doorway. The file room would be a quiet place. It would ensure them privacy, since most of the men only went in there under threat of death.

"Let's go have our talk, Annabelle."

He led her down the corridor and into the small room. As usual, things were a genteel mess. Files were scattered everywhere— in the stacks along the floor, across the lone table, in the two chairs. John reached down and picked up a stack to free up space for Annabelle to sit. He gestured for her to take the seat while he closed the door. What he had to say wouldn't be for prying ears. He didn't want his former sweetheart made uncomfortable in any way.

As he turned from closing the door, he walked straight into her embrace. Her arms went round his neck, pulling his mouth down to hers. Her lips were softer than he remembered. She pressed her body into his as her mouth opened in an invitation.

Once again, everything happening just reconfirmed what he knew when he saw her. His body didn't leap at her touch. His heart didn't race. He didn't want her anymore.

John took her locked hands and pried them apart, returning them to her sides. The narrow room only allowed him to take a small step back but he did so.

"Wait, John. I'm sorry." She smoothed her skirt and took a deep breath. "I got carried away."

"Annabelle, you've thanked me more than enough. I was only doing my job."

"Oh, John." She sighed. "Don't you understand?" She tapped her foot impatiently.

Annabelle didn't remember John ever being slow to

catch on. Maybe the rough time he'd put in on her case had dulled his senses.

"I will be a little more forthright then. Oh, how can I put this delicately?"

He stood before her, a perplexed look upon his handsome features. If anything, the passing years had added to his appeal. Years in the sun had tanned his face, causing a few lines here and there around his eyes. He had been attractive before; now he was devastatingly handsome. His hair was a bit too long for her taste and he could certainly use a shave, but he was still the best-looking man she had ever laid eyes upon.

"What I'm trying to say is… " Annabelle suddenly burst into tears. Her emotions were too raw. So much had happened in such a short amount of time. She had to make him understand. Before it was too late. Again.

"My marriage was a mistake. A dreadful mistake. I allowed Papa to push me into it." She pulled the glove from her hand and tenderly touched his cheek. "It's you I love, John. I've always loved you. I've dreamed of being with you all these years. And now we can be together."

"Annabelle—"

She cut him off, waving away his words with her hands. "No, hear me out. I have spent the last ten years of my life in misery. Except for Johnny and Olivia, my life has been empty. Void of any meaning. But I am free now, John. Finally free. We can be together, as we were meant to be."

She placed a hand on his chest but he quickly removed it. The look she saw on his face confused her.

"It's my turn, Annabelle. I can't do this. I hated you for years, but I know those feelings simply masked my love for you. You hurt me deeply. I thought I would never recover from that hurt.

"But I did. You might be free, Annabelle— but I'm

not. I'm deeply in love. Committed to another woman. I don't want to be with you, Annabelle. I'm sorry."

Her head reeled. The room started growing dark. She thought she might faint.

"You can't possibly mean it," she stammered.

John nodded. "I do. I know we share a history but my feelings for you are in the past. I'm working on building my future now. With someone else."

Annabelle couldn't stop the tears from streaming down her cheeks. "Then why did you want to talk to me? Why did you bring me here and close the door? I thought—"

He interrupted. "I have something I needed to tell you. Something Braden told me just before he died."

"Braden?" She was confused. "What does Braden have to do with us? He's dead. I don't want to worry about him anymore."

"Braden was my half-brother."

Annabelle thought she might faint. She started swaying. John caught her and eased her into a chair. She couldn't believe what he'd just said.

John knelt before her. "Braden told me how my mother gave birth to him after her husband's ship went down. How she became... a little unstable for a while. His uncle took him in and raised him. My mother got better. She moved away and eventually married my father. They—"

"He lied, John." Annabelle was calm now. This was all a bad dream that would go away. She would make everything right. "Braden had a way of twisting lies into truth and truth into lies. He knew how I felt about you. He probably figured you felt the same way.

"Braden knew he was dying, didn't he?" she insisted. "He was going to his death and he did whatever it took to reach out and hurt you. And me. Well, I won't let him keep us apart, John. And even if it is true, who cares? You never knew you had a half-brother before now, so surely you won't miss him."

Her calm tone had now given way to a rising hysteria. She was losing John and it was all because of Braden Reynolds. He was haunting her from his grave. There was too much at stake. She wouldn't let the bastard win.

"John, please. Please." She took his hand and held on to it tightly. "Don't give the devil his due. Don't let Braden win. It doesn't matter that he was your half-brother or that I married him. What matters is—"

"That I love Alena. That's what matters. Do you think I give a damn about Braden Reynolds? I don't. If I still loved you, nothing would stop me from pursuing that love."

He cupped her cheek and gazed at her tenderly. "But I love Alena now. She is my present and my future. After knowing her, I could never love another. Not even you, Annabelle."

The grief that had been absent when John told her of Braden's death now consumed her. Annabelle bowed her head. She had lost John, this time for all eternity. Her anguish threatened to swallow her whole. She thought how comforting death would be after hearing his rejection.

Yet John had given Johnny back to her. She had every reason to live. She had her son. She was rid of Braden. She must be strong. The last ten years taught her she could do whatever it took to survive. She would take those lessons to heart.

Annabelle met his eyes. They were full of concern for her. Oh, how she would miss this man.

"Then I hope I will always have your friendship, John. I would be most obliged to keep it."

He took her hands in his and gave them a squeeze.

His smile was gentle. "You will always have that, Annabelle."

~

ALENA RODE through the arts district slowly. She had gotten directions from a passing cabbie. This city was certainly fast-paced. She was used to a much slower way of life. Men and women scurried along the streets as quick as mice, only with more purpose. Single riders and coaches alike tore down the streets as if their lives depended upon it. Everywhere she went were sounds and smells. The buzz of talk. The aroma of freshly roasted coffee. The laughter of children. It overwhelmed her, much as her emotions did now. She pushed aside all thoughts of John and Jeb, determined not to think of either one of them, else she would shatter.

She got a few stray glances. Raised eyebrows at her attire. One obese matron pointed rudely at her, twittering so loudly that Alena felt a hot blush rising up her neck and onto her cheeks. She realized that to start anew, she must fit into society more. She decided then and there that her days of dressing in Jeb's castoffs were over. She would become a lady. Dress like one. Speak like one. Act like one. She might not be able to control much at this point but she was tired of being an outcast. She would no longer let others dismiss her. She would focus on her future.

Self-preservation was foremost in her mind. She would do what it took to survive.

She slowed Chessy and stared in the window of a gallery on her right. It was painted in a violet pastel. So many of the buildings here were of strange colors, nothing like Rio Vista. Yet she loved the bold use of color in unusual ways. It made her anxious to return to her paints.

The large window held three paintings. One was a still life of fruit in a bowl, while the other two were landscapes. The middle one was her work. A sense of pride and accomplishment poured through her. This is what she did and here it was, displayed for all the world to see.

Alena climbed from Chessy's back and looped the reins loosely on the bar along the street. She went to stand in front of the window, staring at the scene. She remembered it well. It was of the pond Jeb loved to fish in. Sometimes, she accompanied him and would sketch on the bank, basking in the warmth of the day. She especially loved the tree that she had made the focus of the landscape.

Alena glanced at the price tag lying flat in front of her artwork and gasped. The gallery owner thought he could actually get that kind of money? That was impossible. Then she remembered John said she had a growing reputation. How Jeb revealed that she had money in her own bank account from the sales of her work.

She would investigate tomorrow. Right now, she wanted a real bath and new clothes, feminine ones. She thought the bank might accept her more readily if she dressed demurely, as a lady, and not an uneducated field hand.

Where should she start? Alena mounted her horse again and decided to explore the city a little bit. As she rode, she tossed between being thrilled to see it all and yet being dulled to some of it by the pain of losing John to Annabelle. Maybe San Francisco would be a tonic to her soul as she tried to make a new life for herself, one without Jeb or John.

She decided to stay here. Already, an addiction to

San Francisco possessed her. She had read a book once about the author's first trip to Paris. How it consumed him from the beginning. He knew from those first minutes that the City of Lights would always be his home.

Alena determined to create a new life for herself in this bustling city and part from the old, though she still planned to keep the cabin as a retreat. Memories of Jeb were still strong. She couldn't imagine being there without him although she'd spent so many times there alone.

That brought anger bubbling to the surface, knowing all those days and weeks he left her had been to go to that band of cutthroats who had shown no mercy to Braden Reynolds and his little boy. All the people they'd robbed or hurt. For how many years? How many victims?

Alena shuddered, glad to be rid of Jeb. Her feelings regarding him were too muddled now to reflect upon. Disappointment, betrayal, disillusionment— they all fought to take hold of her. She shoved the conflicting emotions far away, determined to focus on the present. When enough time and distance had passed, she would look back on her relationship with Jeb.

She saw a bath house two blocks ahead. Maybe they could also tell her where she might find some appropriate clothing before tomorrow. Alena tied Chessy to the rail, squared her shoulders, and held her head high as she walked inside.

~

JOHN WATCHED the bank from across the street as he sat at a table drinking coffee. He had gone earlier before it opened and spoken with the manager, trying to smooth the way for Alena. She would have no proof of who she was. He had used his badge and status to clear any obstacles she might face.

He still didn't understand why she had vanished without a word yesterday. He'd torn the office apart trying to locate her, questioning every man there about where she had gone. Then he'd ridden the streets for hours, searching for her until long after dark fell. Once he thought he'd caught a glimpse of her and charged down the street, only to frighten a young boy of about fifteen, dressed almost identically to Alena.

Finally he returned home, despondent, racking his brain as to where she might be. He'd thought of her interest in the bank account. That led him, after only a few restless hours of sleep, to meet the branch manager as the man arrived for work. Satisfied that the manager would accommodate any request Alena made, John retired to the café across the street to watch and wait.

The waiting was about to kill him, though. He'd been sipping coffee for two hours now. Where was she? What if he was wrong? What if she didn't show? How would he find her?

John gripped the coffee mug. It was his job to find people. He was damned good at it. He would find her, even if he had to tear this city apart, one house at a time. He wouldn't rest until Alena was by his side again.

A carriage pulled up in front of the bank. John sat up with interest. A woman descended, stylishly dressed in pale blue satin with a matching hat, its feather jauntily swaying in the wind. She adjusted her gloves with an elegant flourish and paid the driver. As the driver pulled away, she stood studying the bank.

It was Alena, transformed into a beautiful woman. No. She had always been beautiful, but this was a new Alena, brimming with feminine confidence and the clothes to match. He knew by the way she tilted her head, by the careful way she looked at her surroundings, that this was the woman he loved. He had never seen her in such finery and had no idea how she'd gotten it but every fiber of his being came alive. It took every ounce of control he had to keep his seat and allow her to go into the bank unescorted.

Still, he wanted to be waiting for her when she emerged. He signaled for his bill and paid it, keeping his eyes on the bank through the windows along the front of the café. John opened the door to a brisk wind and crossed the street.

The time couldn't pass fast enough.

CHAPTER 35

*A*lena pushed open the door to the bank. She saw three tellers engaged with customers at the far end. She didn't know exactly where to go. She supposed the branch manager would be the place to start. She doubted a teller would have the authority to give her the information she needed.

A desk sat off to her right and an office door lay beyond it. A name appeared upon it and Alena suspected it must be the office of the administrator in charge. She took a calming breath and walked over to the man seated behind the desk.

"May I help you?"

His speech was clipped, very businesslike. He eyed her suspiciously, as if she didn't belong there. She was already uncomfortable enough in her brand-new clothes and strange undergarments without this man's condescending stare.

"I would like to speak to the manager, please," she said crisply. "As soon as possible."

The bank's lighting reflected off the man's balding pate. He raised his eyebrows at her. "And you would be?"

"Miss Alena McClaine."

285

His eyes widened. She wondered if he associated her last name with the thriving artist, although she knew he wouldn't suppose she was the actual painter. As Jeb had said, women didn't paint. Period.

"I'll summon Mr. Livingston. Just a moment, please."

He hurried to the closed door and knocked, opening it and sticking his head in a brief moment to converse with its occupant. Then he stepped back as Ichabod Crane walked through the doorway. At least that's how Alena saw him. She had fallen in love with Washington Irving's characters, painted so vividly, and none more so than schoolmaster Ichabod Crane.

The man in front of her was tall and gangly, with sparse hair that went in every direction. He was dressed immaculately, though, and spoke in smooth, cultured tones.

"How do you do, Miss McClaine? Argyle Livingston at your service. Seymour here tells me you wish to see me. Do come in."

He motioned her into his office and offered her a seat. "May Seymour bring you some coffee? Tea?"

Alena was bewildered at such solicitous treatment. "No, thank you." She seated herself in a high-backed oak chair and looked around the office.

"Thank you, Seymour. That will be all."

Livingston re-entered the office and closed the door. He seated himself behind a massive desk void of any papers. Alena wondered what the man actually did all day inside these four walls. Maybe the file cabinets behind him kept him busy or maybe he counted piles of money in transactions that came in. She had no idea how a banker occupied his time.

"What may I do for you, Miss McClaine?"

"I have an account here that was established some time ago for me by... my guardian, Jeb Foster, who has since passed away." Alena paused, willing herself to go on. "This is the first time I have visited San Francisco, but I plan to make my home here. I needed to see what funds have been placed in my account and learn how to access them."

She hesitated, not sure how to approach the next issue. "I don't know what kind of paperwork you might wish to see for proof of identity." She had none, and had not figured out a way to solve this dilemma, much less any type of death certificate for Jeb.

"I wouldn't worry about that, Miss McClaine. I'm sure I can look into matters and have a ready answer for you in the next few minutes." He gave her a broad smile. "Would you excuse me, please? I won't be long."

Alena had worried she would never be able to gain access to the funds which Jeb had spoken of, if in truth they were there. How Argyle Livingston would go about establishing that she could access the account Jeb had set up for her puzzled her.

The bank manager returned in less than ten minutes. "Ah, Miss McClaine. I hope you've been comfortable during your wait."

"Yes," she told him.

Livingston pulled up a chair next to her instead of returning behind the desk and laid out a few items along the desktop. He pointed to the first one. "Here is a copy of your bankbook. This is yours to keep and you will need to bring it with you each time you make a deposit or withdrawal. The bank will also maintain a record of these transactions."

He handed her the book. "Thumb through it and become familiar with what's contained in it. Take your time."

Alena took the small passbook and turned the pages slowly. Each deposit was duly dated and initialed by Jeb, a bold *JF* in the margin numerous times. No withdrawals had been made. As time passed, money placed into the account grew sizably.

She flipped to the last page to see the final amount and almost choked at the figure. She could easily live a lifetime on what was here, more than comfortably. It would be enough to buy a house in the city, even employ a housekeeper. That way, she would be free to paint and read and walk.

Tamping down her surprise, she faced Livingston. "And the other items?"

He lifted another bankbook. "This is an account set up by Mr. Foster seven years ago this month. It's what we call a joint account, meaning you, as well as Mr. Foster, have access to it."

Livingston gave her a sorrowful look. "I am deeply sorry for your loss."

"Thank you," Alena said, her voice barely a whisper, the pain still raw.

"Knowing that Mr. Foster has passed, this account will become solely yours now. You may maintain it as a separate account, or if you feel it would be beneficial to you, we can easily combine the accounts for you. There is no hurry, of course."

More money? Jeb was certainly full of surprises. She reached for the second bankbook and gave it a cursory glance. She feared the money was tainted, blood money produced from his robberies and other illegal activities with the Marker brothers. She would have to ponder how to handle these funds. Maybe John could help her disburse what was there, returning what she could to the injured parties.

But John Harper was no longer in her life. Still, she was certain the U.S. Marshal's Office would be able to determine in part where some of the money should be returned, whether to banks that were robbed or to individuals. Alena would look into contacting them, possibly when she left here. John had said he would more than likely be taking a team out to the Marker brothers' hideout. That way, she could avoid running into him.

"I'll take into consideration whether or not to merge the accounts, Mr. Livingston."

"Very good." He picked up the last item on the desk, a long, narrow envelope. "This contains a key to a safety deposit box. The account was also held jointly. Would you like to look at the contents within the box while you are here?"

Alena stood. "Yes, please."

Livingston accompanied her from the office and across the bank. He opened a door with a key and they went down a long corridor. Another locked door was opened and she found herself in a room that was a maze of gleaming metal.

"Your box number is on the key itself, which simplifies matters," he explained. He showed her and then led her to a bank of boxes. "Place your key in here and I will do the same."

Alena turned hers as the bank manager did, which opened a slot containing a long, cylindrical metal box. The bank executive slid it out for her and placed it on a table in the center of the room.

"When you have finished examining the items within, please return the box to its correctly numbered slot. Once you close the door, it will be sealed. You may enter this room and remove or place any contents into your deposit box during regular banking hours. However, I or another representative of the bank must always accompany you in order for you to access your safety deposit box. Have I made everything clear, Miss McClaine?"

She nodded. "Yes. I understand all the procedures."

"Then I will allow you some privacy. Please stop in to see me before you leave." Livingston smiled at her benignly. "I trust you will remain a valued customer, Miss McClaine."

He exited the room and she sat on the bench next to the table, staring at the box. What had Jeb placed in it? She opened the top and found a letter. Withdrawing it, she saw her name scrawled across the front of the envelope. She opened it and read:

Dearest Magdalena –

If you are reading this, then I must be dead. I'm afraid the circumstances

will be unpleasant, as I intended to destroy this letter once I left the gang.

If I'm fortunate, you had no knowledge of my other life while I was alive.

Maybe I was killed on my last job. So many times I've wanted to part ways

with the Markers. I prayed I would before you discovered my awful secrets.

If I did, I would have already done away with this letter so, once again, my time

must have been up before I was able to return here and do so.

You'll find nothing of value in here, I'm afraid, but you should already have

gained access to your funds. I'm so proud of you, Sweetie Pie. You have come

a long way as an artist. I know you'll attain even more with your talent. Know

that no matter how things ended, I always loved you and your dear, sweet mama.

I wished every day that I had been Margarita's husband and your father. Know in

my heart I always felt it so. Goodbye, my sweetest angel.

THE NOTE WAS unsigned but she recognized the writing as Jeb's. Alena anguished over why Jeb led a dual life. She couldn't imagine what pleasure it brought him. In fact, the letter led her to believe otherwise. She would never understand why, she supposed.

Did she ever really know him? She pushed any regrets aside. She couldn't change things now. It would only bring her more heartache to dwell upon it. It would have to be enough to remember their good times and be satisfied with that.

Alena decided to search through the box's contents. It surprised her that besides the letter, only one item remained. She reached in and lifted out a silk scarf. She brushed the material against her face, detecting a faint scent of some long-ago perfume. She supposed it had belonged to her mother and that was why Jeb kept it all these years.

She placed the scarf and folded letter into her new reticule and pulled the drawstring closed. It was hard getting used to carrying around such a strange item. Already she longed for the comfort and ease of her trousers, but she was determined to make a break with the past and become a lady in every sense of the word. Maybe she could compromise and paint in her pants in the privacy of her own home. She wouldn't want to muss the new clothes she planned to purchase, or stain them in any way. She had been appalled at the cost of one simple gown and the accompanying undergarments, much less the shoes and hat that matched the outfit.

Alena returned the metal box to its correct slot, wondering if she even had a need to keep it. She would think about it later, back at the hotel. She would go to the Marshal's Office now and still be able to make her afternoon fitting at the dressmaker's she had found yesterday. The woman promised her two more gowns would be ready, ones already started that only needed a few adjustments. Alena would then take time to look at material and hats. The thought of what lay ahead made her dizzy. Being a lady was turning out to be more complicated than she'd imagined.

She returned to Mr. Livingston's office, Seymour greeting her much more cordially this time. She supposed Mr. Livingston had informed the clerk of what an important customer she was. Alena stifled a giggle at that thought.

"Here are your passbooks, Miss McClaine. Please feel free to contact me at any point. If you feel you might need the advice of a business manager now that Mr. Foster is no longer able to advise you in that capacity, I would be happy to recommend someone."

"Thank you for your time, Mr. Livingston. You have been most accommodating."

Alena placed the bankbooks within her reticule and walked to the exit. She pushed open the door, having to fight it a bit because of the blustering wind that pushed from the opposite side.

She brought a hand to her hat, certain it might blow off at any second. Did ladies always wear hats? Already, her head felt heavy with its weight. She couldn't wait to remove it.

Alena looked up to hail a passing cab, only to find John Harper standing right in front of her.

Her breath caught in her throat. Why was he here? How had he found her?

She realized that as a U.S. Marshal, he found people for a living. He had heard Jeb tell her which bank held her account and had put two and two together. She wondered how long he'd been waiting for her.

She lowered her eyes, a mantle of sadness weighing her down. A heart couldn't really break. Could it?

Who would put hers back together?

John cleared his throat and reached for her gloved hand. Oh, the warmth that rushed through her seemed almost sinful as he wrapped his hand around hers. Alena knew it was wrong, so wrong, to want another woman's man, but she did. She wanted John Harper desperately, more than the very air she breathed. She pulled away then, hurting too much at their touch. If she could curl up and die along the sidewalk, she would. She no longer wanted to be in a world where John wasn't a part of it.

"Alena?"

His voice was husky, thick with emotion. She reluctantly raised her gaze to his.

His fingers entwined with hers. "You disappeared yesterday," he said. Alena heard the hurt in his words.

"I wasn't really needed. Besides," she took a deep breath and her words rushed out, "you're free now. Free for Annabelle." She felt him flinch.

John tightened his grip on her hand, shaking his head.

"And what would I want with Annabelle?"

Alena looked away, but strong fingers took her chin in hand, lifting it up. She forced herself to meet his eyes. "You'll want to be with her now."

A single tear slid down her cheek. "She made it obvious to everyone yesterday. She might be a new widow, but she's in love with you, John. She always has been."

He brushed away the tear with his thumb. She trembled at his touch.

"Why would I want to be with her, Alena, when it's you that I love."

She drew in a quick breath.

"I've found myself bewitched by a sharpshooter who also has quite a way with a paintbrush. A woman who taught me what true love really is. Your touch healed me, Alena. Not just from the gunshot wound. Not just from dealing with my blindness."

She began trembling, hope growing within her.

"Your courage and intelligence and passion are what I need in a woman. In *my* woman. Don't you know I want to spend the rest of our lives together?"

And then he smiled, a slow, sensual smile that lit up his entire face. It was a smile from the heart, one meant only for her.

A glow replaced the chill, spreading through her like a rising sun ready to shine down on a new day. John Harper wanted her— Alena McClaine— and not Annabelle Reynolds.

As Alena answered John with her own smile, he folded her into his arms. She was caught in a tight embrace from which she hoped there would never be an escape. His mouth sought hers and she became lost in a kiss of passion and promise, one that she hoped would start each day anew and end it, as well.

Alena was ready for a new life. With John. Wherever it took them.

ALSO BY ALEXA ASTON

THE HOLLYWOOD NAME GAME
Hollywood Heartbreaker
Hollywood Flirt
Hollywood Player
Hollywood Double
Hollywood Enigma

Lawmen of the West
Runaway Hearts
Blind Faith
Love and the Lawman
Ballad Beauty

DUKES OF DISTINCTION:
Duke of Renown
Duke of Charm
Duke of Disrepute
Duke of Arrogance
Duke of Honor

MEDIEVAL RUNAWAY WIVES:
Song of the Heart
A Promise of Tomorrow
Destined for Love

SOLDIERS AND SOULMATES:
To Heal an Earl

To Tame a Rogue

To Trust a Duke

To Save a Love

To Win a Widow

THE ST. CLAIRS:

Devoted to the Duke

Midnight with the Marquess

Embracing the Earl

Defending the Duke

Suddenly a St. Clair

THE KING'S COUSINS:

God of the Seas

The Pawn

The Heir

The Bastard

THE KNIGHTS OF HONOR:

Rise of de Wolfe

Word of Honor

Marked by Honor

Code of Honor

Journey to Honor

Heart of Honor

Bold in Honor

Love and Honor

Gift of Honor

Path to Honor

Return to Honor

Season of Honor

NOVELLAS:
Diana
Derek
Thea
The Lyon's Lady Love

ABOUT THE AUTHOR

A native Texan and former history teacher, award-winning and internationally bestselling author Alexa Aston lives with her husband in a Dallas suburb, where she eats her fair share of dark chocolate and plots out stories while she walks every morning. She enjoys travel, sports, and binge-watching—and never misses an episode of *Survivor*.

Alexa brings her characters to life in steamy historicals, contemporary romances, and romantic suspense novels that resonate with passion, intensity, and heart.

KEEP UP WITH ALEXA
Visit her website
Newsletter Sign-Up

MORE WAYS TO CONNECT WITH ALEXA

CPSIA information can be obtained
at www.ICGtesting.com
Printed in the USA
LVHW040540090721
692259LV00007B/458